The
NARROWBOAT
SUMMER

Also by Anne Youngson

Meet Me at the Museum

The
NARROWBOAT
SUMMER

ANNE YOUNGSON

FLATIRON
BOOKS
NEW YORK

THE NARROWBOAT SUMMER. Copyright © 2020 by Anne Youngson.
All rights reserved. Printed in the United States of America.
For information, address Flatiron Books,
120 Broadway, New York, NY 10271.

www.flatironbooks.com

Designed by Michelle McMillan

The Library of Congress has cataloged the hardcover edition as follows:

Names: Youngson, Anne, author.
Title: The narrowboat summer / Anne Youngson.
Description: First US Edition. | New York : Flatiron Books, 2021. | "Originally
    published in Great Britain in 2020 by Doubleday"—Title page verso. |
Identifiers: LCCN 2020047446 | ISBN 9781250764614 (hardcover) |
    ISBN 9781250764607 (ebook)
Classification: LCC PR6125.O946 N37 2021 | DDC 823/.92—dc23
LC record available at https://lccn.loc.gov/2020047446

ISBN 978-1-250-76462-1 (trade paperback)

Our books may be purchased in bulk for promotional, educational,
or business use. Please contact your local bookseller or the
Macmillan Corporate and Premium Sales Department at 1-800-221-7945,
extension 5442, or by email at MacmillanSpecialMarkets@macmillan.com.

Originally published in Great Britain in 2020 by Doubleday,
an imprint of Transworld Publishers

First published in the United States by Flatiron Books in 2021

First Flatiron Books Paperback Edition: 2022

10 9 8 7 6 5 4 3 2

For Mary, the best of sisters

The
NARROWBOAT
SUMMER

I

The Number One

O N THE TOWPATH OF a canal in a town not far from London, not far from the coast, is moored a narrowboat painted dark blue with the name *Number One* picked out in red lettering on the prow. It is tethered tightly to the bank with ropes made wet by the rain and slimy with age, wrapped around pegs bent out of shape by the misaimed blows of a lump hammer. It is still in the water. At either end the doors are fast shut and the windows along the side are latched. On the roof is a skylight, cantilevered up to let the fresh air into the cabin below. Puddles of water on the deck and roof show that it has been raining, but at this moment it is not.

There are two people on the towpath, walking toward each other. One is a tall, relatively plump woman: that is to say, around half the number of women in her age group—she has gone some distance past fifty—would be slimmer and shorter than she is, but she is not so tall or so plump as to be remarkable. In one hand she has an orange carrier bag and on her feet a pair of bright silver running shoes; these might not be out of place on a towpath but are out of place with her black wool skirt and tailored blouse. Her hair is wrapped up in a largely colorless scarf, apparently once purple.

The woman approaching her is shorter and more slender. She is carrying an umbrella in a color often called fuchsia, though fuchsias come in a range of colors. She is holding it at her side—not needing its protection at the moment—but open, as if anxious about the time it would take to bring it into use if she should suddenly need it. Her hair is carefully styled and her clothes might have been carefully chosen to be unremarkable. If so, the choice was successful.

As they approach the moored boat, the sun inserts a finger of light between the clouds and it is all at once a lovely day, at that moment, on that towpath. At almost the same instant, when the two women are close enough to each other for a nod and a smile of greeting, if either or both of them thought that was appropriate—they are complete strangers, so it seems unlikely—at that precise moment, the narrowboat begins to howl. It howls as if it were a mezzo-soprano in mid-aria spotting her husband committing adultery in the stalls while being impaled from behind by a careless spear carrier. Both women stop walking.

EVE'S HANDS WERE FULL OF the debris of a career of more than thirty years. She kicked aside the Strategic Five Year Plan, folded and wedging the door open, to let it shut behind her. What she was carrying now were items so small and insignificant she had overlooked them when she had made a pile of things definitively hers: the books, pen set, files of personal information that could not be claimed as property of the Rambusch Corporation. These had been placed into a cardboard box supplied by the management. The packing had been not so much overseen as attended by Clive, a representative (ironically, because neither word could accurately be applied to him) of the Human Resources department. He stood beside her, rumbling idly like a vacuum cleaner (which he closely resembled) switched on and ready to suck if anything misplaced came within reach of his hose. That had been the day before, the penultimate day. Now, on the last day, she stood in the corridor holding things so odd and familiar they had been invisible. The plastic frog stuck to the side of her computer monitor; the postcard of a building in New York pinned to the cork board; a calendar from an overseas charity with six more pictures of starving children still to come; a mug with a picture of a hedgehog on top of a scrubbing brush and a brown deposit welded to the bottom; a letter opener with what looked like teeth marks in its bamboo handle; a purple scarf that had been tied to the handle of a filing cabinet for so long it had faded along its exposed length and only revealed its original, shocking depth of color on the inside of the knot; a photograph of a team-building exercise, the participants all in hard yellow hats standing under a cliff holding up ropes in triumph, though whether after or in anticipation of an ascent or descent she could not remember. She nearly dropped this in the bin, already full of discarded good-luck cards, but closer scrutiny revealed that no one in the picture was recognizable as an individual—though she could pick herself out as the only woman in the group—so she used it as a tray on which to pile the rest of the rubbish.

The door shut with a hiss from its automatic closure system.

The nameplate—*Eve Warburton: Planning*—swung toward her, stopping inches from her nose. Had she had a hand free, she might have defaced it in some way, but in the circumstances she just leaned forward and gave it a kiss.

"Goodbye, Eve Warburton, Planning," she whispered. "Nice to have known you."

First the scarf then the frog then the letter opener fell from her stack on the way to the lift. She recovered them all and stopped in the lobby to ask the receptionist for a carrier bag. The receptionist went to look in a cubicle in the wall behind her desk. Eve put her pile down on the counter and watched the oil circulating in the installation designed to impress the visitor with the technical brilliance of the Rambusch Corporation's engineering and manufacturing capability, its mastery of pumps, pistons and valves. Her eye caught the plastic sign on it which read:

Constructed from Production Parts

Eve took up the letter opener and levered this off. One final souvenir. She pushed it down the front of her skirt.

The girl returned with a disposable carrier bag from the local sandwich outlet.

"It's all I can find."

"It will do," said Eve. It was hard to stop the pilfered notice sliding out as she loaded a carrier bag with small, odd-shaped items, until the receptionist, interpreting her clumsiness as evidence of emotional turmoil, did the job for her.

"I'm, you know, sorry you're leaving," she said.

"It was time to move on."

"I thought of you, having to work with all those men on the top floor. I mean, no one to have a gossip with and that."

"They didn't have much of a feminine side, by and large," said Eve.

"Oh, I know!" The receptionist came out from behind her barrier with the filled bag. Eve was afraid she might be about to offer a hug, in compensation for Eve's fall from the masculine heights of the fourth floor to mere womanhood.

"Luckily for me, I'm on the masculine side of the feminine spectrum," she said.

She turned left out of the building, toward where her car would normally be parked—indeed, where it was parked—but even as her hand reached into her pocket for the keys, she remembered it was no longer hers. Company property. She could call a taxi or catch a bus or walk. She had no intention of going back inside the building for the rest of her life, and this ruled out a taxi because the number of the local firm was in her surrendered company mobile. It was raining, but she did not want to hesitate in full view of the receptionist, so she began to walk. It was a long way, in kitten heels, from the Rambusch premises to the edge of the industrial estate. It was a fairly hefty hike up a hill to the first bus stop on the main road. The notice filched from the lobby display impeded her stride, so she took it out and thought about lobbing it over a hedge but on second thought put it in the carrier bag. The rain falling on her head slid in large drops down her perfectly conditioned hair into the top of her blouse, into her ears and her mouth. She took out the faded scarf and tied it over her head. She felt like a bag lady; she rather hoped she looked like a bag lady. It could be a new career.

When she reached the first bus stop she leaned against it, resting her feet until a bus arrived and she bought a ticket into town. Once there, she went into a bookshop and found an Ordnance Survey map of the area showing all the paths and alleyways so that she could plot a route back to her flat on foot, avoiding the main roads she normally drove down. She went next door to a shoe shop and bought a pair of running shoes. These were handed over in a brilliantly orange and substantial carrier bag, big enough to take all her belongings from the office, the kitten heels and the notice. From the map, she found that the quickest way home was to start down the towpath. Just as the rain was stopping, she set off.

Walking toward her was a woman her own age. Between them was a dark-blue narrowboat, apparently deserted. The name painted in red lettering on the prow was *Number One*.

ON THE WALK TO THE hairdresser it began to rain, which was something Sally had not foreseen. Raindrops, she reflected, were falling on her head, although the song was entirely inappropriate in her current circumstances.

"My word," said the hairdresser as Sally dripped on the mat. "You didn't come prepared."

Sally had known Lynne for over twenty years. Twenty years of a relationship conducted in reflection, meeting each other's eyes in the mirror. They had talked about everything in that time. They had exchanged information about children, holidays, kitchen appliances and plumbers. They had shared opinions about soap operas, brands of ice cream, chewing gum and British Summer Time. They had discussed renewable energy, interest rates, the Middle East and mobile phones. It was always a shock to her to stand up—after she had been shown a glimpse of the back of her head and had the cut hair brushed from her shoulders, the nylon coverall whisked away—to find that she was taller than Lynne. How could someone who had filled the mirror so emphatically for half an hour or more be so dumpy an individual in the real world? She only came to this part of the town to visit the Kut Above, and had never seen Lynne in the street. She sometimes wondered if she would recognize her if she came across her queuing for a prescription in Boots. And yet, she thought of Lynne as her friend, and had done so ever since the day she had said she would rather be called Sally than Mrs. Allsop, and Lynne had agreed.

Sally had something to say on this visit; with Lynne's face in the mirror to frame the story, she could say it and, in saying it, fix it.

Lynne combed Sally's wet hair, persuading it into a smooth and elegant shape unlike its usual wispy incoherence.

"Just tidied up a bit?" she said, as she always did.

"I wondered about highlights," said Sally. "Not today, of course. Next time, maybe."

Lynne said it would be a fiddly process. "And I'm not sure what color you'd use. Your hair's so fair, and so fine, it would be hard to find a color that was a strong enough contrast, without going completely over the top."

"Pink," said Sally. "Or turquoise."

"Of course, but you wouldn't want that. We could get away with a nutty brown, if you're set on the idea."

"But I do want pink or turquoise, I haven't made up my mind which."

"Well," said Lynne. "What's brought this on?"

"New beginning," said Sally. "Fresh start. My new career as a single person." The scissors and comb became quite still. Lynne was staring at her in the mirror. "I told my husband last night that our marriage is over. There is no reason why anything, from this moment forward, should be as it has been up to now."

"I'm so sorry," whispered Lynne. "Do you want to talk about it, or is it too painful?"

"I'm not at all sorry and I don't mind talking about it, but it's the future I'm more excited about."

"It must be difficult after twenty-five years? I mean, you didn't seem unhappy. Maybe I've had it wrong all this time, but I really thought the two of you were close. Did he . . . ? I mean, you know . . . After all, men—"

"Duncan is entirely blameless," said Sally.

Lynne remained still; almost rigid.

"But you must have, well, emotional issues?"

"The only emotion I feel is relief," Sally said. "And that isn't an issue."

"But why?" said Lynne. "There must be a reason?"

"I was bored."

Lynne's face, as she brought the scissors and comb back into play with something close to aggression, was becoming quite red, and it was possible she looked cross though Sally had no way of knowing what she looked like when cross, because they had always tended to agree with each other. Sally saw that Lynne, far from admiring her resilience and self-determination, wanted her to be in need of sympathy—as a victim or as the guilty party racked with guilt. She had not foreseen this, and she considered the narrative Lynne was hearing. She was leaving her husband;

she had not been abused; she had not been rejected; she did not feel guilty. Yes.

"You obviously don't approve," she said.

Lynne clamped her lips together and kept her eyes on Sally's head, cutting Sally's hair as if there was a looming deadline after which it would set solid.

"No, I don't, but of course I don't know anything about it. I just know that being married isn't easy and it's up to us all to work at it and not just throw up our hands and walk away as if it never mattered in the first place."

"On the other hand," said Sally, "it's sometimes harder to endure the everyday than it is to cope with a big trauma."

"If you say so."

"I think I'll have my gap year now," said Sally. "Twelve months of doing something I wouldn't normally and probably won't ever do again."

"Like what?"

"I haven't decided. I expect something will turn up."

It was still raining when she left the Kut Above. She stepped into a corner shop and bought a folding umbrella in a shade of pink she thought might be an exact match for the highlights she was imagining. She would be going somewhere else to have them done. After all, was it not important to change every aspect of her routines? How else would she be able to identify those hooks and burrs and combinations that held her, like the flag on a flagpole, free to flap about but not free to drift or soar?

The umbrella was less easy to manipulate than the label had promised it would be, but it kept the rain off her hair, which had the bounce and body only Lynne had ever been able to give it. The rain stopped as she crossed the canal bridge and, on an impulse, she took the steps down to the towpath. It was possible to walk most of the way home by this route, but she rarely did. It was muddy; there were no shops; the people who lived in the boats moored alongside had more than the average householder in the way of untrustworthy dogs, dubious houseplants, bare feet and rusty bicycles. It being an unusual route for her was one good reason to set off down it today. Another was that it was longer. It would delay her return to the house. She had told him she was going because she wanted peace; she wanted silence and the chance to think. But the silence consequent on announcing that decision was surprisingly hard to bear. And she could not decide where, exactly, she wanted to go.

So she took the long way back, along the towpath, walking slowly and, because she no longer needed it, swinging the pink umbrella by its strap. Walking toward her was a woman her own age. Between them was a dark-blue narrowboat, apparently deserted. The name painted in red lettering on the prow was *Number One*.

EVE WARBURTON AND SALLY ALLSOP stood still on the towpath, halted by an unearthly crescendo of sound. They looked at the boat, until the noise died away, then at each other.

"Was that human?" asked Sally.

Eve said she hoped not. "But whatever it was, it doesn't seem right to ignore it."

Sally advanced toward the *Number One* and bent her knees to look through the window. The noise began again, accompanied by the thud of something solid being propelled with force against the glass. She staggered backward, lost her balance and sat down on the worn and wet grass of the towpath. Eve skipped sideways to avoid her but became entangled in the open pink umbrella. As the wailing died away again, they were left sitting side by side facing the boat.

"It's a dog," said Sally.

"Are you sure? Could it have been a child, do you think?"

"Not unless they've started breeding them with black-and-white fur and floppy ears."

"Well, that's a relief. Dogs I can cope with. Children terrify me." Eve stood up and looked at the skylight on the roof. "You'll have to slide through that hatch to make sure it's all right," she said. "I'm too fat."

Sally made no effort to move.

"I'm sorry to have to tell you that my expertise is entirely in the field of children," she said. "It's dogs that terrify me. There is no way I'm going to dangle my legs into a space occupied by a dog—a rabid dog, for all I know." Eve stood with her hands on her hips. "Why is it," said Sally, scrambling to her feet, "that it is perfectly acceptable to say you don't like children but admitting that you don't care for dogs always makes people look at you just like you're looking at me?"

"I'm not looking at you the way you think I'm looking at you. I'm not really looking at you at all. I'm thinking."

The noise came again, rising to a peak of unutterable anguish and dying away. The weight of the dog's body hammered against the window. They took a step back and looked up and down the empty towpath and over their shoulders at the motorists passing across the distant bridge.

"We can't do nothing," said Eve.

"We could just walk away," said Sally.

But she did not walk away. She stayed where she was, watching Eve climb onto the rear of the boat, which rocked gently, and inspect the fastenings on the solid little door leading off the platform where the driver would stand, holding the tiller, if the boat were moving. Eve abandoned the back and went to the front, an open well protected by a canvas cover held taut with studs. She began to unclip these, one by one, and Sally, seeing this was going to be a slow business, went to help her. When they had released one side and folded the cover back, Eve climbed into the well. The doors at this end had glass in them, a scaled-down version of the doors you might find leading into a conservatory at a stately home. The dog began to howl again, on a more tragic, personal note. Eve took up a heavy metal tool lying on one of the benches that lined the wall and broke the glass. It became eerily quiet.

"What's happening?" asked Sally, from the towpath.

"I'm reaching in to release the . . . Oh! Quick, catch him!"

Seconds later Eve was splayed awkwardly across the side of the well, Sally was once again in a sitting position on the bank, and a bundle of black-and-white fur and floppy ears had already passed the bridge and was accelerating down the towpath.

"Bugger," said Eve.

Sally lay flat on her back and began to laugh.

"I'm sorry," she said. "I know it's not funny, but I woke up this morning determined to stop being so bored and boring, and not to keep on doing the same things I always do. And look, something has happened to me that has never happened before. Quite spontaneously."

"Breaking into a boat and releasing a manic dog has never

happened to me before, either," said Eve, "but I was just racking it up as another experience in a totally shitty day. You must be the sort of person who always looks on the bright side."

"I don't, usually. But today, I'm embracing change. For a change."

"I don't mind embracing it, but I do like to have a choice of whether to change or not. When someone else decides for you, it's harder to look on the bright side."

Eve was still sprawled in the well, wedged against a gas bottle with a couple of folding chairs impeding her feet. Her orange bag had fallen on its side and hanging out of it was a plastic notice which read: *Constructed from Production Parts.*

Sally, reaching down a hand to help her up, asked what it meant.

"Nothing at all. It is meaningless. That's the point. Constructed and produced are synonyms. It is meant to imply that the parts are not prototypes, but prototypes are produced, as well. Sorry, I'm being cross and pedantic. More importantly, what do you think we ought to do now?"

THEY WERE SITTING ON THE benches in the front well discussing the options—whether to run away, like the dog, or to run away but leave a note; or whether it was imperative to take some positive action, such as chasing the dog or seeking out the owner—when they became aware of a rhythmic sound coming closer. Looking out from under the awning they could see a figure advancing toward them along the towpath. An exclamation mark: tall, narrow, black and slightly menacing. The sound was the steady thud of wellington boots, the regular smack of a leather satchel against a waterproof coat, and an underlying whistle of breath drawn in and let out.

They scrambled out of the boat and stood waiting for this finger of doom to pass by. It didn't. Setting down the satchel on the ground, the woman—for close up she was recognizably though unconventionally female—looked from one to the other. Her face was the color of marmalade and so mapped with wrinkles it was hard to see how any cosmetic enhancements, in the unlikely event she wanted to apply them, could be smoothed on to its corrugated surface. Her lips were thin and appeared, until she opened them to speak, like one more set of horizontal wrinkles.

"You've been on my boat," she said. "You'd better explain why." The voice was an audible version of the face.

"I'm afraid I've broken your door and let the dog out," said Eve.

"There didn't seem much else we could do," said Sally. "It was howling."

The boat owner opened her mouth a little wider and bared a set of uneven teeth. She ran a gray, textured tongue over them and nodded.

"People who think the dog is howling because it's in pain," she said, "usually report me to the RSPCA, or the Canal and River Trust, or the Environment Agency, or the police, or anyone else they can think of who might be interested in giving me grief. It makes them feel righteous and it passes the problem on. I like your approach better. If the dog's in pain, smash a way in and sort it out. I like that. I'd say you cared more about the dog and less about the law. I like that, too."

"We thought it might be dying," said Sally.

The old woman shook her head. "He was showing off, that's all. I'm the one who's dying."

She picked up her satchel and stepped onto the rear of the boat, unlocking the doors.

"Well, I should give you some money to have the glass replaced," said Eve.

"It's not worth it. The cost of repairing anything on a boat is higher than you could believe, given everything is so small and should logically be cheaper. I'll probably nail a bit of wood over it until I come across a piece of glass the right size."

"We could come in and sweep up the mess," said Sally.

"You can do that, yes. And you can have a cup of tea with me. I'd like that. I've taken a fancy to you already."

Inside, the boat was sparse, neat and workmanlike. The cabin they entered as they descended the steps from the rear deck was the kitchen. It had a cooker and cupboards, a table and two benches, a plastic washing-up bowl in the sink and a kettle on the hob. There were no ornaments and no ornamentation. The wood-paneled walls were empty except for a map and a row of hooks from which hung a torch, a whistle, a dog lead and a first-aid kit. The old woman reached into a cupboard and handed them a dustpan, brush and bucket; they carried these through the boat, accepting shared responsibility for the mess, or a shared reluctance to stay alone with the owner in the kitchen.

The second cabin had a board attached to the wall, which might have been a bed or a couch though it had no covering to make it inviting to sit on or lie on, with lockers underneath. There were three shelves containing books. Between this and the next cabin were a washbasin and a cubicle with a door, which was shut. In the front cabin were two slatted bunks covered in rough blankets, tightly tucked in; these blankets represented the only soft surfaces on the boat. Sally and Eve swept up the shards of glass from the otherwise clean floor and returned to the cabin, where the old woman relieved them of the pan and brush, the bucket and its contents, disposing of them behind the cupboard doors.

"My name is Anastasia," she said, laying out three white mugs and three teabags, and indicating they should sit down on one of the benches. The kettle whistled throatily.

"Oh," said Sally, "what about the dog?"

"He's called Noah and, before you ask, it's got nothing to do with boats. It just begins with the sound I find myself shouting most often."

"No," said Sally. "I meant, shouldn't we be worried about where he's gone? Go looking for him perhaps, or report him missing?"

"Look," said Anastasia, lining up the teas on the table, "stop worrying about the dog. Nothing will happen to him. That dog will be dogging me to the end of my days and beyond, I shouldn't wonder. He will come back. Not many certainties in this life, but that's one of them."

"Oh," said Sally. "My name's Sally."

"Eve," said Eve.

"Sally," said Anastasia. "And Eve and Anastasia. An E and an A and an S. Which spells SEA, I suppose. Not much sense in that. A Y would be handy, to make us EASY. You don't have any friends called Yolanda you could introduce?"

"My middle name is Yasmin," said Sally.

"Perfect. Here we are, then: Easy!"

The tea was so strong Sally and Eve took small sips, letting the tannin into their systems in gradual doses. Anastasia drank hers like a pint of beer, in large gulps, with relish.

"Actually," she said, putting the empty mug down, "I may not be dying. Dying may not be inevitable. There is a chance that what's wrong with me now can be made to go away and I may still have the opportunity to die later, of something else. But making the effort not to die would be quite complicated and I'm not sure I can work out how to accomplish it. So it might be easier to go for it, and die from what I've got now."

"And what is that?" asked Eve.

"They don't know exactly, or they do know and they're not going to tell me until they have scanned it from every angle and have biopsy results on anything they can scrape or squeeze or slice out of me. That, you see, is the problem. In order to have a chance of not dying, I have to keep going back for this appointment, that appointment, this procedure, that procedure, such-and-such an operation, belt and braces, follow-up treatments. And to do all that, I have to stay here."

"Surely you must stay here, then. At least until you have a clear diagnosis and understand your options," said Sally.

"I can't," said Anastasia. "I can't afford to. If I stay, I have to pay for a mooring, if I can find one, or keep moving between temporary moorings, and I haven't the money for the one, and who knows when the invasive this and the radiated that will make me too weak to manage the other. Plus, I've got the boat to look after. To get all the certificates needed to renew my license to be on the canal, I have to have the engine serviced and the bottom blacked. I can't afford any of that either, but I know someone with a boatyard in Chester who will do it for me for free, but I need it done by the second week in August. It would take me at least four weeks to reach Chester from here, and that would be without any rest days, so I need to start now. There it is. If I want to live, I have to stay here. If I'm going to carry on living the way I do, I have to go to Chester."

"There must be some way round this," said Eve.

"Oh, there is. I need someone with nothing better to do for, let's say, the next three or four months, and a house I can borrow to live in while they take the boat to Chester and back for me."

"And you don't know anyone like that?" said Eve.

"With a house and time? Not likely, is it?"

"I don't have anything better to do for the next four months," said Sally, "but there's someone living in my house."

"You couldn't do it alone anyway," said Anastasia. "I can, but you couldn't."

There was the slightest sound from the rear of the boat, a mere hint of a tap or a scratch. Anastasia sat up and turned her head. It was the dog, returning with as little noise as possible.

Once fully in the cabin, he turned out to be a medium-sized, terrier-like animal with a rough whitish coat with black blotches, long legs, a barrel-shaped body, floppy ears, extremely bright brown eyes and a swirl of black on his face that looked remarkably like a question mark.

"Yes?" said Anastasia. The dog lay down, put his head on his paws and raised one eyebrow and ear, then the other. "You know what I think." The dog appeared, with a judicious blink, to acknowledge that he did, indeed, know what she thought. Nevertheless, she told him, in a bellow that made Eve flinch and Sally, already uneasily shifting on her seat, jump. "You're a complete disgrace. Why anyone who had the first notion of dog breeding wouldn't have seen you for the disaster you are at the outset and hit you on the head with a spade I JUST DO NOT KNOW. I'm going to do it myself, one day. One day."

There was a watchful silence for a moment, then Noah subsided onto his side and went to sleep, almost immediately starting a chorus of whiffling snores that formed the background to the conversation.

"As it happens, I have a flat I live in alone," said Eve. "And in truth, I'm not sure I can think of anything to stop me using the next four months to travel about on the canals."

"Am I right in thinking," said Anastasia, "that you have absolutely no idea how to drive a boat? Have either of you ever set foot on a canal boat before your assault on the *Number One*?"

"No," said Eve.

"Nor me," said Sally.

"But you expect me to trust her to you, do you?"

"No, of course you couldn't," said Sally.

"Hang on," said Eve, "I'm getting confused. Didn't you tell us only a minute ago that you needed someone to do you a favor, and now you're talking as if you would be doing us a favor."

Anastasia sucked her teeth and slowly unbuttoned the waterproof coat she was still wearing.

"I suppose you could do it together, if I taught you the basics. But are you good enough friends to put up with each other?"

"We're not friends at all," said Sally.

"We've only just met. Rescuing your dog," said Eve.

"That is probably all to the good," said Anastasia. "You could be most of the way to Chester before you found out how annoying the other one is."

There was a long pause. Then Anastasia began to smile; although the corrugated severity of her face meant it was not immediately clear that this was the expression she had in mind.

"I'm not at all sure . . ." said Eve.

"What about the dog?" asked Sally.

"He'd come with you."

"This is ridiculous," Eve said. "You only met us five minutes ago and you don't know the first thing about us. Wouldn't you want to check on us in some way? Make sure we're not alcoholics or drug dealers or something?"

"Here's the thing," said Anastasia. "Most of the people I know in the boating community are alcoholics or drug dealers or simply wasters. But they do know how to handle a boat. So of course I have thought of asking someone I know to take the *Number One* to Chester for me, while I live in his or her boat here in Uxbridge. Now you two turn up; never seen you before and you don't know how to handle a boat. But from where I'm sitting, I don't have either of you down as abusers of any kind. So as I see it, I have a choice between tapping a competent person I wouldn't want on the *Number One*, or two total incompetents, who haven't given me any reason to object to them. And, let's face it, that is one more choice than I had earlier today."

"We're an unexpected gift," Sally said.

Eve turned sideways and looked at Sally. "Are you seriously thinking of doing this?" she asked.

"I have no idea. It's too much for me to think about. But I'm definitely not doing it on my own."

Anastasia and Sally looked at Eve. Noah stopped snoring and raised his head an inch or two and looked at her, too.

"We could think about it," Eve said. "Put a plan together. Work out the details."

"We could," said Sally. "Think about it, I mean."

Anastasia went beyond a smile into something that seemed to be laughter.

"Easy," she said.

EVE COULD THINK OF NOTHING at all to think about. The bend ahead was five hundred yards away and it would take about ten minutes to reach it. Between now and then, there was nothing that clamored for attention. No change in the trees growing down either side of the canal; no hazards that would challenge her ability to remember to push the tiller to the left to move the boat to the right; no plans to make for what would happen next. That morning she had woken on the hard bed made up on the bench in the middle cabin, conscious of not having decided, the night before, what to wear. The anxiety was acute until, wide awake, she realized it was irrelevant. She had no need to worry because she had almost no clothes to choose from and it mattered not at all what she wore. Nor could she think of anything else to worry about. It was worrying.

Hearing the chink of mugs as Sally came through the cabin with two cups of coffee, it occurred to her that she might worry about how long it would take her to find this stranger intolerable. What would be the amalgam of habits, opinions, idiosyncrasies and character defects which made everyone she had ever known impossible to live with, sooner or later. But for the moment, she had not spotted what these were, and there was, therefore, no point worrying about it.

. . .

It had taken ten days from meeting Sally and Anastasia to this, the first day of the journey. The decision, in retrospect, had been made in those ten minutes on the *Number One*, but Eve was a planner and she had nothing but contempt for people who rushed into things without taking the time to think them through, weigh the advantages and disadvantages, map out the steps, make contingency plans for the most likely risks along the way. So while the idea of moving out of her flat and onto a boat had seemed like a gift, the present she most needed—that is, a chance to walk away, avoid making any other decisions, silence the analysis of the past that would not let her sleep at night, yet to reach out and accept it without further thought— was beyond her.

She had gone home along the towpath and washed the mud off her new shoes. Then she went through the bag she had brought from the office and threw out the frog, the postcard, the faded headscarf, the filthy mug and the damaged letter opener. She looked at the two things left, the framed photo of a team-building adventure and the stolen notice about production parts. Then she threw out the notice: its internal inconsistencies were symptomatic of the circulating arguments running around her head, the apparent logic that appeared to lead to a reasoned conclusion that turned out to be the same place as the start. She kept the photo, as a fitting memento of the uniformity of the society she had left, and a happy reminder that she did not exactly match, was not truly one of them.

That sorted, she opened her laptop and began to put together the Easy Plan, as a way of reaching a conclusion on whether it was or wasn't a stupid idea. She laid out the milestones on the critical path, studying the implications of each—how hard would it be to achieve, how serious would the result be if it were not achieved, or if its critical success factors could only partially be met. At the end of this, late at night, with the last glass from a bottle of Chilean Merlot at her elbow and the street outside her open window quiet at last, she went over the results and realized there was nothing to stop her from agreeing to the plan. There was no step she was unwilling or unable to take. This moment was the high point of the next ten days.

The following morning, she took the plan to the pre-arranged meeting at the *Number One* and laid out copies in front of Anastasia and Sally. Anastasia picked hers up and wriggled her lips, hummed a tune and put it down again.

"That much is obvious," she said.

Sally looked down at hers as if it were an exam paper. Finally, she looked up.

"Does this mean we're going to do it?" she asked.

"It means I can't see any reason why we shouldn't," Eve said. "How about you?"

"I need a bit more time," said Sally.

As they left the boat the day before, Eve had detected in Sally a suspicion of the "let's just go for it" attitude she so despised. Now she feared the opposite: that Sally would turn out to be one of those people who, when the plan had been put together and agreed by all parties, took fright and could not be persuaded to set off along the path. She understood one thing, though, as a result of Sally's reaction. She herself really, really wanted to do this.

What had seemed possible while sitting on the *Number One* with those two extraordinary women in front of her, felt like a fantasy to Sally—worse, a joke, ridiculous—as she put her key into the lock of 42 Beech Grove. Just the idea of framing the words she would have to use to explain what she was thinking (dreaming) of doing was beyond her. The house was so emphatically the same. The disposition of its contents, its particular smell, the minor blemishes on its walls and floors, the angle at which the sun fell through the kitchen window onto the tiled floor, were mocking her with their familiarity, their permanence.

Yet she had said the most unthinkable words already. She had sat beside Duncan at the kitchen table and told him she could no longer go through the motions of being the person everyone thought she was happy to be: wife, mother, classroom assistant, resident of 42 Beech Grove. As she talked, Duncan's eyes never met hers but stayed on the cover of a magazine lying on the table between them. A *TV Guide* for the next week with a photo on the cover of one of those women with perfect faces and a name beginning with K—Katie or Keira or Kylie. A flake of crust from the bread she had cut to make sandwiches at lunchtime had landed on the photo and was obscuring one of the famous K's front teeth. It made her look as if some disease or lack of hygiene had led to the formation of a yellowish crust on the perfection of her pearly white molar. Sally reached out a hand to brush it away, because it didn't seem fair to leave her like that, but stopped the movement, not wanting to let it appear she had allowed her attention to be diverted, in the middle of destroying her husband's life, by a stray, disfiguring crumb.

Duncan was a man who never stopped talking, who shared his every thought with her as it came into his mind, and she had expected a torrent of words. Instead, he said, "I need to think about this," and left the room. Only later did she realize he had left the house. She heard him come back in the middle of the night and go into the room that used to be her son's bedroom when he lived at home. All he had said to her since, as he left for work in the morning, was: "You know I love you." That was it. All day, having her hair cut, meeting Anastasia and Eve, forming the plan for the *Number One*, walking home, she had been tasting freedom. But the house whispered to her, as she put the new, pink umbrella in the pot where the other umbrellas lived, did you think it would be that easy? Did you really think you were getting away?

She let the evening pass. Nothing was said, on any topic, by either of them. They ate a meal Sally had cooked in an unnatural, uncomfortable silence. After all, Sally thought, no rush; Eve might not agree to go, and she felt the bitter taste of disappointment at the thought.

Then she went back to the *Number One* and Eve came up with a piece of paper that made it all real. Sally could make no sense of the plan—it was all nonsense, too complicated, she thought, too much detail for what would be simple, once they got started. If they could only decide to start. And in the end, even that turned out to be simple. She said to Duncan:

"I've met a couple of women who want me to help them take a canal boat up to Chester."

"Are you going?"

"I thought I might."

"It's up to you, obviously." He licked his fingers and picked up the last crumbs of cake on his plate. "But it sounds like a good idea. You should do it."

Her relief that he did not have an opinion, need to discuss

the ins and the outs, want to analyze the pros and the cons, as she had expected, was tempered with a fear that it was too easy. He had not believed her when she said the marriage was over, was thinking this would be "a little holiday" that would make her see sense and the problem would go away.

"It will give you time to sort things out," she said, collecting up the empty plates. "What you want to do. About the house and so on."

"Lots to do, yes," he said. "Lots to think about."

The next day she went back to the *Number One* and declared her readiness to go ahead with Eve's Easy Plan.

THEY ALL HAD THINGS THEY felt they needed to do first and they went their separate ways to do them.

Eve had thought of her life as full. She had made sure of filling it, and the surest way of achieving that was to be always looking ahead, planning for the next change. So in theory, this should have been a simple process for her. Going away for a few months—she was used to doing that. But previously, any change she had made had been within a structure she understood; it was not until now, on the verge of changing everything— where she lived, how she spent her days, who she spent her days with—that she understood the boundaries that had enabled her to make decisions easily, because the choices were limited and familiar.

Her childhood had set the pattern. The only child of peri- patetic parents, she had bounced between boarding school, her mother's family in the rural Midlands, and Dubai or Hong Kong or wherever else her father, a civil engineer, had found work building bridges. Each of these environments had been unlike the others. Her school had been highly polished, a place of hard surfaces and restricting walls and intermittent silence and clatter. Wherever her parents lived was hot, full of color and texture, and—because she was never anywhere long enough to know it—unknowable. Her grandmother and her mother's extended family lived their lives out of doors, in a green landscape which was always, in memory at least, cold and wet, but where every house was a pocket of coziness. She fitted in to each of these places. She knew where she stood. Even if she sometimes felt she belonged nowhere.

So it had been at university, then at Rambusch. She would have said, as one of an insignificant minority of women in both places—she studied mechanical engineering—that she fitted in, and as she worked her way up the hierarchy at Rambusch, from design engineer to team leader to project manager to director level, she had begun to think she did belong. Until she found out she didn't. Her career, like her childhood, had been spent on the move: from one plant to another, one office to another, one project to another. She'd always known that in a month, a year, two years she would be somewhere else doing something else, but inside the scaffolding that was Rambusch. She had managed her relationships in the same way. Never expecting or wanting permanence, always looking past the man she was with in anticipation of what came next, which might (and she was fine with this) be solitude.

She made choices all the time—which role to accept, when to start and when to end a relationship—but always knowing the boundaries, the parameters. Now she was without boundaries, and this meant she had an infinity of choices and no certainties.

It was unsettling. She did not want to accept being unsettled. As she stood in her flat wondering what to do next, she found herself looking in the direction of the bin where she had thrown the notice from the display in Rambusch's reception area. She had been constructed from production parts, all this time, while thinking she had chosen the life she led. When she had as much free will as the hydraulic fluid that kept the display moving, going round and round in a purposeless loop.

Now was not the time to waver, she reminded herself. She would do what she always did, and did well: look for practical solutions to practical problems. She went through her flat selecting what to take, what to leave, what to throw out. She went through her contacts selecting who to tell, who not to tell, who to delete. In both cases, the first category was the smallest.

Sally had to go to the school where she worked as a classroom assistant and arrange to have the rest of the term off. She walked there; she always walked there. Her life was made up of such repetitions. She was a victim of routine, but as soon as this thought occurred to her, on the walk to the school, she repudiated the word "victim." If she had been trapped, it was because she had allowed it to happen. She could step out now because she was not a victim; she had control.

She did not anticipate any problems in securing leave— unpaid, of course. The school was looking for ways to save money, and the child who had been her special charge was in hospital for an extended stay. She would miss him; the way he rolled his head against the back of his wheelchair to look up at her; his smile, which might not have looked like a smile to anyone else in the classroom but that let her know he was happy, despite his inability to control his own limbs or articulate his thoughts. She would have missed him more, though, if she had stayed to the end of term, his absence not pasted over but emphasized by the chatter and clamor of those children lucky enough to have been born without a disability. She would miss them, too, of course, but they did not need her. Any more than her own children needed her now.

Her daughter and her son had reacted to her decision to leave their father in the ways she would have expected them to react. Amy had talked at her—much as she had thought Duncan would do, when she told him, but he had not. Amy had lost herself in a tangle of emotions expressed largely in recalling incidents from family life ("You were happy *then*, weren't you?") and in comparison with other mothers who had or had not behaved as she was behaving ("I mean, I'd always expected *her* to do that!"). Beneath all this was the question Sally could not yet fully answer to her own satisfaction: why?

Mark, the quiet one, had said little but looked sad. She found herself starting to apologize to him, but stopped herself. She had no idea what was causing the sadness he was not expressing. Though so much more like her than Amy was, he was the bigger mystery to her.

The conversations with Duncan continued to be eerily short, abnormally to the point. Arrangements for paying the bills; the addresses of the post offices they would pass en route where she would pick up her mail. He had accepted, without argument or analysis, that she was going on this trip. How much more than the trip he had accepted, she could not tell.

When she arrived at the school, Sally found the Head was, or was pretending to be, disappointed and angry that she was

leaving early. This was unexpected. Sally kept calm by looking at
a drawing of an octopus, colored pink with yellow spots, pinned
up on the wall. Behind, Sally thought, the Head's head; she felt
childishly pleased with this thought. Whatever the woman said,
it was so much noise. Nothing was going to stop her now.

Anastasia, it appeared, had set about throwing things out.
Though the boat had looked to be empty of everything not
strictly necessary, or even emptier, yet when they arrived at the
end of the first day of preparation for a review of the next steps,
there were several trash bags to be carried to the nearest bins.
But her main concern was to introduce them to the boat, and
all its workings.

"It's called the *Number One*," she told them, "because that
was what the people who owned their own boat and plied for
trade up and down the canals were known as. Professionals, in
other words. I expect you to bear that in mind. You might be
amateurs, but I need you to take the business of managing the
boat as seriously as if you weren't."

Starting at the stern, where the engine was, lesson one was
maintenance. Eve had assumed she wouldn't need to concentrate to absorb this part of the tour, given her familiarity with
the moving parts of machinery more complicated than the old
Perkins diesel that drove the boat. Anastasia, however, was so
detailed, so insistent and so certain they would let her down,
Eve had to jog up the towpath to a garage on the main road
and buy a notebook in which all of this, and subsequent lessons,
could be recorded.

After the maintenance came the driving. They traveled a
mile north, through a lock, turned round and traveled the mile

back. The weather had given itself a shake and was dry, bright and breezy. Within half an hour, Eve had gone from outrage at being expected to move forward so slowly to a happy contempt for motorists driving across the bridge they passed beneath, who thought such speed was necessary.

They moved on to equipping the boat with what was needed to provide Eve and Sally with a level of comfort and utility that was, if not within sight of what they were used to, at least within faint hailing distance. Anastasia was tight-lipped about their list of essentials, and gave herself the right of veto over anything coming on board. Out of Sally's range of kitchen tools for chopping, slicing and mincing, only two knives made it past the gatekeeper.

"What, you think it's so important to have more than one way of chopping things up you'd risk pounds of metal and plastic smashing my cupboard doors every time you hit a lock gate? Which will be every time you go into a lock."

Her washing line was also rejected.

"It'll go overboard and wrap itself round the prop before you've gone a dozen miles. And you don't need it. I have my own system, which is utterly foolproof. Or I hope it is. I don't think I've let a fool near it before now."

Eve was prevented from taking her hair dryer, iPod dock and electric toothbrush.

"The batteries aren't connected to the national grid, as you'd realize if you used your brain."

They both brought quantities of books and both had to take most of them home again.

"You're meant to be going to Chester, not sitting in an armchair surrounded by unnecessary, unsecured ballast."

They spent a day moving Anastasia into Eve's flat. This was superficially simple because she could fit all she needed into two carrier bags, but it felt delicate. She began to diminish as she walked away from the boat. She never looked back at it, as they went down the towpath to the bridge where Sally had parked her husband's car, but the effort involved in leaving it was engraved in every wrinkle, every unyielding fold of practical fabric, every wheezing breath. In the car, she seemed smaller than she had been, as though this contact with a high-speed, terrestrial world was drying out some vital fluid. Noah came with them, to avoid someone else being ambushed by his unearthly pleas for release, and even though he rattled around in the rear compartment commenting on the experience in falsetto, Anastasia said not a word of reproach.

At the flat, Eve and Sally went into the kitchen to make lunch. They could hear Anastasia moving round, muttering. When they came out with the plates of sandwiches, she was in the middle of the living room, looking aggressive and thus reassuringly more like the woman of the *Number One*.

"There's some things you're going to need to do for me before you go, because I don't have the strength to do them for myself."

It took most of the rest of the day to strip the flat of all its softness. Eve would have described her own style as verging on minimalist, but as they sat drinking tea in the environment Anastasia finally declared acceptable, she realized how wrong she had been. She liked the result. Whenever she took on a new department at work, she had applied the "zero budget" approach to identifying the essence and eliminating the padding. Start from the assumption that there is no money and no staff, then

assume there is just enough of both for the first essential function to be delivered with maximum efficiency: how much and
how many would that be? Add the second essential function,
and so on, leaving the inessential on the shelf and emerging
with a lean and powerful organization. That at least was the
theory. Egos, politics, long-established rights, employment law
and other flies had always prevented her from applying the oint-
ment smoothly. Now she thought the same principle could be
adopted in relation to her living quarters. Remove everything
and stop adding things back in when a state of perfect function-
ality had been achieved.

As they cleared up in the kitchen, Eve said to Sally: "Anastasia's not a woman who holds back from expressing an opinion."

"I admire that," Sally said. "I've gone through life working
out what it is that the person I'm talking to would like me to say,
and saying it. I'm forever being nice."

"There's nothing wrong with being nice. I have a tendency
to be a bit confrontational. I'm thinking I must try to be more
like you. Nice."

"I'll try to be more like you, then. Direct."

When the rearrangement was complete, they played Scrabble.
Eve was better at Scrabble than most of her friends; Sally was
as good as she was, as far as she could judge. Anastasia was in a
completely different league. Not only did she know words they
had never dreamed of (aecia), she was able to pull off tricks like
adding "esca" to the beginning of "late," and managed to use all
her letters making "subterfuge" out of "fug." It was a pleasure,
Eve told her, to be beaten by someone with such a mastery of
the game.

"There's a set on the *Number One*," said Anastasia. "If you practice, you might improve. Don't lose any of the tiles. I'll be counting them when I get the boat back."

After Sally left, Eve took Noah out and walked along the damp railings in the local park. Another dog barked in the distance and Noah lifted his head from a smell and looked in that direction, then up at Eve.

"Not worth your valuable time," she murmured. "Not a dog worth bothering with."

He wagged his tail as if this agreed precisely with his judgment, and went back to the smell.

That night, Eve slept on a futon in the room she used as an office. She slept deeply, but in the morning she remembered half-dreams of a lean, upright figure in a long, plain nightdress moving past her open door from bedroom to kitchen and back. In the daylight, Anastasia's eyes were red and her steel wool hair more tangled and scratchy than usual.

"Are you going to be all right?" asked Eve.

"No. I told you. The chances are I'm going to die, no matter what."

"I meant, living here."

"You know the answer to that, too. If you're trying to find out whether I'm regretting the Easy deal, then yes, I am. But however much I want to run out of here back to the *Number One* and carry on as if I'd never bothered asking the bloody doctor about the symptoms, I've come to the conclusion that that would be giving up—and giving up is not what I do. I could say I wouldn't be able to live with myself afterward, but of course the chances are I wouldn't have to. But I wouldn't even fancy dying with myself, if I'd let myself down."

"That's a relief."

"You want to do this?"

"I do."

Anastasia smiled.

Finally, Eve and Sally moved onto the *Number One*. Eve, with Anastasia's example so close by her elbow, took changes of underwear, trousers, T-shirts and jumpers. She left behind all her jewelry, her makeup, her high-heeled shoes and anything which needed to be hung up on a hanger. Neatly put away, all these things were a way of life she had stepped out of but could so easily, with the opening of a wardrobe door, step back into. If she chose.

Eve expected Sally to come festooned with suitcases and overnight bags packed with all the clothes she owned, but she was wrong. Sally arrived on foot, with a rucksack and a carrier bag.

"I just walked away," she said, climbing onto the boat. Eve knew what she meant.

So here they were, en route, with a bend ahead and the sun shining, the rumble of the engine beneath their feet and the breeze created by their passage ruffling the surface of the coffee in their mugs.

2

To Ricksmanworth

ROUND THE BEND WAS a boat, moving toward them, the impossible length of it filling the canal, the man driving it a fingerpost on the distant rear. Everything that Anastasia had said about how to manage the *Number One* rose up in Eve's mind and made no sort of coherent pattern. Go to the left or the right, slow down or speed up, reverse or idle. Even which way to push the tiller became, in that moment, a decision she could not make. The only fact related to the driving of a boat she could be sure of was that it pivots around the midpoint, so moving the front one way will swing the stern the other. At that moment, this felt like a needless and distracting piece of information, like knowing the force effect of two objects colliding at a given terminal velocity, but not knowing where the brakes are.

The figure on the approaching boat bent toward his control panel and sounded his horn. As if, Eve thought, I'm too busy admiring the countryside to notice he's there. She pushed the tiller to pull the front of the *Number One* to the right of the other craft. It started to pivot, as the laws of physics and Anastasia had decreed it would. The front moved out of the way of what she could see was a beautifully painted and polished boat with a man in a form of fisherman's smock standing on the rear watching her, from beneath the brim of a sou'wester-shaped hat, with unwavering calm. The name picked out in gold on the front of the boat was *Algernon*.

As the bow of the *Number One* moved, just in time (a phrase Eve used to use with smug confidence in her industrial days when it was applied to the trivial matter of logistics rather than the life-and-death matter of driving a boat), so the rear swung out as if desperate to deliver the blow to *Algernon*'s paintwork that the front had avoided. *Algernon*'s owner, or possibly Algernon in person, shifted his tiller slightly and Eve, correcting one error with another, opened the throttle to drive the *Number One* through the gap he had created. A collision was avoided and Algernon (he looked like one) chugged past, a slight smile visible between the upstanding collar of his smock and the drooping brim of his hat.

"First day?" he asked, as he went by. "I'd reverse now, if I was you."

The advice came too late. The front of the *Number One* slid into a patch of overhanging willows and changing to reverse made no difference, as the propeller thrashed about in insufficient depth of water to move in any direction. She put the lever in neutral and the boat settled more easily in what water there was, shifting position just enough to allow the willows to sweep aside one of the folding chairs from the front well that they had put on the roof in anticipation of a quiet, sunny lunch in an hour or so. It dangled above the surface of the murky water, full of mud and debris from the *Number One*'s maneuvers, then dropped and sank with barely a bubble to mark its passing.

Noah came rushing up the steps to join Eve and bark at the departing rear end of *Algernon*. The man at the tiller turned his head and raised his hat. Sally came out at the front of the boat, batting aside the willow branches, and said: "Supercilious bastard," which Eve assumed meant Algernon rather than herself. But none of the moral support offered by her crewmates made any difference. She stood, engine idling, and thought: this is Tuesday. I'm meant to be in a Program Planning Meeting, checking the milestones on new product launches. Had she been there, where she ought to be, Eve would have known what she was doing. But instead, here she was, demonstrating to the world—that is Algernon, Noah and Sally, but most of all herself—that she was completely out of control.

Sally was working her way down the side of the boat, sweeping leaves and twigs back into the water as she went. Eve wanted (what had become of her?) to cry, but diverted herself into anger, preparing herself to despise Sally for whatever platitude she was going to utter when she reached the stern: whatever soothing nonsense she was putting together as she minced along the narrow ledge, it would be enough to justify the rage Eve felt mounting within her.

Sally dusted her hands on her jeans and said, "Do you think the frame of that chair is magnetic?"

"What?"

"The frame. We have a magnet on a string, remember, for fishing dropped keys and paddles out of the canal. I wondered if it would work on a folding chair."

"I made a complete fucking balls-up of that," Eve said.

"I'd have hit him," said Sally.

"I bet you wouldn't. I bet you would have steered round him and exchanged pleasantries about the weather."

"No, I meant I would have wanted to punch him on the nose, if I'd been you. But also, I probably would have hit the boat. Let's go fishing."

It took so long to retrieve the chair that Eve calculated it would have been cheaper, had they been paying themselves the minimum wage for doing it, to go and buy a new one. They began by rocking the *Number One* from side to side to free it from the mud, then started the engine and inched it cautiously back and forth over the target area. They used the magnet on a string, and the boat hook to probe the depths, with Eve trying to make sure her jeans weren't exposing any underwear as she hung over the side, and Sally trying to stop Noah licking her face as she hugged a tree trunk to keep the boat steady. Passing boaters behaved appallingly, slowing down and offering to help or wishing them luck. But the satisfaction of seeing the chair finally break the surface at the end of a boat hook and land, dripping and slimy, on the roof, was worth the sacrifice of all the time it took and all the humiliation endured. During the battle to recover it, the *Number One* had begun to feel like their true domain, the three of them its ruling tribe. At least, Eve felt so. She knew so little of Sally.

THEY WENT TO THE PUB, leaving Noah behind. Sally had accepted he was harmless, but she still found him hard to overlook. Whenever he brushed against her leg or stood on her foot she was reminded that she didn't like dogs. Every time Noah caught her eye, she could tell he was noticing that she didn't like dogs. So they left him behind. There was a football match on the TV in the pub but there was little passion for the game, or for this particular match, among the audience. They sat in a loose arc round the screen and talked among themselves, roused only occasionally to expressions of disgust or admiration. Eve went up to the bar. Sally chose a window seat with a view of the backs of the watchers' balding heads and a distant, oblique angle on the footballers. She tried to recall what, in the life before, she would have been watching at this moment on the set at 42 Beech Grove. It was hard enough to remember what day of the week it was.

"I take it you don't want to watch the game," said Eve, coming back with their drinks.

"I don't. I don't mind if you do, though."

Eve shrugged. "I tried to become interested in football. There was a time when I wanted to be one of the boys, before I realized they were not a club worth aspiring to join. I made a real effort to work out what it was all about, and to care about one team above all others, but I couldn't do it. I went along to a few games, in company with an expert, and even that didn't do it for me. So little happens. I'd rather watch snooker. At least in that game, every tap on every ball counts. In football, they can tap the bloody thing back and forth for a full eighty minutes and not a single touch makes a jot of difference at the end."

"I've never watched it," said Sally. "Live or on TV. I've always assumed I wouldn't like it—which isn't very impressive, I know."

"Your husband isn't a fan?"

"No."

On the screen, a goal was scored, or almost scored, or was scored and disallowed. A cluster of blue shirts and yellow shirts dispersed into their constituent parts and a yellow shirt filled the screen, in close-up, supporting a face which could have stood for the model of Christ in agony in a Renaissance painting. The audience half rose from the arc of seats and exclaimed and subsided again, resuming whatever conversation had been interrupted.

"So it wasn't because he was a football bore?" said Eve.

"What wasn't?"

"The walkout. The big break. The 'had-it-up-to-here' moment."

"No. No it wasn't, actually. I never intended to tell anyone this, because it is both strange and trivial, but it doesn't seem to matter now, so here goes. It was *Crocodile Dundee Two*. Or it might have been *Three*. Have there been three?"

"No idea. For the sake of mankind, I'd hope not."

"Exactly. Let's call it *Two*. We're watching *Crocodile Dundee Two* on some TV station for zombies and there's a bit at the end where the hero summons help from his Aboriginal friends to save his wife or the planet or his favorite raccoon hat."

"Wrong continent."

"What?"

"Raccoons. North American."

"Oh. Well, can't have been that, then."

"Sorry."

"It's all right. Crocodile Dundee tells whoever is with him in the middle of the outback, where there is nothing but bare rock and stunted trees and snakes, that he is going to make a phone call. He takes up something like a stick on a string and he whirls it round his head, faster and faster, and it sets up a cadence of sound, rising and falling, making a noise but no sense. Unless you were an Aborigine in the bush, presumably. And as I listened to it, I thought: this is like my husband's voice. Going on and on, rising and falling and creating a noise which is somehow impossible for me to listen to or understand. And I thought: enough."

On the screen the match ended and the watchers drifted away. It was quiet in the pub and Sally had the relaxed feeling, which often came to her in public places, of being alive and safe but without responsibility for herself or anyone else. She had a fondness for supermarkets, where there were always lights and people, where it seemed impossible that death, decay and emotional trauma should exist.

"Did you explain to . . . What is his name, by the way?"

"Duncan. No, of course not. I'd still be there now, trying to make him understand. I just told him I no longer wanted to be married. To him or anyone else."

"How did he take it?"

Sally thought back to the day before she met Eve, the *Number One*, Noah and Anastasia, sitting at the table with Duncan and the celebrity photo obscured by a crumb.

"Quietly," she said.

As they walked back along the towpath in the dark—Anastasia would never have forgotten a torch—Eve asked whether there was anything else, apart from the tendency to drone on, that would justify Sally in taking the step she had.

"Well," said Sally, "he used clichés and—what would you call them?—sayings, aphorisms. Then he'd substitute some rubbish word for the ending. Like 'Too many cooks spoil the Stabat Mater' or 'More haste less polymyalgia.'" Eve laughed. "After a bit," said Sally, stumbling on a piece of rough ground and grabbing Eve's sleeve to stop herself falling, "it stops being funny."

"I'll have to remember that," said Eve. "Many a true word spoken in spaghetti."

"As they say," said Sally.

"What?"

"That's what he would add. 'As they say.'"

"As, indeed, they say. Now, where is the boat?"

As if she had pushed the button on a remote control, Noah set up an unearthly howl, guiding them down the line of moored boats to the *Number One*.

EVE WOKE UP WHEN A shaft of sunlight, striking through the overhead skylight, caught her in the eye. She pulled the curtains open. She habitually wore outsize T-shirts which habitually rode up over her thighs as she slept. She bought them, cheap, wherever she could find them, and most of them were decorated with slogans celebrating long-gone events or achievements that had been celebrated by relatively few people. The one she was wearing this morning said "Northampton East Ladies' Darts Tour 1998" in burgundy letters on a pink background. A badly drawn hand holding a dart of mammoth proportions and doubtful perspective gestured over her left shoulder. She remembered none of this as she reached for the curtains and drew them back.

She had a view of still, slightly scummy but nevertheless sparkling water and a fringe of trees on the far bank. Noah, who was asleep on the floor beside her, reared up and opened his mouth as if in preparation for one of his trademark howls. Instead, he yawned, revealing discolored but functional teeth and a pink tongue. He stretched, a version of dog yoga. Eve wondered whether she might not take up yoga again, in the orderly constraints of the boat. She looked at the thigh exposed by the darts team T-shirt and thought: perhaps jogging.

Noah caught her eye and, so it seemed, jerked his head in the direction of the back of the boat. She rolled out of bed and went through the kitchen, up the steps, slid the hatch cover back and stepped out onto the rear deck, taking hold of the roof to keep herself steady.

To the right and to the left, along the towpath either side of the moored boat, were fishing rods, extended over the canal at random angles between 90 degrees to horizontal. Each rod was attached to a fisherman. Every fisherman's head turned in her direction. Eve let go of the roof of the boat and tugged at the hem of her T-shirt.

"Good morning," she said, to the nearest rod.

"Going soon, are you?" he said.

"I'm not dressed yet."

"That's as maybe, but your boat's blocking Aaron's station. Isn't it, Aaron?"

"Huh," said a youth standing beside him. The crotch of Aaron's trousers was nearer to his knees than his waist, and his knees were not a great distance from the ground.

"And Jason's!" shouted someone else, from farther down the forest of rods.

"And Carl's!" said a voice from the other direction, the speaker obscured by the back end of the *Number One*.

"Your fucking dog's eating my bait!" yelled Aaron.

The *Number One* rocked slightly and Eve rocked unsteadily with it. From the front of the boat, fully awake, fully dressed, setting her feet faultlessly between the fishermen's bags, baskets, boxes and stools, stepped Sally.

"Don't worry," she said, picking Noah up and holding him uncertainly at arm's length. "We're going almost at once." Noah hung limply from her arms and submitted to being handed over to Eve, who dropped him into the front well.

"You'll be cleaning that up, I hope," said the fisherman who had spoken first, indicating where Noah had deposited the contents of his bowel on the worn section of the path where it stood the best chance of attaching itself to a passing foot, like an opportunistic seed looking to find fresh ground to take root.

"Of course," said Eve. Collecting dog feces had not featured in their instructions from Anastasia and it fell outside her experience.

"Here," said a fisherman, and held out a flesh-colored bag.

Sally took it and, with a motion too quick for Eve to follow, collected the little brown pile, tied up the top of the bag and handed it to Eve—who almost dropped it, not anticipating the feel of the plastic and the soft mass of the contents. She looked up to see Sally smiling at her, a secret, joyous, complicit smile.

EVE: Anastasia? Are you there?

ANASTASIA: I picked the thing up, didn't I?

EVE: It's just . . . you didn't say "hello" or anything.

ANASTASIA: It's a machine. I couldn't know who would
    be there.

EVE: Well, it's me. How are you? I mean, any news?

ANASTASIA: Thursday. Test results.

EVE: Oh. Good luck with that.

ANASTASIA: If you're going to waste my time with meaningless phrases, you'd be better employed polishing a bit of paintwork.

EVE: Sorry.

ANASTASIA: Is there any paintwork left to polish?

EVE: We did have a little contretemps with another boat.

ANASTASIA: You mean you hit it.

EVE: No. We missed it.

ANASTASIA: Details?

EVE: We came round a bend and there was this boat in the middle of the canal, and I couldn't quite remember all your instructions. But I promise you, I didn't hit it.

ANASTASIA: What did you hit?

EVE: Trees.

ANASTASIA: Much damage?

EVE: No, only a few scratches. And one of the chairs fell in but we managed to fish it out again.

ANASTASIA: I knew you weren't competent to deal with the unexpected. You'll just have to remember to expect it.

EVE: We'll try.

ANASTASIA: Maintenance regime?

EVE: Yes, oh yes. We're doing that. No worry. Ticking and dating the boxes as instructed.

ANASTASIA: Where are you?

EVE: Hang on. Sally, where are we? Oh, Bridge 174, apparently.

ANASTASIA: As I suspected. Pathetic progress.

Call ended.

EVE: Anastasia? We got cut off.

ANASTASIA: We'd finished talking.

EVE: No, I just wanted to say, about Thursday, what will be will yoghurt pot.

ANASTASIA: Is that complete nonsense?

EVE: It is.

ANASTASIA: Good. Easy!

THEY HAD AGREED TO TAKE turns cooking.

"I should warn you, I'm not used to cooking for other people," Eve said, "unless it's in full-on entertaining mode, and I'm not about to do that sort of thing in these circumstances."

"What sort of thing?" asked Sally.

"You know, three courses, at least one of them using ingredients you can only buy in Waitrose or an Indian shop on the other side of town."

"I am used to cooking for other people," Sally said, "but I've never used ingredients I couldn't buy in Asda or done more than two courses. Or less, come to that. Duncan likes his puddings."

"Please promise me you will not make puddings," said Eve. "I'd only eat them."

Sally cooked first. She sliced and chopped and threw everything into a pan and then turned it out what felt like seconds later, with a mound of rice, on to two plates.

"That was quick," Eve said.

"I never hang about," said Sally. "I seem to have been in a rush my whole life and now I don't know why. I don't know what it was that was so urgent I always had to wear shoes that fastened with Velcro so I didn't have to waste time on laces."

"This is delicious," said Eve, shoveling it in. "I'm going to have to find a way of cooking that is in the middle ground between the dinner party and the ham sandwich. Actually, I'm looking forward to it."

"Tell me," said Sally, "about leaving your job. What happened?" Eve did not reply at once, busy spearing the last grains of rice with her fork. "Or don't tell me, if you don't want to."

"You're being conciliatory again," Eve said. "Stop it at once. I was trying to work out whether I could tell you what happened without any bitterness, like you told me about the end of your marriage. Bitter, self-justifying people—such a bore. And I think, when I go over it in my head, I'm at risk of morphing into one. So this is my chance to stand back and be objective.

"Right. What happened was, Rambusch was taken over by an American conglomerate. I was part of the management team that put together all the performance data to support the takeover, the historical figures and our short- and long-term forecasts. Nothing we put in the documents was wrong, though we massaged the statistics a little. We chose scales for the graphs that made the fluctuations in performance look less dramatic; we presented the forecasts as a midpoint between best and worst case, when in fact they were between the in-your-dreams best and something not as bad as there was an outside chance it would be. But we told the truth.

"Anyhow, it all went swimmingly and we got big bonuses and settled down to be nice to our new owners. Only our new owners turned out to believe that if something goes wrong, the correct response is not to find out why and then to try and stop it happening again, but to find someone to blame. I can't pretend there wasn't already a flavor of this in the Rambusch Corporation. We, the management, were never very tolerant of people who appeared not to be taking their jobs seriously enough, but we were prepared to accept that screw-ups occurred when everyone had been doing their best, and that what lay behind the problem was a process failure or a market failure, or an unforeseeable combination of circumstances. The new parent company didn't think like that. If we presented figures that showed quality defects had risen from 0.8 percent to 1.1 percent against a target of 0.5 percent, they would ask which of us deserved to be fired."

"I can't imagine having to cope with that," said Sally.

"No. Believe me, it's draining. The way round it, as far as my colleagues were concerned, was to lie. If you never showed the figures getting worse, there was nothing to blame anyone for, and their jobs were safe. By the time the truth came out, they would have been able, so they thought, to find a scapegoat. Then they could claim to be as shocked as their new bosses, while reassuring them that the people responsible had gone."

"You were the scapegoat," said Sally.

"Not exactly. The quality wasn't my responsibility, but it was my job to provide updates to the plan and so I was the one signing off on the lies. And there were plenty of good reasons for the dip in quality that were no one's fault: floods, strikes at suppliers—that sort of thing. Look, this isn't boring, is it? I mean, you didn't go into all this detail when I asked you how come you walked out of your marriage."

"It's not boring," said Sally. "And I like the logic of it. This happened, and this was the result. I couldn't explain walking out on Duncan like that. I wish I could."

"Well, I wanted to tell the truth and describe all the problems to the board and my colleagues didn't want me to. They were beginning to talk like their new masters, claiming the managers responsible for quality and the manufacturing plants must be made to do their jobs properly and the fault rate would miraculously improve, and we would be able to justify the blip retrospectively by pointing to the underperforming subordinates who had been shaken up.

"I couldn't go along with it. I am prepared to tell a good story, but only if I feel I can back it up when challenged. And I said so. I was used to being heard, in that company, and to being listened to as an equal. I had never held back in the past, if I felt strongly about something, and if anything, this had worked in my favor. But this time I wasn't criticizing business decisions, I was telling them what I thought about the way they were behaving. What I thought about them. No going back after that. All of a sudden, I just wasn't one of them."

"Did you still want to be?"

"Ah, the right question. I don't know. Maybe I'll be able to tell you the answer by the time we get to Chester."

As she cleaned her teeth in the tiny space in front of the tiny basin, Eve tried to recall the impotence and, because of the impotence, the anger she had felt through all the conversations about whether she would be happier in another (subordinate, nonexistent) role, or whether she felt her future lay elsewhere. How on earth, she thought, bracing her feet against the movement of the boat caused by a passing wash, could it ever have mattered so much?

SALLY WAS AT THE HELM. Eve sat beside her on a locker and looked around: at the sky, a fading vapor trail the only mark on its blue surface; at the reeds growing in the water where the bank had broken down, bowing to the *Number One* as it passed; at the moored boats, carrying their badges of entitlement, their warning notices and padlocks; at Sally. Sally was watching the canal ahead. She was wearing a pair of brown corduroy jeans and a beige T-shirt. Her hair was neat, on the blond side of brown; her features were even and unremarkable.

Eve picked up the Nicholson Guide lying beside her.

"Where are we?" she asked.

"Just passed Bridge 175," said Sally.

Eve studied the Nicholson. "I've been thinking, anyone called Yasmin ought to be bold and colorful and unconventional. You need a complete makeover to bring out the inner Yasmin in you."

"I'm not sure it's there. Truly, I'm not. I know I talked about highlights, but all that's a bit of wrapping paper. I'll still be the same old parcel of nothing very exciting underneath."

"When I joined Rambusch," said Eve, "I was wearing M&S separates and behaved like it. You know what I mean. Or you may not, but the clothes I chose for work were diffident. They had that 'not wanting to offend-ness,' a sort of 'don't want to stand out-ness.' The men all strutted about in suits and striped ties and pointy lace-ups and behaved as if they expected respect, demanding attention. I got the reaction I wanted, and so did they."

"I can see where this is going, but you aren't a diffident person and I am. I'm a definite M&S separates person."

"But what you see now is where I've got to, not where I was. You don't know how much I had to grow into the arrogant bitch I succeeded in becoming."

"So you went out and bought a suit and high heels and started to strut? And that worked?"

"No, actually, it didn't work too well because it wasn't my style, but it was a step on the road."

"And you think I ought to take the first step on the road to becoming Yasmin by jazzing myself up?"

"I do. Let's stop in Rickmansworth. It's a couple of locks and a mile away. It looks big enough to have a few charity shops. We'll find something outrageous for you to wear."

The moored boats stretched out for some distance before they reached the town, a trailing string of floating habitation guiding them into where the solid houses of solid citizens began. Eve, who was driving, throttled back as instructed by Anastasia to avoid the wash rocking the boats they passed. It also meant she was able to compare the *Number One* with the alternatives lined up along the towpath. Many were smarter, one or two were scruffier. None, she thought, managed to look as authentic as the *Number One*, quite as sensible and workmanlike. The scruffy boats were proclaiming the determination of the owners to be alternative. The smarter ones were all, to a greater or lesser degree, displaying in miniature the native habitat of the house owners whose holiday homes they were. The hire boats, at least, were uniform and bland, whereas some of the worst excesses of the privately owned were shockingly twee.

They found a space on a mooring near the road leading into town.

"Does it make you feel like a gypsy, driving into a new town in your home and walking about as a stranger?" Eve asked.

"No," said Sally. "Not really. But it does feel like being on holiday. Are we on holiday?"

"I would say so."

They found a charity shop where Eve picked out everything in Sally's size—and more things were in her size than any other—that was brightly colored, seriously patterned, unconventionally styled, or all three. Sally took an armful of these into the curtained cubicle and came out wearing a black skirt with an asymmetric hemline and a broad band of red swooping from top left to bottom right. On top she wore a silver sleeveless T-shirt under a red T-shirt with slashes in it, and a black bolero jacket with embroidered flowers. There had been no one in the shop when she went into the changing room, but by the time she came out an elderly couple and a determined young woman had turned up and were clicking the hangers on the racks. Everyone—the strangers and Eve—stood still and looked at Sally as she struck the curtain aside and strode out among them. The color began to rise in her face.

"Nice jacket," said the younger woman, turning back to the trouser rail. "I wish I could get away with something like that."

"It suits you," said the older woman.

Sally ducked back into the cubicle and, having checked the other shoppers had left, came out in an Indian cotton sundress.

"I knew you were a Yasmin," said Eve.

On the next street they passed a hairdresser who was able to do highlights, if they came back in an hour. They ate lunch in a café, then Eve went back to the *Number One* and swabbed all horizontal surfaces, inside and out, until Yasmin returned, the bright pink flecks in her hair brightening up the drabness of her clothes.

"That'll clash with the red T-shirt," said Eve.

"Good."

3

To Milton Keynes

ON EITHER SIDE OF the canal were fields, pasture, hedges, sheep. If there were buildings and roads, they were penned in behind the contours and the trees and might as well not have been there. Sally was at the tiller of the *Number One*, wearing a turquoise top, her head tilted up as if the color in her hair had weight, was lifting her chin in counterbalance, forcing her to take a longer, loftier view. There was a boat moored ahead, just before a bridge. It was the sort of gray that is the faded remains of other, more purposeful colors. On the rear deck and the roof were bundles of wood, a wheelbarrow, plastic drums full of soil and dead or wilting vegetables, tarpaulins, lengths of rope and hoses, randomly cast down. The name on the stern, fittingly, was *Grimm*. Sitting on the grassy bank by the bridge was a slight figure which stood up as the *Number One* approached and held up both arms in a curious, imperious gesture. Sally had already slowed for the bridge and the moored boat, and now reduced speed further. She could see that the figure was female, wearing a summer dress in a style from the fifties, full-skirted, tight-waisted. Her hair was cut short and square and stood out round her head at the same angle as her skirt stood out round her legs, making her look as if she was composed of triangles.

Eve came up from below.

"Help," said the figure when they were within earshot. She said it with no volume or emphasis, more a command than a request.

Sally put the *Number One* into reverse and they came to a halt, the bow nudging the bridge, the back a few feet behind the gray boat, which was shorter in length.

"What sort of help have you got in mind?" asked Eve.

Noah, who had been lying on his back with all his undercarriage exposed when Eve left the cabin, appeared through the door, right way up and moving at the speed of an empty plastic bottle approaching a weir. He skipped from the *Number One* to the back of the other boat, to the towpath, and had buried his nose between the legs of the figure on the bank by the time Eve had finished her question. Toppling backward under the pressure of paws and muzzle, the girl sat down and folded her arms round the wriggling body of the dog.

"Noah, Noah, no, no, Noah!" she shouted.

Another boat began to inch through the bridge toward them, and Sally reversed and maneuvered the *Number One* to sit alongside the towpath behind *Grimm*. The oncoming barge cruised past them, the middle-aged couple on the stern staring at the tangle of dog and girl on the grass.

"I said," repeated Eve, "what sort of help?"

"Oh," the girl stood up and shook herself. Noah dropped from her lap and lay down on the towpath, at once, so it seemed, asleep. "It won't go." She jerked her head toward the gray barge, bobbed hair flaring out then landing, strand by strand, back in the same position. "Where's Anastasia?"

"In Uxbridge."

"How can she be in Uxbridge when the *Number One* is here in front of me? It's way, way too far to walk from there to here, so how can she be in Uxbridge?"

"Nevertheless, she is," said Eve.

"Who are you, then?" asked the girl, bending down to grip Noah's muzzle with both hands and blowing up his nose.

Sally provided both their names. Eve wasn't sure that was what the girl meant, but she seemed satisfied.

"Trompette," she said.

Eve was convinced she had misheard this, that the girl had managed to wrap up a sneer in some phrase in French or a nonsense word.

"Trompette?" said Sally.

"Yes."

"Are you on your own on the boat, Trompette?"

"No. There's Billy."

"Where's Billy?"

"Oh, yes, he could sort it," said Trompette, as if responding to the next question rather than the last one. "But he's smashed."

"I see."

Noah had wandered off down the towpath in search of smells.

"When you say it won't go," said Eve, "do you mean the engine won't go, or it won't drive the boat?"

"The engine's all right," said Trompette.

Eve stepped onto the back of the gray barge and opened what she now knew was called a weed hatch, which gave a view of the rudder. The shadow of the bridge and the muddiness of the water meant she could see nothing at all. She sank her hand down into the opaque wetness, watching her spread fingers as they took on the green then the brown of the water until they were deep enough to be without light at all. It felt slimy, viscous, surprisingly warm. And empty. She lay down on her stomach and reached farther in. She found a soft, ticklish frond, seized hold of it and pulled upward. It broke the surface to reveal itself as a strand of rope—which was a relief as there were other, more organic possibilities in her mind as her hand made the upward journey.

Only a foot or so of the rope cleared the surface; the rest remained tethered in the depths.

"Do you remember what Anastasia said about the washing line?" she asked.

"I do," said Sally. "She said we'd only let it trail over the side and it would get wrapped round the rudder."

Trompette was sitting cross-legged on the cabin roof eating an apple which she had produced without apparently disturbing her triangular clothing or entering the boat.

"That's not a washing line," she said. "That's a mooring rope."

"She warned us about that, too," said Sally.

Eve looked over the side of the boat and saw that only one rope, tied to the roof rail, was being used to hold the gray barge to the bank.

"Are you short of a mooring rope, by any chance?" she asked.

Trompette flicked her apple core into the air. Noah came hurtling down the towpath and arrived in time to catch it as it fell.

"Looks like it," she said.

"Well," said Eve, waving the loose, frayed end she still held, "there's your fault. From what Anastasia told us, the only way to sort it is to cut through it, strand by strand."

There was a pause. When no one else had spoken or moved for some moments, Sally said:

"Will Billy do that? When he's not smashed, I mean."

Trompette lay down flat on her back. Noah lay down on his stomach.

"He could, but you see we need a pump-out. I want to move now."

"You shouldn't have let the fucking rope trail in the water, then, should you?" Eve pointed out. "And never mind about Billy, can't you do it?"

"If I had to," said Trompette.

Eve looked at the scummy water then at Trompette's triangular perfection, and then at Sally, who smiled at her. Then she lay down on her stomach again.

It took an hour with her arms in the water for Eve to clear the tangled rope, using a knife Trompette found for her, a wooden-handled clasp knife with a very sharp blade. There was some satisfaction in it. The sun on the nape of her neck, the small triumphs as pieces of rope came loose, the narrow limits to the problem—three square feet of water three inches from her face—and the weight of Noah's body propped up against her legs. As well as the feeling of triumph when the last piece pulled free. Eve closed the knife and slid it into her jeans pocket. She put her arm into the water one last time and ran her fingers over the smooth surface of the shaft.

"Done," she said, standing up.

They moved off in convoy, the *Number One* ahead of *Grimm*,

Sally steering the one and Trompette, looking pert and unper-
turbed and architecturally still, at the tiller of the other. Billy
had yet to appear. Eve was sitting cross-legged on the roof of
the *Number One* looking at the view, which was open and un-
dulating. Noah was leaning against her left knee, reminding
her, via a small but insistent ache, that she had given up not just
yoga but going to the gym. On the other hand, she never used
to walk anywhere except along corridors and across car parks,
and she'd been striding down towpaths for what felt like miles
since the journey started. It was hardly surprising her joints and
muscles were sending out distress signals.

The locks on this stretch of canal were wide enough to take
both boats together. At the first lock, Eve scrambled onto the
bank and emptied it, opened the gates, let the two boats in,
filled it, opened the gates to let them out, closed the gates.
There were two gates at each end, and though Anastasia had
said it was possible to push open the opposite gate with a boat
hook, she had advised against this until they were more sure-
footed. Instead, Eve had to jog from end to end, then cross the
closed gates to reach the opposite side. Sally gave her encourag-
ing smiles. Trompette didn't.

At the second lock, Sally did the work. She raised the paddles to fill the lock, first on one side, then on the other. She
leaned against the last one, preparing to let them down again,
carefully, as Anastasia had directed.

"You need the key to turn the shaft so the sneck releases. If
you let go, the paddle will drop and the key will spin round and
fly off and cripple you. I don't want cripples in charge of my
boat. So hold the key and turn it until the paddle is down."

As the *Number One* and *Grimm* sank down with the falling

water, Sally became aware of a drumming sound. She leaned in closer to see if it was rising up from the mechanism working the lock, then looked round to see if it was the wind snapping a taut wire or a branch beating on a roof.

Dum Dumdedumdedumde. Dum. Dum. Dum Dumdedumde-dumde.

Trompette was standing with the throttle in her hand ready to move forward once the lock was full and the gate open. As she guided *Grimm* out, the drumming increased and what seemed to be a lavatory brush rose from within the boat in time to its beat. All Sally could see was the tortured bristles of a wiry head of hair and the flash of white hands paddling the taut skin of a conical drum. The figure moved from the stern to the roof in easy, feline movements, settling himself in the same space among the debris that Trompette had occupied earlier.

"A boat which is the *Number One*," he said, "and two women who are not Anastasia."

"She's in Uxbridge," said Trompette.

"Uxbridge?"

"So they say."

❧

SALLY: Hello?

ANASTASIA: You're shouting.

SALLY: Sorry. I was ringing to see how you got on at the hospital yesterday.

ANASTASIA: I went. I waited. I was talked at, very seriously, came home again and thought about what had been said.

SALLY: What did you think?

ANASTASIA: I thought it would be helpful if I considered my body as a fridge.

SALLY: A fridge?

ANASTASIA: Exactly. In a fridge, unwanted deposits build up. Mold, ice crystals, puddles of water, that kind of thing. The fridge keeps on doing what it does only too exuberantly, or not exuberantly enough. Now, if I owned such a fridge, I would get in there with the scraper and the bleach and the sponge and I'd chip and swab and mop. Then I'd see if I could work out what caused the problem, and fix it.

SALLY: I'm following.

ANASTASIA: What I wouldn't do, is throw the thing away. If I couldn't fix the problem and it happened again, I'd scrape and swab and mop again. And again. And finally, I would decide the fridge was no longer a fit thing to take up space in my boat and I'd throw it out.

SALLY: Yes. I see that.

ANASTASIA: So, I made up my mind to let the professionals scrape and swab and mop and try and fix the problem rather than throwing myself away at the first sign of a malfunction.

SALLY: Do they think they can?

ANASTASIA: How should I know?

SALLY: What do they say?

ANASTASIA: What they say is blather. It's what they don't say that is relevant.

SALLY: Right. What didn't they say?

ANASTASIA: They didn't say I'd live for years, but then again they didn't say I'd be dead in six months.

SALLY: Well, that's hopeful.

ANASTASIA: No it isn't. The only reason not to give me the first piece of information is because it is unlikely to turn out to be true. There are numerous reasons why they might not have mentioned the second piece of information, of which the possibility of it not being true is only one.

SALLY: No, but had it definitely been true, I suspect they would definitely have said it.

ANASTASIA: I try not to indulge in naïve optimism. And the *Number One*?

SALLY: What? Oh! Everything's great. We're writing down everything in the logs, the maintenance, the distance, the top-ups, that kind of thing. And we've got a chart, just so you don't think we're not telling you everything. So far, Eve is ahead, or behind, if you see what I mean. She's bumped the front going into three locks and under one bridge and I've hit the front four times and the side twice. We carry out an inspection every night when we stop and, so far, we don't seem to have caused much damage.

ANASTASIA: Good.

End of call.

SALLY: Anastasia? Did you ring off?

ANASTASIA: You'd told me what I wanted to know.

SALLY: Yes, but you hadn't told me everything I wanted
     to know. Any news on when they might be planning
     an operation?

ANASTASIA: No. And if there was, I wouldn't tell you.

SALLY: Why not?

ANASTASIA: Cards, flowers, visits, bunches of grapes.

SALLY: If we promise to do none of that?

ANASTASIA: I'll know in the next few weeks.

SALLY: Easy!

ANASTASIA: Easy!

NOAH DISAPPEARED. OVER THE PRECEDING days, miles, locks
and bridges, Eve had conceived a fancy that she had formed a
relationship with Noah capable of being described as ownership.
The dog, she thought, clove to her. The word had cropped up in
a Scrabble game the night before. Eve had found a place to put
it and had contemplated it smugly while Sally thought about her
move, recognizing its neatness (so much more satisfying and
less messy than "cleave") and aptness to the warm weight of fur
and limbs even then asleep on her foot. Then Sally put down
"astonish," with an "s" at the end of "clove," scoring 82 points
and completely destroying the symmetry of the moment.

Noah slept in Eve's cabin, looked earnestly and hopefully
into her face when it was time for him to be fed. Further, and
more tellingly, he had been known to come when she called
him. Sally, he ignored. This notion of a relationship, of some
piece of flesh made warm by circulating blood to which she was
emotionally necessary, had cheered Eve every morning as she
opened her eyes on the whiskered face tilted to one side, and

each night as she fell asleep to the sound of the whiffling snores coming from the floor beside her. When they met Trompette, Noah's performance with the maiden in distress had been as cruel a shock as the time when, as a teenager, she had assumed a boy she fancied was asking her to dance at a friend's party when in fact he was only holding out a hand to take her dirty plate away from her. How easily, she bitterly reflected, was she lulled into complacency.

But despite this, he was hers, and she was his. And as they were eating lunch, it came to Eve that he had gone. She had made lunch. She had always tried to minimize the time she spent in the kitchen, in her previous life, but had found she was beginning to enjoy preparing such simple dishes as were within her capability, in the orderly, constrained space of the *Number One*'s kitchen. So she was distracted over making an effort, and did not notice he was not there until the food was on the plates and they had begun to eat. Whatever was on the table, Noah would be a constant, uncritical observer, chin on paws and eyebrows raised one after the other as his eyes swiveled from plate to plate. And now here he was, absent.

"Where's Noah?" she said.

"As if I would know," said Sally. "Or care." She sniffed the air. "It still smells as if there is a dog on the boat, but that doesn't mean there is."

Eve went up onto the towpath and began to call the dog. They were moored with other boats, most of them occupied, and her cries of "No-ah, No-ah"—with the emphasis despairingly on the first syllable—mingled with the sound of music and chat and laughter. She stuck her head through the hatch of the *Number One*.

"I don't expect you remember when you saw him last?"

"About an hour ago," said Sally.

"I'm going to look for him."

"You know that's a waste of time!" Sally shouted after her. "Anastasia told us: he'll come back."

"I know," called Eve. "But I'm going to look for him anyway."

She walked back the way they had come, past other boats, under a bridge, over a lock, out into the featureless miles of overhanging trees and open pasture. She counted her steps and called his name every hundred paces. She passed a pair of lovers welded together in the shadow of a leaning chestnut. She overtook a solitary man then a solitary woman who might have set out together but were now resolutely apart. Two bicycles, wobbling onto the uneven grass to avoid her, then a jogger came past in the opposite direction. She diverted round a mother, toddler and buggy feeding an inharmonious gathering of ducks. For a long while she saw no one. A heron lifted slowly from the water's edge ahead of her as if it resented the need to move for her convenience. Spirals of tiny flying insects drifted along the surface of the canal. In the distance, the sound of a helicopter became audible, then louder, then dipped away.

"No-ah! No-ah!" shouted Eve. But he hardly ever came to her calls. He was a dog who made eye contact. If he wanted her to do something for him, if she wanted him to do something for her, they would catch each other's eye.

A piece of hawthorn twig became caught in her sandal and she stopped to remove it. She had no idea how far she had walked, but nearly an hour had passed since she'd left the boat. It seemed, simultaneously, impossible that she would ever find the dog, and almost certain that he would be around the next bend. She licked her finger and wiped away the smear of blood from the scratch inflicted on her by the twig, and kept walking.

"No-ah! No-ah!"

She passed two more bridges and started down a straight stretch with a lock in the distance. There was a dog running toward her, but it was the wrong dog. It bounded past her, all yellow and hairy. The owner came up. He was old, gray and bent, a slow-moving, crooked figure wearing a hat with a brim, a suit and tie and polished lace-up shoes. For a brief moment, Eve forgot about Noah as she tried to imagine what would lead a man to choose such clothes to walk his dog along a canal towpath. As she wondered, the dog barked, and another answered it.

The bank on the other side of the canal was steep and covered in scrub, and there, right on the edge, where the ground gave way to water, was Noah. He was almost vertical, with his front paws dug into the mud and his back end up in the air, but his tail was wagging and he looked ready for anything.

"Noah, Noah!" shouted Eve, the emphasis falling on the second syllable. The other dog owner stopped beside her.

"Can he swim?" he asked.

"I don't know, I don't know," said Eve, struggling to release her phone from the pocket of her jeans. "Stay there, Noah," she commanded. "Stay there."

"His options would seem to be limited," said the man, who clearly had a dog too pernickety to risk the undergrowth.

Eve dialed the number of her flat. When the receiver was picked up, she said: "Can Noah swim?"

"All dogs can swim," said Anastasia.

"Is that a 'yes'?"

"All dogs can swim," repeated Anastasia, "but not all dogs do swim."

"And is Noah a dog that can and does, or a dog that can but doesn't?"

"I've never seen him do it."

"He's on the wrong side of the canal in the middle of nowhere and I don't know how to get him back."

"Tch, tch," said Anastasia. (Eve later tried to reproduce this sound for Sally, but it was unrepeatable.) "What did I tell you the first time we met? The dog will always come back."

The other dog began to bark at a jogger in the distance.

"Silas!" shouted his owner, with the emphasis on the last syllable.

Noah was still in the same position, alternately barking and wagging his tail. Eve squatted down on the very edge of the path. She was not a natural squatter and the position was hard to hold but it made her feel closer to Noah, even if forty feet apart in the horizontal plane. Also climbing into the opaque brown water remained a possibility, and it appeared more achievable when she was this close.

"Noah, Noah," she whispered. Noah wagged his tail. Then the weight of Silas, who clearly thought she was at his level to play with him, being a dog of no brain, fell against her and pitched her sideways. She put an elbow out to break her fall but it missed the edge of the towpath and she momentarily felt herself to be rolling toward the water. She corrected the movement at the expense of all dignity and sprawled, face down, with her legs splayed out and her hands grasping at tufts of grass. Something that felt and smelled like a very wet dog started nuzzling and bumping her. As she tried to push it away she caught sight of a leg on the edge of her vision and it was white, not yellow; short, not long. Not Silas; Noah.

She rolled over and let the dog jump on her, all four, wet and slimy legs and the wet and slimy tongue and the dog's breath of him on her chest and her face. She folded her arms around the dripping bundle and hugged.

"Are you all right?" asked Silas's owner. "Do you need any help?"

He didn't look a robust enough figure to supply any help, had she needed it, so she shook her head, rolled over and sat up. Then she began to cry.

"Steady on," said the man.

"How ridiculous is this?" sobbed Eve. "I haven't cried in public since I was eight, when Miss Clutterbuck told me to pull my socks up in assembly and I thought she meant it literally, so I did."

"I don't have a hanky. Or a Kleenex."

"No need. I have a T-shirt." She wiped her face on it.

He walked back with her toward the *Number One*, Noah skipping along ahead of them as if he was the sort of dog accustomed to orderly strolls after dinner, and Silas lagging behind to examine every blade of grass.

"Did you really do that?" asked the man.

"Do what?"

"Pull your socks up?"

"I did. They were only little white ankle socks, so I couldn't pull them up very far. Everyone laughed."

"Everyone?"

"It's true. The teachers, the other children, the caretaker. I wouldn't be surprised if the bust of the founder wasn't having a quiet snigger."

Noah looked back at the sound of their laughter, then shook his ears and ran on.

"You know," said the man, "when people leap into water to save a dog, and someone drowns, it is always the owner, never the dog."

"I don't think I would have drowned. Not in a canal. I can swim."

"I don't suppose you would. That's not what I'm saying."

"No, I see. The dog always comes back. That's what Anastasia says."

"I thought I might have recognized the dog. I will be turning round now, but do give my regards to Anastasia. Tell her you met Parnassus."

"Is that your name?"

"No, it's the name of the boat which I live in whenever I can escape from the carefulness of my daughters. They think I should be spending my retirement walking to and from the newsagent in my slippers."

"I think I might have spotted that as we came past. Rather elegant? Mainly black and simple?"

"How kind of you to say so. It is my pride and joy."

He raised his hat and Eve lifted a hand and they parted.

IT WAS HOT. MOVEMENT WAS too much effort; everything was still. In the ripple of the *Number One*'s wake the weeds and reeds lifted and fell and were motionless again. Around the middle of the afternoon they reached a lock, beside a road bridge and a pub. The pub had a large garden and a children's playground and was pulsating with people, colorful as to clothing and exposed flesh. There was no escape from the sun below the lock, but above it they could see a line of trees, so they went through. There was no need to put in any effort as an embarrassment of helpers was ready to open and close the gates and the paddles. Anastasia had directed them to refuse all such help as the general public could not be trusted to operate the paddles safely and let the water in, or out, gently enough to avoid damaging the boat. But Anastasia was no doubt impervious to heat and indifferent to exposing her summer wardrobe to close scrutiny by the frequenters of pub gardens, and Sally and Eve were neither impervious nor indifferent. So they stayed on the boat, smiling and trying not to hit the lock gates.

Grimm was moored above the lock; there was no sign of Trompette or Billy, but there was what could have been an old sheet hanging from the roof on the towpath side and the public strolling past all stopped to look at it. Eve and Sally moored the *Number One* farther off, under the trees, beyond the official moorings so there were no bollards and they had to hammer stakes into the unyielding earth. They put the sparse mattresses from the cabin on the roof and lay, drinking lemon squash and taking bets on the color of the next boat to come past. After half an hour only two had, and they were both the wrong color.

The sun was beginning to drop and the heat, though still gripping, was less extreme, so they stood up and walked down the towpath to look at *Grimm*'s sheet. It had red letters painted on it, which read:

Canal Stories
Hear it Here
Tonight

When the light was fading and the crowd in the pub had thinned out, Billy came out of *Grimm* and walked down the path, beating his drum. He walked from *Grimm* past the pub garden to the lock, along the lock and back. Then he set out again, only this time Trompette, a crisp little butterfly all in white, followed after him with a handbell which she rang at every fifth beat. Every tenth beat, she called out: "Story time!"

People began to wander toward them. After four passes, they had a small crowd assembled: sitting on the lock gates, on the grassy towpath, on the low wall round the pub garden, on folding chairs and cushions. Eve sat on one of the bollards beside *Grimm*, but Sally did not feel ready to commit herself to this experience, so she held back, leaning against a post a little nearer the *Number One*, a little farther from the crowd.

It was still daylight but, after the drum stopped beating, *Grimm* began to look mysterious, in its grayness and stillness, with a largely silent crowd around it. Sally could not see Trompette, only Billy. He was standing on the back of the boat with a Chinese lantern, unlit, which he placed on the edge of the roof. He jumped to the towpath and held his arms up; the one or two murmurs in the crowd were cut off and it became still.

Billy began:

Let me tell you a story—a true story. It happened here, on this towpath; maybe not on the very same section of this towpath as you are sitting on now, but close. Just about here, or hereabouts.

Somewhere you've passed or will pass.

It's 1847. Think back. In a hundred years, the Second World War will be over. Thirty-two years ago, the Battle of Water-loo was fought and won. Queen Victoria is on the throne and she's twenty-eight years old and married to Albert. This is the Grand Junction Canal and it has been open for upward of forty years. A masterpiece of engineering ingenuity. And toil. Hours and hours of hard work, months and years of hard living.

As he spoke the last sentence, Billy seemed to bend under the weight of the words. He was wearing a loose, coarse jacket, a handkerchief round his neck and clips on his trousers, immediately below the knee. Now he took a flat hat from his pocket and set it on his head. There was an illustrated history of the canals on Anastasia's shelf of books and Sally recognized the figure of Billy as a character from the photographs; any one of the bargemen captured by an early camera, standing by his boat or his horse. When Billy began to speak again, his voice was rougher, more melancholy. As he talked, he trudged up and down the towpath past the watching faces to the bollard where Eve sat, and back again.

It's October. You can feel the chill through your worn coat, the wind gets under your neckerchief and cuts you to the bone and you're bone-tired. Your name is Isaac Bridges and you work for Bissell's in Tipton, taking cargo to London and back. From Tipton to London by canal is 154 miles and there are 69 locks. You've walked those 154 miles, worked those 69 locks, taking a boatload of iron to Paddington Basin. It took you seven days. You've unloaded your iron and loaded up the hold with corn, and you're on your way back to Tipton. The barge is heavy and the horse is sleepy and you're walking along behind him, driving him forward. You're thinking of the inn you'll be stopping by tonight, picturing the tankard of ale that'll be waiting for you, tasting the bitterness of it and the strength of it on your tongue as you go on putting one foot in front of the other, keeping the horse moving. And there, in your mind, is the end of the day; the moment when you lay yourself down next to your wife, Ann; you're thinking of the comfort and softness of her as the miles go by. It's her stout little figure you can see at the tiller of your boat—or you could see her, if you had the energy to turn your head sideways and look.

Billy didn't turn his head to look, but the audience did, as surely as if he had lifted a finger and pointed, to make them take note of the hunched, shapeless bundle of clothes that was suddenly—or was it sudden? had it been there all along?—at the tiller.

You've walked as far as . . . say hereabouts. Between Cowley and Braunston. Coming toward you is another barge. Laden, low in the water. Another horse pulling another rope. This is no surprise. You've passed several boats already, traveling toward London, and you've crossed smoothly. There are rules; the right way to do things. These rules are written down, pinned up in the toll houses at the locks, but you don't need reminding. You know how to do it.

The boat going toward Tipton—yours—keeps to the towpath side. The boat going toward London—his—moves over to the opposite side. Your horse keeps to the side of the towpath by the water's edge. The other horse passes on the hedge side and, as the horses and boats meet, the London-bound boatman lets his rope go loose. Your horse steps over it. Your boat floats over it. The other boatman waits till you are clear of it then takes up the slack and goes his way. That's the way to do it.

Only the boatman coming the other way doesn't do it. His name is William Hickman, though you don't know that until later. He's only been working this canal a few months and you've never seen him before. He's younger than you. As you walk toward him, you call out—you're pretty sure you will have called out—"Pull your horse to the hedge side!" But William Hickman keeps his horse by the water's edge. His boat is on the far side of the canal, as it should be, but there is no room for you to pass his horse on the canal side of the towpath. It all comes upon you too quickly. You have no time to think. There's a horse where it shouldn't be, two ropes strung across the path going opposite ways. You lift yours up and over his horse's head—what else were you to do? You pass him, but it's all wrong, it's all wrong. You're trying to hold your rope up and look round to see what is happening behind you. You see William Hickman's rope sweep across the roof of your boat. You see Ann, caught up, swept off her seat. You hear the splash as she is dragged backward into the canal by a rope that has her caught up in its strong, wet grip.

There was a splash. Something moved on *Grimm*'s roof—too quick to see what, or by whose hand—and the woman-shaped bundle was jerked off into the canal. The audience gasped. One or two even took a step toward the canal, but Billy was there, between them and the edge of the towpath.

"Stop the horse, stop the horse!" you shout. Then you jump into the canal, of course you do. There's Ann, with her long skirts, her petticoats, her shawls wrapped round her and over her head to keep off the chill—it's October, it's near the end of the day. You jump in and your brother Alfred, who works for Bissell's, too, and is following along behind with another boat, another cargo, comes running up to help you. You reach Ann, loosen the rope, try to hold her up—she's not helping herself—grab the end of the rope Alfred has thrown to save you both. You reach the bank; pull Ann out, the whole weight of her, the plumpness of the body and the wetness of the clothes. You look up and see William Hickman standing, watching, a little way off. When he sees you out of the water, he clicks his tongue at the horse and walks on.

"You'll pay for this," you say, or maybe you only think it.

Billy moved aside and there, on the towpath, was the wet bundle of clothes that might have been Ann Bridges.

Well, is that the end of the story? Is it? Oh, no. Not for Isaac, not for William, not yet for Ann. She is taken to hospital, hardly conscious . . . But wait a minute, what about William Hickman? Shouldn't we hear his story, too? Imagine you're William, for a moment. Indulge me.

He straightened up, loosened his necktie, tilted his hat at a different angle and was at once a fitter, jauntier man.

You've tried a few things in your life and done well at them, but nothing has quite suited you, you haven't found something to stick to. You've always been a laboring man; you've worked with horses, and with boats, the first on the farms, then the other in the port and on the rough, rough sea. You've not long started in the canal business—you know boats, you know horses and you're just beginning to think this is the right line for you. You're quick; you get a move on, work hard, don't drink or fornicate more than the next man—maybe less, because you're always looking ahead, ready to spot the next chance coming along, and you won't succeed in getting a hold of it if you're forever nursing a headache, or dreaming of the lock-keeper's daughter.

So here you are. It's October 1847, and you're driving your horse along the towpath somewhere between Braunston and Cowley, keeping one eye on the boy you've got steering the boat—you're not sure he's to be trusted—and the other on the horse, making sure it keeps up a good pace. And along comes old Isaac Bridges, plodding toward Tipton, head down. You don't know him, but you know his type. His horse is in the middle of the towpath and you slow your pace a little, waiting to see which side he's going to go. Oh, you know the passing rule all right, but you've noticed not everyone obeys it, so you don't make assumptions. You watch to see what this dozy old beggar is going to do. He doesn't call out to you—you're sure of that, nothing wrong with your hearing—and he seems to be drifting toward the hedge side, so you keep on the water's edge. What else are you supposed to do? You're new to this game, don't know the people; it's not up to you to shout instructions to a man who's probably been up and down this towpath every week since it was first built.

Old Isaac wakes up as you pass him and lifts his rope over your horse's head. He seems to be in a complete muddle, fusses

over the rope, not watching where he's going, what he's doing.
You're distracted, too. There's more slack in your rope than there
would normally be because you checked your pace, and you were
preparing to drop it down, if Isaac had taken the path he should
have done. So the rope isn't taut, and so isn't high enough out of
the water to clear Isaac's boat. There's his wife, all wrapped up
like a woman who has to wear all her clothes on her back be-
cause she's no space to store them. Dozing away like Isaac. Your
rope snakes over the top of the barge toward her. You think—
and this is something you can't prove, and you'd never get Isaac
and that brother of his to back you up, but you think that Isaac's
rope also comes adrift from the mast it's fixed to for towing. You
think that's what was bothering him, fussing about on the bank.
So, and this is important, you don't think it was your rope caught
round the old lady. No. When it was all over, your rope was
lying loose in the water and you think it was Isaac's own rope
that grabbed old Ann and jerked her off her perch.

After the splash—two splashes as they go in one after the
other—you stop your horse and wait to see them hauled out
onto the towpath like two parcels of dirty washing. Then you
move on. You thought that was the end of the story. But it
wasn't. Except for Ann. Time to shed a tear for Ann.

Billy took off his hat and pointed to the bundle. Trompette
appeared with a wheelbarrow that normally sat among the other
debris on the roof, loaded the wet clothes into it, and wheeled it
away as Billy kept talking.

She's on the bank. She's not looking too good so a cart is called
and she's taken to hospital. The doctor comes. Looks at her

wrist, sees the mark of a rope on her skin. Shakes his head over her. Two days later, she dies. The doctor says it was shock, and mortification from the wound to her wrist traveling all the way up the arm to the lungs.

Poor Ann. Poor Isaac. No more soft, warm cuddles in the cabin. No more hot food ready for him on a cold night. No one he can trust to steer the boat while he drives the horse. And poor William. The police catch up with him on the canal close to London. Where else would he be? They arrest him for manslaughter. It's 1847. Manslaughter—you could go to the gallows for that. You could find yourself in a transport ship and lucky to reach Australia alive—or unlucky to reach Australia alive, who knows?

There's a trial. Old Bailey. Judge in a wig. Isaac tells his story. William tells his story. The doctor says Ann had an injury to her wrist. She stopped breathing. There it is. Now, ladies and gentlemen of the jury, gathered here together on this towpath in this century, what is the verdict? Does William go free, sail away on the canals of England for another thirty years of hard, honest toil, or does he have his new career snuffed out? You decide.

Billy picked up the lantern from the hatch and lit the candle inside; held it up. The glow was bright in the warm dusk of nearly-night.

Let's say this lantern is William Hickman, body and soul, and you hold his fate in your hands as I hold this lantern in mine. What will you do? Let him go, to float away down the canal into whatever adventures await him, or put out his light, send him into oblivion? Come along, now. You've heard the evidence. Hands up for guilty.

No one spoke, at least not aloud and clearly.

All right, then, not guilty. Is that your verdict? Hands up if it is.

Now the audience became livelier, raised their voices to the friends standing next to them and to strangers nearby. But the majority of hands went up. Billy smiled.

Not guilty, you soft-hearted liberals! There he goes, see, you've let him loose and you've no idea where he will go or what he will do next, be it harm or good.

He let go of the lantern, which lifted and drifted—slowly, for there was no breeze—above the canal toward the lock. Sally watched it go and noticed a solitary figure of a man walking down the towpath toward the group around *Grimm*. He was deeply familiar in the way he walked, held himself, the way his hair bobbed as he moved. But she did not let the name into her mind. It could have been an illusion of the light, the night, the strange story of Isaac and William, the drifting lantern passing over the man's head and vanishing behind a hedge—although it cast so little light the evening seemed darker when it was gone.

Billy spoke for the last time.

If you think you are better than the judge in his wig in the Old Bailey in the nineteenth century, if you think you have

more understanding and tolerance and compassion, you would
be wrong. He found William Hickman not guilty, just as you
have.

Billy and Trompette circulated among the crowd with up-
turned hats, collecting money. The people moved off toward
the road and the pub, discussing the story, leaving Eve on her
bollard and Sally leaning against her post. Through the chatter-
ing throng walking away from them emerged the man Sally had
noticed, walking toward them. He sidestepped Eve and stopped
in front of Sally, looking at her closely as if, in the dark and the
strangeness of the location, he could not be sure who she was.

"Eve," said Sally, "meet my son, Mark."

"Well," said Eve, "that's a bit of a turn-up for *The Rubáiyát*
of Omar Khayyám."

MARK WAS A SLIM BUT solid-looking young man, easy in his
movements. Eve suspected he had come to entice Sally back
to the comfort and familiarity of Beech Grove, and prepared
herself to despise him. She decided at once there was nothing
of Sally about him, so he must be a true chip off the block of
Duncan. But he was so easy a companion it was hard to maintain her distrust. They had already eaten but walked back to the
pub with him and had a drink while he ate. Eve had assumed
mother and son would want to be alone, but they had both
paused on the towpath, looking back over their shoulders (on
second thought, he did remind her of Sally), and it was Mark
who said, "Aren't you coming, too?"

He worked for the Forestry Commission, he told her, in

between shoveling an enormous portion of fish and chips into his mouth. He was coming to the end of a Graduate Training Scheme and was ready to take up whatever role he was assigned, anywhere in the country. He loved trees, he said, in all their variety. He loved that he had been trained in practical skills as well as management skills. He liked that he worked outdoors, and he liked the pace of it, which was measured, as befitted the majesty of the forests.

More often than not, when Eve talked to other people about their careers, she found she rather regretted not having had the chance to experience what they were experiencing. Other people's lives, particularly if they were passionate about what they did, sounded so interesting, even though she knew that they were telling her only what was good, and how it worked in theory, leaving out the dullness, irritation and inefficiency that were inescapable in any organization, as far as she could see. So she was captivated by Mark's account of the program he had completed and the openings ahead of him, and by the end of the evening had completely forgotten she'd ever thought he was an agent provocateur sent to disrupt their trip on the *Number One*. He was also completely unlike her picture of Duncan.

"You should stay with us for a few days," she said. "You could tell us about all the trees we pass."

He laughed. "You don't need to know that," he said.

Sally was up early, washing her sheets in the sink. The dog and Eve conspired to stop her sleeping—Mark had been given Eve's bed, so Eve had moved into the other bunk in the rear cabin and Noah had come with her—and she detected an odor of dog on the pillowcase. It was almost a pleasure to know that Mark was leaving today, though she could not remember having enjoyed his company so much since he was a bundle without motive powers, snuggled against her chin.

"I'm thinking of buying a Kindle," Sally said as soon as Eve appeared.

"What?"

"So I can read during the hours I have to spend in the dark listening to you and the dog snoring and grinding your teeth."

"I knew I did that. I should have warned you."

"And one of you farted. Often. Maybe both of you."

"For a married woman, you're very intolerant of other people's sleeping habits."

"Duncan was a good sleeper. Maybe I'd have left sooner if he hadn't been."

The morning was cooler; a breeze was shaking the sheets on the washing line, which was a piece of string strung between the tiller, through the holes in two, tall, hinged rods located on the roof and put into the upright position for the purpose, to a cleat on the front of the boat. This was Anastasia's way of drying washing and her temporary crew were proud of it. None of the other boats had come up with a better way of solving the washing/drying problem; they festooned their craft and the towpath with any number of makeshift, unstable, unsightly and inefficient contrivances having loose ends and trailing parts. Or they cheated, by having an electric dryer for example, or using a laundrette, or tolerating very dirty clothes. Anastasia's system was a masterpiece of countersunk screws, brass bolts, snecks. The sheets were held in place with pegs fashioned from pieces of metal; Eve described the process she guessed had been used to fabricate them, but Sally was not concentrating. Although she listened. Once or twice she had caught herself treating Eve's voice like Duncan's. Letting it saw through the air somewhere just out of reach. But mostly, it was no hardship to listen to Eve. Whatever she said was relevant to the confines of their new lives.

When she was not able to sleep, Sally drew the map of the boat in her mind, beginning at floor level, remembering every angle, every surface, every fixing. Moving up to knee level, to waist height, to head height. One night, she had to go and check the position of the flush in the toilet to prevent her brain snagging on its undiscoverability.

Mark was catching the bus. They examined Nicholson together, found the most convenient bus stop and spent the day moving at the *Number One*'s pace toward it. Mark took his turn at working the locks and driving the boat, but mostly he lay on the roof watching the banks slide past, or jogged down the towpath, disappearing from view and reappearing farther on, ready to step on board. Each time he materialized from the darkness under an arch it was a shock, but when he was on the *Number One* he fitted himself neatly around them. It was only as they were walking up the village street to the bus stop that Sally realized: if he had come to say something to her, it had not been said.

"You haven't said anything," she said, as they sat on a wall beside the post with its sparse information about the bus service, "about me leaving."

"When I came," Mark said, stamping on an empty crisp packet bowling past in the strengthening wind, then putting it in the bin attached to the post, "I meant to talk to you about it, but then I didn't know where to start."

"At the beginning."

"Well. I was cross, you know? When you told me. Funnily enough, I felt as if it wasn't fair on me. All my life I've had a mum and a dad who were married to each other, when lots of my friends didn't, and I thought it wasn't right you should suddenly turn me into someone from a broken home. That wasn't who I was."

"Oh, Mark!"

"I know, I know. I couldn't help it, though. Then I thought I was being selfish and the one who had a right to feel cross was Dad. I couldn't picture him in that house without you, so I went to see him, thinking he'd be in bits. And honestly, he wasn't. He was more . . . bemused, like someone who's spent the whole of his life waiting for the next episode of a soap opera on TV only to find it's been axed. It was as if he was just waking up and looking round and wondering what had happened."

"I can imagine."

"And then Amy came round, full of outrage—I expect she had a go at you, too."

"Oh yes." Sally smiled at the thought of having this calm, considered conversation with her daughter. Amy had battered her with the words which came to her as she opened her mouth, and would have done again, she felt sure, if she had come to visit.

"But Dad didn't really seem to join in. So I thought I'd better come and see for myself what was going on from your side before I worked out what I felt."

"And what did you see was going on?"

"What you're doing, it suits you. Not the hair, of course, that's pretty gross. But the break, the way of life. So I've decided not to fret about it. Or about whether it's an interlude or a definite change of direction. I'll wait and see."

"That's what I'm doing," said Sally.

EVE WAS LEANING ON THE post that supported the tap that was supplying water through a length of green hose to the tank on board the *Number One*. It was a hot day and she was wearing a pair of shorts she had bought the day before; another tipping point had been passed in the rebalancing of her life. She had weighed the importance of looking something less than comical against the need to be cool, unencumbered, accessible to sun and breeze. How she looked was a handful of dust when set against how she felt.

The sun was shining so brightly it was hard to look up without being blinded by the sharp and ever-shifting sparkles off the water, the polished surfaces on other boats, the white-painted lip of the wharf opposite, so Eve was studying her feet, and her absurd legs, and the line of the hose crossing the path in front of her. She was listening to the water falling into the tank and waiting for the note to change, which would mean it was nearly full and she could turn the tap off.

A commotion broke out to her left and she closed one eye as a precaution, squinted toward it with the other. A group of young men were approaching a hire boat moored farther down the bank. They were laden with drink; cans held together with plastic halters in their muscled, tattooed arms, and carrier bags hooked into the fingers of their broad hands. They were loud, and dazzling: the whiteness of their uncovered arms and legs, the sheen on their football shirts, the silver of the cans catching the sun as they struggled to carry their load onto the boat. Eve looked away, waited for the splash, wished she had bought a sun hat along with the shorts, a pair of sunglasses. She suspected she might have made up the muscles, and the tattoos, and perhaps even the drink.

At length, after further shouting but no splashes, the bank and the boat parted company and all the arms and legs and bottles and cans seemed to be aboard and the boat was traveling, or drifting, in Eve's direction. The *Number One*'s water tank, unregarded, had filled and overflowed. Eve turned off the tap and disconnected the hose and was looking down, coiling it neatly in the shape of an ammonite, when the clamor of young men's voices turned into recognizable sounds. Almost a whole sentence.

"Hello! Hello there, beautiful!"

Eve raised her head from the hose to see who they meant. They were looking in her direction and there was no one on the bank except her. She laughed. The men laughed back, calling and whistling and drinking and ignoring the progress of their boat, which was moving gently toward the wharf opposite. There was a jolt as it struck the concrete. Eve held her hand to her mouth in expectation that, this time, one of them would lose his hold and fall. None of them did. The two or three perched on the narrow ledge running along the side of the boat each managed to hold on to the roof rail with one arm and keep one foot connected, windmilling their other arms and legs in a chaotic parody of the cover of the Beatles' *Help!* album. Which Eve owned, or had done, though who knew what decisions Anastasia was even then taking about what was, or was not, necessary to an orderly existence.

The activity on the hire boat transferred to the far side. The crew, if they could be called such a thing, seemed to have concluded that this was a suitable destination and settled down to tackle the rest of the bottles and cans. Eve finished coiling the hose. She fetched a mop and swabbed up the spilled water. She went down into the cabin and straightened everything that was, however marginally, squint or crumpled. She drank a glass of water, slowly, standing at the side hatch watching two male mallards squabbling. She began a shopping list on the pad hanging up for the purpose.

Sun tan lotion
Sun hat

She thought about it for a while, considering what else she could possibly want, looked at her toes, wrote:

Nail varnish

Then crossed it out.

She took a book and went outside to the helmsman's seat on the rear deck. From across the canal a renewed commotion indicated that the young men had wearied of their mooring, or had run out of beer, and were on the move again. They persuaded the boat into the middle of the canal and hung there, slack-mouthed and sleepy, then continued their progress toward Eve.

"Hello, beautiful," said one, with a sorrowful note in his voice as though he had fought and lost and was bearing it with dignity. The rest backed him up with a few uncertain whistles.

The boat gathered speed, which might have been because the

man holding the tiller intended it to or because his or someone else's knee had nudged the throttle. The boy at the helm did not alter course but continued straight ahead toward the bank they had recently left, where a line of bushes and small trees overhung the canal. His crew became loud and incoherent as the first branches smacked them on the head, but it was too late to prevent the bow traveling, full tilt, into the undergrowth where the one young man at the front was completely lost from view. All the others began to laugh, wildly, and it seemed to Eve to be a number of minutes before anyone put the boat into reverse. As it slid backward, she waited for the empty space to be revealed where the body at the front had been, but there he still was, a compact ball covered in debris.

As the boat made steady progress toward the next bend, they all turned and waved. The one at the front, brushing himself off, lifted his head and shouted:

"I love you!"

"We all love you," agreed the one at the back.

They left the surface of the canal spotted with twigs and leaves, floating among bubbles rising from the mud like so many fish eyes coming up to see what had happened that was so extraordinary.

It was a mystery to Sally how, one moment, it was necessary to take the boat up and up and up, then, rounding a bend, to find the next set of locks waiting to drop the *Number One* down and down and down to continue its journey. Water, after all, generally fell in one direction.

"It's to do with the watershed," Eve said. "The point where the rivers that feed the canals start running down to the sea."

This didn't sound too convincing—either the explanation or Eve's way of delivering it—so Sally let it go and thought, instead, it was like the walks and cycle rides they used to go on when the children were small, because Duncan felt that was what families did together. He had been an only child of elderly parents and had grown up longing for what he believed was a normal family life. Sally had quite enjoyed these walks because they meant she was not doing any chores, and she had time to think. But it always felt like something they were doing because they ought to be doing it, rather than something they wanted to be doing. When Mark found their pace too slow for him and began finding his own way of exploring the countryside, the rest of the family let the practice lapse. But the thing Sally remembered most clearly was the sinking feeling as she approached a hill, whether going up or down, because, even if it was down, it would be up on the way back. So it was on the canal, only there was no more effort involved in going into an empty lock and rising to the top than in going into a full one and dropping down to the bottom.

Later she noticed Eve reading one of Anastasia's books on the construction of the canals, and it did not surprise her when Eve admitted that she had been wrong about the watershed. Canals, it seemed, like footpaths, went up to a summit and then down again, and provision of water was just one of the problems to be tackled by the early canal builders, which they had come up with so many inventive ways of overcoming.

⌒

EVE: Hello?

ANASTASIA: Where are you?

EVE: Oh. Bridge 126.

ANASTASIA: What have you been *doing*?

EVE: We've been going carefully. You wouldn't want us to behave recklessly, now, would you?

ANASTASIA: There's reckless and there's cautious and I want you to be on the cautious side of reckless. But then there's idle and there's active and I'd expect you to make at least a small effort to get over the line and be halfway toward active.

EVE: You're barking at me.

ANASTASIA: Well?

EVE: Oh, well. I would say we have moved off cautious and are working our way to the midpoint between that and reckless.

ANASTASIA: Which you should never cross.

EVE: Which, I promise you, we will never cross. And it honestly doesn't feel as if we've been idle. We've had a visitor.

ANASTASIA: Who?

EVE: Sally's son.

ANASTASIA: She's not being seduced back, is she?

EVE: No. He didn't try, and even if he had, she wouldn't have listened. I'll prove it. Sally! Anastasia's worried Mark might have tried to change your mind about the trip.

SALLY (*faintly*): Impossible.

ANASTASIA: Good.

EVE: Also, we met some friends of yours.

ANASTASIA: Now I'm worried. Friends? What friends? Ludicrously overused word, "friends."

EVE: I know, you're right. We met some people who know you.

ANASTASIA: Of course you did. Most people who live on the canal know me. Boat?

EVE: *Grimm*.

ANASTASIA: Number of people on the boat?

EVE: Two.

ANASTASIA: It's time Trompette walked away.

EVE: Funnily enough, Sally thinks the same.

ANASTASIA: What's funny about that?

EVE: Nothing, nothing. How are you?

ANASTASIA: Still possibly dying.

EVE: Of course, but otherwise?

ANASTASIA: Not dead yet.

EVE: Good.

ANASTASIA: Easy.

SALLY TRUDGED UP TO THE next lock, swinging the key in her hand, watching where she put her feet because it had rained and she was wearing sneakers that were not waterproof. When she reached the lock, there were two boats in it, coming up, and several people waiting to open the gates, or just hanging about. Sally went up to a woman leaning against a gate beam.

"I can open the gate," she said, "if you want to get back on board."

The woman shook her head.

"Neither of these is mine," she said. "I'm waiting to come up."

So Sally crossed over and repeated the offer to the man on the other gate, who accepted it. The two boats and their crews negotiated their way out of the lock and the *Number One* came in. When they had shut the gates, the woman said to Sally:

"Isn't that Anastasia's boat?"

"It is."

"Is she on board?"

"No. She's entrusted it to us to take up to Chester."

As she spoke, it occurred to Sally how strange it was that Anastasia had trusted them in this way. The woman she was talking to was a decade younger than she was, she guessed, and was wearing shorts with sturdy boots at the end of her long, muscular, tanned legs. She looked so thoroughly competent. And yet—Sally looked down into the emptying lock where Eve stood, hand on the throttle, head turned to watch the distance from the lock gates—hadn't they also begun to look as if they knew what they were doing? Anastasia's instincts, she thought, might not have been wrong.

"You know," the woman told her, "I owe it to Anastasia that I'm living the way I do."

"Oh?"

"Yes. I took up boating because I had reached one of those 'had-it-up-to-here' moments. You know what I mean—wrong job, wrong partner, etcetera, etcetera. And I happened to be living on the canal at the time because I couldn't afford a house, so I just cast off and kept going. I loved it all summer, then winter came along. I was that close to giving up. I was fighting my way through the snow on the towpath with a can to fetch water because I was frozen in and couldn't move the boat to the tap, and I was thinking I would never, ever be warm again. And I met Anastasia with her dog. I told her I was fed up of being cold and I was thinking of going back to where I could have a hot bath and go to sleep with the central heating on, and she ignored what I'd said and asked me to tell her what I could hear. Right at that moment. So I listened for a bit and I could hear the ice creaking on the canal and Anastasia's dog snuffling and far, far away, the hum of traffic. Then she asked me what I could see. This was on the Kennet and Avon Canal and it was flat but such gentle countryside, huge sky, every tree covered in frost and lit up by the sun. It was so beautiful. Anastasia said I had to work out which I wanted to have as normal and which as an occasional treat—the silence and the beauty, or the hot bath and the warm room. That was five years ago, and here I still am. Never regretted the decision. Or not often."

"Are you alone on your boat?" asked Sally.

"Yes. For the moment. Not always, but mostly."

"Do you want me to hang on and help you take it through the lock?"

"Oh, no!" The woman laughed. "I'm perfectly self-sufficient."

WHEN THEY REACHED MILTON KEYNES, Eve caught a bus into town and bought a bike. Sally would not come with her. Eve was unsure why this was. Although she felt she knew Sally by this time and had grown fond of her, there were still moments when she detected frictions in the working of Sally's machinery, a hesitation that could be a symptom of an imminent break-down, or merely a bit of dirt which would pass through. Eve was not implicated in this malfunction, she believed, but she couldn't see a way of running a diagnostic check and effecting a repair. It occurred to her now that there might be a problem with money.

The boat bills—fuel, pump-out, gas—were paid from a tin into which they each put an equal amount of money each week. The amount and the tin had been provided by Anastasia. They had procured their own tin and set their own limit for food money, adopting the same approach, but in this area of joint banking, Eve had begun to cheat. She found two things to be true and suspected a third—she ate more, she was more self-indulgent and, or so she believed, she had more money available to her. So when she went shopping she bought more than the tin paid for. Sally never mentioned this and Eve did not know if she chose not to or if she had not noticed.

On the matter of bikes, Eve felt able to say:

"I expect you think if you had the money you wouldn't waste it on a bike."

"I do have the money," Sally said, "but spending it on a bike would be a complete waste as I never learned to ride one."

The bike shop in Milton Keynes was enormous and completely full of bikes, on the floor, on shelves and hanging from the ceiling. The staff were all young, lean, busy and wearing T-shirts. The customers were indistinguishable from the staff, except that most of them had brought their bikes into the shop with them and were holding them lightly by the saddle or handlebars like mothers who had brought their toddlers to a clinic. Eve noticed that, although she stood out from the crowd by being older, fatter and unaccompanied by a bike, she appeared to be invisible.

She toured the stock. She had last bought a bike at the age of twelve when her purchasing decision had been based on color and basket type. Only a few of the bikes in the Milton Keynes shop had baskets. The bikes with baskets were in colors that were probably called Dawn Sky or Midnight or Lemon Candy. Eve looked at these first. They were cheap and simple in construction, as far as she could tell: the shop was dark. She lifted the Midnight one off its stand, wobbled under its weight, stepped backward and collided with an androgynous elf in Lycra shorts.

"Careful!" said the elf, feeling the drop handlebars on its racing bike as if they might have been bruised in the encounter.

This piece of blue scaffolding masquerading as a bike was not what Eve was looking for, but when she tried to restore it to its previous position the slot where the wheel had fitted moments before had clamped its teeth together and resisted her attempts to put it back. She wheeled it, weaving a path through the other bikes, to a desk where a man with muscles but no hair and a name-badge identifying him as Clyde was just finishing a phone call.

"Do you want to buy that?" he said. His tone was so neutral it was loaded with the unspoken subtext: I can't believe anyone would want a bike like that . . . but there again, now I come to look at you, I can believe *you would* want a bike like that and, frankly, it's probably what you deserve.

"No," said Eve. "It's an overweight, under-engineered piece of crap. I don't know anything about bikes, but even I can tell that much. I can tell you what I do want to buy, if you like."

"Go ahead," said Clyde, still not quite looking at her but allowing his focus to home in on the area she occupied.

"I want a bike that is relatively light, relatively easy to ride on the road but also capable of going along towpaths, is not going to break, costs less than a thousand pounds and is available for me to ride away today."

"Ladies' bike, is it?"

"What's the advantage?"

"Easier to get on and off."

"Disadvantage?"

"Either heavier, or less structurally rigid."

"Not a ladies' bike."

Clyde looked straight at her and smiled. The light level, the muscles and the name had deceived her. He was no younger than she was. She smiled back.

An hour and a half later she was cycling down the wide, empty path beside a divided highway on a silver hybrid with eighteen gears and no basket. The first hour had been spent trying out the options on the stretch of path outside the bike shop. The last half hour had been spent fitting the accessories—panniers, lights, a sheepskin saddle cover—proposed by Clyde as essential to meet her specific needs. In the short time since the decision was made, her relationship with the bike had begun to grow and was now, after only a few hundred yards in the sunshine, as intense as any she had known. She lifted her feet from the pedals in an excess of joy, as she remembered having done on her first date at the age of fourteen when a boy called Theo had invited her to go with him to explore a disused flour mill. She felt as completely happy as she had been then.

She realized she had missed the road that led to the canal, braked abruptly and fell off. She landed on the soft, soft grass beside the empty path—oh, heaven that is Milton Keynes—but her bike fell onto the tarmac. She picked it up and felt its frame for dirt and scratches. They had both escaped unharmed. She cycled up to the *Number One*, ringing her bell. Sally put her head through the hatch.

"Look!" said Eve. She was still astride the bike; she had not yet worked out the best way to separate herself from it in the limited space, with the added hazards of ropes and bollards.

"Woman and bike as one," said Sally. "Please tell me it hasn't got a name."

4

To Norton Junction

ANASTASIA: I'm going to come and visit you.

EVE: What? I mean, hello, Anastasia, that would be lovely.

ANASTASIA: Of course it won't be lovely. It will be excruciating for all of us, but I can't look at these walls any longer.

EVE: How will you get to us?

ANASTASIA: On a train. Jacob is going to organize it for me.

EVE: Jacob?

ANASTASIA: You must know your own neighbor.

EVE: Yes, naturally, I do. I just didn't realize that you did.

ANASTASIA: I met him on the stairs. I'd paused for a rest and he thought I was some poor old sack and I thought he was a young man who would only be interested in buying, selling and taking drugs.

EVE: Well, he was wrong.

ANASTASIA: We both were. He's been very helpful, him and his computer. I can go to London on the Tube and catch a train to Long Buckby and there is a bus to Long Buckby Wharf which is where you will meet me.

EVE: All right. When?

ANASTASIA: The day after tomorrow. Or possibly the day after that. Just be at the wharf when I get there.

EVE: Any idea what time of day?

ANASTASIA: No. Jacob knows all the train times, but I haven't made up my mind which one to catch. So just wait for me.

EVE: We'll be there.

ANASTASIA: If you're not, I'll sit by the wharf and make a nuisance of myself.

EVE: That sounds like a plan.

SALLY WAS IN CHARGE. THEY had been through the lock that marked the end of the model suburb that was Milton Keynes and then Eve had cycled ahead down the towpath, leaving her in sole possession of the *Number One*. It was three miles before the next lock and, until then, there was only the bass rumble of the engine; fields, hills, the sort of tufty white clouds children were supposed to draw (but rarely did, in Sally's experience) in a blue sky.

Several boats passed by, heading in the opposite direction. A hire boat with what looked to be three generations of the one family, all zipped tight into orange buoyancy vests, talking at full volume in accents she could only place as being from somewhere to the north. An immaculate, privately owned boat with traditional decoration on the chimney, crewed by a couple wrapped in waterproofs as if they had no confidence in the brightness of the day, having been misled too many times in the past. A boat that looked lived in, lived on, with two sturdy brown women in the stern, looking relaxed. They raised their mugs to Sally as they passed, and she wondered whether she looked, to them, to be like them—in control and happy. Because she was.

She let her mind drift over the word that occurred to her, noticing the roof of this last boat. "Clutter." An Anastasia word. In her Beech Grove existence, she would have thought "untidy," not having the notion of there being too much of anything, only of things not being in their place. A strand of pink hair blew across her face and she stuck out her bottom lip, blew it away. There was something desperate about the pink hair and the ridiculous clothes, she now thought. She had needed to test her resolve on the bridge that led from Beech Grove to Chester, or wherever else she might be going. She had rushed too far; she didn't need to be so crudely distant from the shore she had left.

She stood up, ready to throttle back as she approached a bridge and moored boats. "Thrupp," said a sign on the wharf. Sally added this to "clutter" as another word she liked the taste of and would never have spoken, even to herself, before. When she reached Yardley Gobion (was she creating these names from the depths of her happiness, or had they always existed?) Eve was waiting for her. A bit red in the face, a bit damp and muddy.

"I hit a bump," she said, climbing aboard as Sally slid the *Number One* into the side. "And fell off."

"Are you all right?"

"Chipper. I bounce, or so it seems."

They moored up, went to the pub and ordered fish and chips, then found a table in the garden. As they sat in the sun, occasionally batting a wasp away, Eve asked Sally what she was thinking about. It was a question Duncan had often asked and Sally had invariably answered with some triviality which had not been at the top of her mind at the time, but now she answered honestly.

"I was picturing my hand reaching up for a ceramic storage jar, pale green, pink rose pattern round the base and rim, labeled 'Tea.' Again, and again, and again. Then waiting for the kettle to boil, for the water to flow out of the kettle into the teapot. Waiting for it to be ready to pour, cool enough to drink. All these minutes of time not long enough to do anything else with, but cumulatively, a lifetime in which there is not time to do anything except wait."

Eve said: "I filled every minute. If I went to fetch a coffee from the machine in the office I would take my phone with me and make a call on the way. If there was an agenda item in a meeting that was nothing to do with me, I would read the emails my PA printed off for me or a report I had to edit. Sometimes, I admit, I thought about things that had nothing to do with work. Whether to reorganize the furniture in my bedroom; whether to go with friends to the Algarve. But these things need thinking about, so it didn't feel like a waste of time to be thinking about them."

Sally said: "I have never had to go to many meetings, but whenever I did, I was always waiting for it to finish so I could go and get on with something else. Even though there was never very much I had to be getting on with."

"What do you feel when you're waiting for a lock to empty?" asked Eve.

"Ah, peaceful."

"So do I."

"We're a pair, aren't we?"

After a while, Eve said: "So what are you waiting for now? For the journey to be over?"

"No. I'm in a suspended state. I can't tell you how restful that is."

The food came and Noah lay on Eve's foot, watching each forkful, shuffling to his feet whenever her finger and thumb closed on a chip, in expectation that her hand would travel not to her mouth but to his.

"Look at the dog," Eve said. "He is faced with two irreconcilable alternatives and he's too dumb to realize it. Oh, the innocence of dogs!" She lifted a chip and, keeping an eye on Noah, put it slowly into her mouth.

"What?" said Sally, who had been watching a toddler at a nearby table. The child was clutching her knickers and Sally was waiting to see if the mother would notice in time.

"Noah knows that you don't like dogs and I do, so it makes sense to ignore your plate and put all his energy into watching mine. He thinks: this is my best shot at getting a chip."

"That sounds about right."

"Ah, but what he has failed to factor into his decision is that I'm greedy and you're not. And if that is the case, you are the more likely source of leftover food." She waggled her fork at Noah. "I am going to eat all of it," she told him.

"Here," said Sally, passing her plate over. "I've had enough. You can feed him some of mine."

"Result!" whispered Eve in Noah's ear, and flipped a chunk of fish and batter into his waiting jaws.

There was a flurry of activity at the toddler's table, adults reaching for table napkins, mother whisking the wailing child off into the pub. Eve looked round.

"What's happening over there?" she said.

"The little girl's just wet her knickers," Sally said.

"How do you know?"

"I've been waiting for it to happen."

"I would never have noticed."

"No, but I probably wouldn't have noticed the dog was waiting for a chip."

Eve put the bike back on the roof and retreated to the cabin to digest her lunch and marvel over the sensation of having undertaken strenuous exercise in the recent past. Sally carried on driving the *Number One* through the expansive landscape, watching the front wheel of Eve's bike rotating slower and slower until it finally stopped and there was nothing moving on the boat, just the water curling away behind it and the scenery sliding past.

A long, straight stretch of canal gave Sally a view of a bridge in the far distance. The Guide told her a river (the Toye, another strong, plump word to add to "clutter," "Thrupp" and "Yardley Gobion") had joined the canal, and she was aware of a slight current, a little more resistance to the boat's passage.

She watched a heron lift off the bank and tuck its long legs up for a flight over the field; she nodded to a man wearing a hat, walking along the towpath, and he lifted the hat in acknowledgment. She wished she had a hat of her own to afford this courtesy to other passersby and fellow boaters. She mused over the origin of the word "boater" as applied to a hat, though this was not the sort of hat she had in mind. She wanted something soft, shapeless, drooping; the opposite, in fact, of a boater, but appropriate to the boater that she was. If Eve had been there, she could have shared this whimsical thought. But she might not have done.

She was smiling, in any case, as the once-distant bridge came closer and closer. There was a figure standing beside it, quite still, so at first she took it for a buttress. When it became clear it was a person, she thought "fisherman" and was not surprised it had not moved in all the time it took her to reach it. There was a series of locks beyond the bridge and Sally steered the *Number One* into the bank so she could rouse Eve and make a cup of tea before they started the climb. The man who had been so motionless now pushed himself off from the bridge and came along the towpath to where she was winding the center rope round a bollard to hold the boat steady against the bank. He was a smooth, slight man, with wispy hair and a small, neat beard. He was wearing rather old-fashioned clothes—a tweed jacket, wool trousers, gaiters—and he had a rucksack on his back. No fishing rod. He did not speak to Sally but walked along peering through the windows of the *Number One*.

"Where is Anastasia?"

"Not here, I'm afraid."

He came right up to her, where she was looping the spare rope out of harm's way, and she saw he was older than she had thought. Though smooth, his skin looked brittle, spotted, worn.

"She's not dead, is she?"

"No. She's staying in Uxbridge and we're taking the boat to Chester for her."

"Why?" he said. He was standing too close.

"To have the bottom blacked or something like that."

"No, why is Anastasia staying in Uxbridge?"

"Well . . ." He was making her uneasy. His eyes were rather bloodshot and she was catching the whiff of someone whose clothes and hair were not clean. He felt tense, too anxious for what her answer might be. As if telling him Anastasia was ill might push him over the edge into despair and she would be the one responsible.

The rear door of the *Number One* rattled open and Eve and Noah climbed out.

"Where are we?" said Eve.

"Bridge 55, Lock 20," Sally said.

Noah stopped on the edge of the deck and put his head on one side to consider the man standing, still too close, beside Sally.

"Ho! Noah!" the man said.

Noah had a look around and sniffed the air then jumped down onto the towpath and advanced on the stranger in a subdued version of his normally ecstatic greeting of old friends. The man bent and scratched behind the dog's ears. Noah rolled over and exposed his belly, which the man tickled. This ritual complete, Noah set off up the towpath like a dog with rats and rabbits on his mind.

"You were telling me," the man said to Sally, "why Anastasia is in Uxbridge."

"She's just having a few tests," said Sally.

"And we're having a holiday," said Eve, stepping off the boat onto the towpath. "Who are you? We'll have to let her know we've met you."

"Well, well, well," said the man with something close to a giggle, all anxiety gone and a sort of pixie-like charm replacing it. "She's indestructible, Anastasia, wouldn't you say? In-des-truct-ible. I pity the poor doctors, indeed I do. Now, my name is Arthur and I'm hoping you two ladies will give me a lift."

"A lift?" said Eve. "Where to?"

"Norton Junction."

"We're meeting Anastasia at Norton Junction in a couple of days," said Sally.

"*Are* you?" said Arthur. "Champion, champion. I'll work the locks, of course. To pay for my passage, as it were."

"We only travel at walking pace," Eve said, "never mind the locks. Wouldn't it be quicker to walk?"

"Oh, but I'm an old man, my dear. The legs, you know, the legs and the poor ruined feet. They do long for a rest."

"Are you asking us if you can sleep on the boat?" asked Sally. She sounded shrill, but she was unsure if Eve had detected the odor the man was carrying about with him; although she knew, from experience in the classroom, that she would cease to notice it after a while, she was not keen to go through the time until this state was reached. Also, she did not want him on the boat. Or anywhere near the boat. And she thought this was small-minded of her, and this in turn was making her irritable and miserable.

"No, no," Arthur said. "You young ladies need your privacy. I've a tent here in my rucksack. But a bit of hospitality, now, that wouldn't go amiss. A shared crust, a brew. What do you say?"

"What would Anastasia say?" asked Eve, which was the question Sally had been pondering. But it wasn't a question that troubled Arthur. He laughed and moved his feet in what might have been, Sally thought, a caper, though she had never been sure what that was.

"She wouldn't say anything, my lovely ladies, she'd nod, and I'd nod, and there we'd be, as we have been year on year since you two had pigtails and gingham frocks. Sharing the work; lightening each other's loads. We have a history, Anastasia and me. Now"—he detached his rucksack and heaved it onto the rear deck—"if the water's hot, I could do with a shower before I set to with the windlass on this next set of locks. And I'll put the kettle on as I go past, shall I?" And he was gone, leaving Eve and Sally standing on the bank looking at the spot where he had recently stood.

"What do you think?" asked Eve.

"He smells. Had you noticed?" They were both whispering because, though he was unlikely to hear them from inside the boat, Arthur gave the impression of a man who would catch you out, if you let your guard down. Eve shook her head.

"The shower is a good idea, then, is it?"

"It is."

"Do you think we should phone Anastasia?" Eve asked, then instantly shook her head. "No, probably not."

Arthur came out of the shower looking smoother and pinker and wearing clothes no less old-fashioned but more casual: a pair of fawn trousers and a white shirt. He smelled of Sally's lemon soap but his clothes had a metallic, chemical old-man-and-musty-wardrobe tang. Though his odor was no longer actually offensive, Sally still found him repellent. He looked even more slippery, even more likely to leave the boat by one door and reappear, without a sound and when least expected, at the other. He was fluid; though his movements were jerky he appeared to transpose himself from a position, upright, to a position, seated, by some trick. Sally went back over the moments it had taken him to go from being a complete stranger to a member of the crew, drinking tea with them, to work out whether there had been anything she could have done to stop this happening. There wasn't. He had asked for a lift and she could have said "no," but she was sure this would have made no difference to the outcome.

Eve was clearly interested in him. She wanted to know where he came from and where he was going, but he waved these questions aside.

"Later, ladies, later. We should get going up the locks and delay the chat until such time as the work is over."

He was off the boat and up at the first lock with a windlass at the ready before Sally had the cups stacked in the sink.

"He does skip about," she said.

"He could be useful," said Eve. "Shall I take over driving?"

Before—before Arthur—whichever one of them had been working the locks had covered quite a distance. And this time there was a boat ahead of them but none coming the other way, so they had to empty each lock before the *Number One* went in. But if the work was less, with Arthur scampering back and forth on the other side, the fact of his presence, of his scampering, made stressful what was normally a pleasant, undemanding task. When Arthur hopped back on board for the short journey to the second lock, Sally called out to Eve that she would walk. She reached it before they did, and hung over the gate, waiting for the lock chamber to empty, and watched the *Number One* approach, Eve at the tiller and Arthur, a stick-like figure glued on to the gunwale, holding the rail with one hand.

They worked five of the locks this way, a major road crossing between two of them reminding Sally of the hurry to move forward she had left behind. After the last of the five, there was a stretch to the outskirts of Stoke Bruerne and the next lock. Sally climbed aboard the *Number One* and said to Eve:

"We'll moor in Stoke Bruerne, shall we?"

"I thought so," Eve said.

Arthur, perched on the gunwale still, said: "There's nowhere to pitch a tent in the village."

Sally was standing with her back to him. Eve, at the tiller, was facing him.

"Well . . ." Eve began, then caught Sally's eye. If Sally had shaken her head, Arthur would have detected the movement, so she mouthed the word "NO" instead. "We'd better wait until we've gone through it, then," Eve said.

"There's nowhere between the village and the entrance to Blisworth Tunnel."

"Before?"

"Just here will do."

EVE WAS FASCINATED BY ARTHUR. She was used to being in rooms full of men and confident of being able to categorize them in an instant by their dominant characteristics and then, after a brief acquaintance, by the subsets, those details of attitudes, values, interests that went to make up an individual. She rarely found herself, after lengthy or even intimate knowledge of a person, to have been mistaken in her first assessment. Occasionally, someone who presented as arrogant, patronizing and misogynistic had later revealed all his uncertainties and lack of self-esteem in ways both direct and indirect. But even after such revelations, and after she and they knew she had been told and had retained a memory of the person this person truly was, even then, the dominant behavior was the same as before. So, to all practical purposes, she was right.

But Arthur eluded her. It was not just that he shape-shifted from one moment to another, appearing sturdy and feeble, strong and weak, old and in the prime of his life, in the time it took to respond to his last remark or turn back to him from looking away; or that he moved as rapidly from appearing needy to appearing to be in control, from being tragic to being childishly happy. At no point did he begin to conform to any of the types she had met before.

She would have liked to discuss all this with Sally, but at first it didn't seem possible. Arthur was so present, even when absent. But when he was setting up his little tent under the hedge beside the towpath, she asked Sally what she thought of him.

"He makes me uneasy," Sally said. "I don't know why, so don't ask me."

Eve thought this was as abrupt as Sally had been since they started out.

"I can see why he would," she said. "He never seems the same, one moment to the next. But he's harmless, surely?"

"Probably," said Sally. "I don't feel as if I want to touch him, or be alone with him. I have no idea what he might say or do next."

Eve felt this was rather unsatisfactory. It worried her, as it turned out she felt responsible for Sally's well-being, for keeping her moving forward away from 42 Beech Grove. She turned away. Sally touched her arm.

"And actually, I'd rather it was just you and me on this boat," Sally said. "That suits me."

"It's only for a day or two," Eve said, but she was absurdly pleased by this remark.

It was Sally's turn to cook and she walked into the village to buy more sausages, as sausages were what she had planned and there were not enough for three. Eve offered to go on the bike. Sally said no. Arthur offered to go but Eve could see he didn't mean it, was not even trying very hard to look as if he meant it. So Sally went. After a few steps she stopped and came back.

"You're not a vegetarian, a vegan, kosher, halal, on a gluten-free diet or allergic to some everyday ingredient, are you?" she asked Arthur.

"No," he said, looking meek. "None of the above."

Having set his tent up, Arthur produced a harmonica from his rucksack and sat cross-legged on the roof of the *Number One* playing tunes that were fast, then slow, that dipped and dived as Arthur himself did, but that sounded to Eve like the right soundtrack for the day, for the place. She had the technology to play any of the music on her phone, and had imagined they would drift down the canals to the sound of Bach or Beethoven, move round the cabin cooking with a bit of Alanis Morrissette, settle down in the twilight to listen to something slow and mellow from Kate Bush or Simon and Garfunkel. In fact, they never had. It had never felt appropriate to drown out the sounds of the canal, all the whispers, gurgles, whistles, rustles, cries and songs of the water and the wildlife and the fringe of vegetation. But the folksy, harmonious, unfamiliar tunes that Arthur was playing, they were a fitting accompaniment to the canal's music.

Then he began to sing. Folk songs that told stories. These had always confused Eve because she never knew whether she was supposed to be captivated by the story or by the music and the voice, and she never seemed to have the capacity to appreciate both. Arthur had a lovely voice, though, so she concentrated on that; concentrated so hard she was startled by a round of applause from a group of young people passing by on a hire boat she had not heard approaching. Arthur gave a victory trill on the harmonica and bowed extravagantly. Then he started another, slower, sadder song and all the sadness and pathos of it seeped into his face, his stance, his very way of being.

Sally came back and started making a noise with the pans in the kitchen, so Eve went outside and joined Arthur on the roof.

"You don't live in a tent on the towpath, do you?" she said. "You must have a home."

"I do, I do. It's in Uttoxeter."

"That's one of those places I could never pinpoint on a map," said Eve, thinking it was the sort of place she'd expect Arthur to live. Not easily summed up.

"I know where it is," said Arthur. "No need for you to know as well."

"You haven't walked from Uttoxeter, though, have you?"

"Now," said Arthur, holding up a finger. "Stop with the little, creeping questions. Ask me what you want to know."

"What are you doing here?"

"Good, good. I'm escaping. What are you doing here?"

"I'm escaping, too."

"As I thought. Tell me what you are escaping from."

Eve noted the imperative replacing the interrogatives she had used and determined to copy this when her turn came.

"I've been sacked. So I have to decide what to do now, and I find I've forgotten how to make that sort of decision. So I suppose you could say I'm escaping from the future. Tell me what you're escaping from."

"Killjoy and Snubbit. They employ me as an accountant, and Killjoy, Snubbit and all their employees, clients, the figures they generate and the boxes I slot them into are bearable only for so long. How long? you are going to ask. I can't tell you. It varies. Less than a year, more than three months, as a rule."

"That can't be their names."

Arthur swiveled from his hips and looked at her and she felt she had wasted a question, as she had a feeling the number of questions he would answer was finite, and she would not know what the final number was until he told her she had used them all up. So she said: "I don't have any previous experience of canals as an escape route."

Arthur appeared to do a little jig on the spot, though he remained sitting down.

"The best, my dear, the very best. The calm of them, always and never changing."

"Only as an escape, though," Eve said. "Not a way of life."

"If I had no job," he said, "and no responsibility for anyone but myself, I would want to stop escaping and start living."

"On the canal?" said Eve, confused into another question.

Arthur, when she glanced across at him, was wearing his most tender, his most melancholy, his most serious expression.

"A canal is nothing but a man-made watercourse," he said. "A miracle of engineering created to make or maintain wealth."

"So not the answer?"

"That depends on what the question is. There can't be an answer until you've defined the question."

Eve was relieved when Sally stuck her head through the hatch to tell them supper was ready.

"That was quick," said Arthur, suddenly looking and sounding like a skinny old man who wanted to be looked after.

They ate the meal in an awkward silence. Sally and Eve had fallen into the habit of having a book or a newspaper or a crossword or Sudoku puzzle to hand at mealtimes, but they only turned to these amusements when they had discussed the food and, if that sparked any topics of more enduring interest, only when these had been exhausted. With Arthur there, it seemed rude to line up a diversion which would look as if they were planning to avoid talking to him, but Eve could think of nothing at all spontaneous to say about sausage, peas and mash, so said nothing. Sally, who was normally happy to start the conversation by mocking her own culinary efforts, also said nothing. And Arthur, as if no food had passed his lips for at least a fortnight, could only have spoken if he had been prepared to do so with his mouth full. Eve tried to catch Sally's eye, but she kept her head down.

After the last sausage had been eaten (by Arthur), Sally looked at him and said: "Pancakes?"

Arthur's slippery face formed itself into a smile that was

clear, uncomplicated, utterly charming, and Sally smiled back—
how could she not?—and began making batter. Eve cleared
the dishes into the bowl in the sink and sat down again. They
had reached an agreement, early on, that when one person was
standing up and moving about, the other should sit still. Eve
had pointed out that this was the sensible approach; she was
happy to relax into idleness and watch Sally work when it
was Sally's turn to be working. Sally had had to be reminded
at first that no one would judge her if she did not wash up at
once, or sweep the crumbs from the table as soon as the meal was
done. Eve had observed the transition from rigid compliance to
cheerful acceptance and had chalked it up as another step in the
unwinding the trip was achieving.

As Sally whisked the eggs in a bowl, Arthur began to feel
about in the storage cavity below the bench she had been sitting
on. He took out all the games—Scrabble, Cluedo, chess, two
packs of cards, Monopoly and Uno.

"Now, then," he said. "Which of these do you two ladies
play?"

"Not until after the pancakes," said Sally, sounding just like
Eve's mother. "You'll make them sticky."

"Oh, no, no, no," said Arthur. "Stickiness. I should think not.
What would Anastasia say?" He turned to Eve and dropped
his voice. "She is all right, isn't she? She is coming back to the
Number One?"

"I told you," Eve said. "She's meeting us the day after tomorrow at Norton Junction."

"You did, of course. It's an old man's folly, to fear disaster."

After the pancakes had been eaten, Sally and Eve did the
washing-up, following their usual ritual. One washed, one sat

and dried as the dishes were passed over. The one washing sat down and the one drying stood up and put everything away. It was like the callisthenic exercises Eve used to do during a secondment to Japan: simple, relaxing, purgative. After her return home, she had never done them again. She felt sure that, in the same way, if ever she re-entered her old life she would go back to a random processing of the tools for cooking and eating on the basis that there was always something else she could be doing. But in this space, with Sally as a partner, she liked the pattern they formed and the resulting tidiness was a constant source of pleasure.

While they cleared up, Arthur went out onto the towpath and rummaged around in his rucksack, accompanied by Noah, who had the air of a dog keeping an eye on Arthur, though whether in hope or fear it was impossible to tell. As soon as the last dish was put away, the last crumb swept up, Arthur re-materialized in the cabin, turned out to be sitting just where he had been before, with the games stacked at this elbow, looking from one to the other with his eyebrows raised.

"We play Scrabble," Sally said.

"Are either of you any good?"

"We both are," said Sally.

"As good as Anastasia?"

"Not quite. But we have been playing a lot, so we may have improved."

Arthur put the tips of his skinny little fingers together.

"The thing we must get straight," he said, "before we begin, is our several attitudes to winning and losing. Only once we know this can we choose the right game to play. The game that will preserve, you understand, harmony."

"Doesn't everyone have the same attitude?" said Sally. "Everyone wants to win, no one wants to lose."

"That is like saying everyone wants to live, no one wants to die, and assuming that, in stating so much, you have penetrated to the very heart of an individual's approach to life and to death."

"Let's start with you, then," Eve said. "What is your attitude, Arthur, to winning and losing?"

"Too fast, young madam, too fast. I think we need to define our parameters, understand what it is we mean when we talk about how we feel in the matter of winning, or of not winning."

"Sounds good," said Eve, who liked definitions and parameters.

"We don't keep the lights on after ten o'clock," said Sally, "to avoid draining the battery."

"Right! Right! Let me transport you, then, to the moment a game is over. Now, imagine you did not enjoy the game, because it was too long or too confusing, or you had cramp and no room to move your foot to get rid of it, or you were worried about whether the cake you had left in the oven was burning or whether someone else around the table might be about to be sick, or you hated one or all of the other players to the point of distraction. It doesn't matter why. If you won, would that cast a retrospective light on the experience that transformed it into something worthwhile? Something you later reminded your fellow players about with a happy nostalgia: 'Do you remember when we played Monopoly for eight hours and could barely move at the end?' and they would all groan, but for you, it is a memory worth preserving, rose-tinted, because of your victory."

Eve started to speak but Arthur held up a hand to stop her. "No, wait. Hold that person, who might or might not be you, in your mind, and consider now a game that has passed as enjoyably as you could have hoped. Laughter, teasing, plenty of swift action. But you lost. Do you care? Do you make a mental note to suggest a different game next time, one you believe gives you a better chance of winning? Or do you think, 'Never mind, it was fun.'"

"I'm the first type," Eve said. "I admit it. Whether I enjoyed myself or not. I'm really only playing to win. But without, hopefully, the post-victory gloating. I don't think I do that."

"You do a bit," Sally said. "But you still enjoy the game, whether you win or lose, don't you?"

"Up to a point. What about you? You don't care much, one way or another, do you?"

"I don't care about winning," Sally said. "But I hate to come last, or, if there are only two players, to be too far behind whoever wins . . . We're talking here," she said, turning to Arthur, "of a game involving some level of skill, aren't we? No one minds losing at Snakes and Ladders because they never threw a six to start."

"I mind," said Arthur. "Good game, boring game, hard game or simple game, outcome a lottery or outcome a result of skill, tactics, cunning moves and blocking maneuvers. I want to win."

That surprises me, thought Eve. Then she thought how ridiculous to think that when everything about this man surprised her.

Sally and Arthur remained looking at each other, as if a challenge had been laid down and each was waiting for the other to respond to it.

"How about," Eve said, "you teach us a game we haven't played before. Then you are sure to win and we won't mind losing because we were always going to."

"Can you play cribbage?" said Arthur.

Neither of them could, but some way through the explanation of how the game worked, Sally declared that not only could she not play cribbage but it was unlikely she would ever want to play cribbage, and she climbed out of the *Number One* to take Noah for a turn along the towpath. Eve, however, was enthralled by it. She liked the simplicity of the game and the complexity of the scoring—which they had to do with paper and pencil, lacking the pegboard that, Arthur said, was one of the joys of playing it, often a work of art in itself as well as a visual presentation of relative positions. Eve became so involved that it was only with the dimming of the light that she realized it was late, that Sally should be back by now, that she was sitting inches away from a man she had met only a few hours ago and who she could not begin to understand and who was therefore capable of anything. She shifted away from him, instinctively.

"Battery-saving time," she said. "I'll have to say goodnight."

Arthur swept up the cards they had been playing with. "You have the makings of a cribbage player," he said.

"You mean I might one day become good enough for you to refuse to play me?"

Arthur made a noise between a snigger and a cough. "Not likely," he said. "But you might be good enough to be worth beating, after a year or two."

Eve went outside to look for Sally and found her sitting on a bollard, Noah at her feet.

"Lights-out time," she said.

"I know," said Sally. "That's what I was waiting for."

It was a still night and the mooring was remote from houses and roads so the rhythmic snoring of Arthur in his towpath tent was audible inside the *Number One*. Eve lay her head on the pillow in the expectation of being kept awake by the pattern of sounds from the bank, but the rules of cribbage running round in her head proved enough to send her to sleep despite it.

IT RAINED. A SOFT, MISTY drizzle that dampened the surfaces but appeared to be no inconvenience until it soaked through layers quicker than expected and made everything that needed to be touched in the process of moving a boat—the tiller, ropes, rails, lock keys—slick and slippery.

Sally stood by the open side hatch looking at the downy drops of moisture on Arthur's zipped-up tent. She had made a pot of tea and wrapped a towel round it to keep it warm; now she was trying to decide whether to go over and leave a mug where Arthur could reach it from inside his cocoon. She could not understand what she felt about Arthur this damp, gray morning. He was like a violin, playing tunes that were never the same, in tone, in mood, in tunefulness, so it was impossible to know, before it came on stage, whether to dread or look forward to the sound it would make. As she stood there, with her mug of tea, she was inclined to feel sorry for him, in his tea-less, cramped and, for all she knew, not quite waterproof shelter. On the other hand, she was fearful of what would happen if she approached, if she called out and announced she was there. She had no idea what he would do, her imagination not reaching the end of the possibilities; it snagged on the idea he might emerge, in one movement, partially clothed or even naked, aggressive or, worse, too welcoming. He was, as she had said to Eve, so hard to pin down.

She lifted her mug to her lips and at that moment the zip on the tent slid upward and Arthur rolled out. He was wearing the same clothes as the night before and looked like a cat unfolding itself from the place it had chosen to sleep in. Sally was just thinking that there was nothing threatening about a waking cat (unless you happened to be small enough to be its prey) when Arthur appeared down the steps from the rear deck, shaking drops of water off his jacket.

"Tea?" she said.

"You are a lovely lady."

"And breakfast?"

"Lovelier and lovelier."

He seemed diminished this morning, a little, gray figure who stayed hunched over his mug while Eve and Sally did their morning tasks. He waited to use the bathroom until it would be no inconvenience to them; he scuttled over to his tent and collapsed it, so it seemed, in a single movement; having stowed everything in his rucksack, he came back on board and sat, hunched and silent, at the table until it was time to move.

There were two more locks to work before they were clear of Stoke Bruerne. Eve offered to do them without him, as she was wearing waterproofs.

"No, no," he said. "I must earn my passage."

They gave him what Anastasia had described as the emergency poncho. It was enormous and orange and not, she told them, suitable for prolonged use because the wearer of it had to be ever vigilant to avoid trapping the flapping fabric in any number of dangerous and damaging ways. It was not an emergency and it was not pouring with rain, but Arthur accepted the loan of this garment, scarcely smaller than his tent, and appeared unconcerned about looking ridiculous—which he did. Sally, at the tiller, was at liberty to observe passersby taking a second look. She found herself keeping a watchful eye on him to make sure he heeded the advice, which he had treated with indifference, to make sure nothing snagged as he skipped from gate to paddle, from paddle to gate.

They reached Blisworth Tunnel. It was, said the book, 3,075 yards long; long enough for the light at the end to be visible only in the best conditions, from the right angle, in the right light. It was not obvious where the end lay, as the *Number One* approached its dark mouth. It was close to two miles, Sally thought, a walkable distance, a distance she regularly walked from 42 Beech Grove to the school where she worked. She tried to imagine the journey ahead as if it was the walk to school on a particularly dark morning when the street lights had been turned off. She listed for herself the markers that broke up that walk, the post box on the corner, the perfectly trimmed yew hedge halfway down the next street, the place where an old plane tree caused the pavement to narrow and the surface to ripple under her feet. But as she steered the bow of the *Number One* through the opening into the narrow space under the arched roof, she stopped thinking about getting to the end—of the imaginary walk, of the tunnel—and focused on the experience of being inside it, the only illumination the *Number One*'s headlight. Being anywhere else became unimaginable.

There was no towpath, just the arch of bricks spanning the inky, lapping water, smacking the sides as the *Number One* sucked it up and pushed it aside in its passage. Sally had thought, as she approached the tunnel's mouth, that she should take off her waterproof, which would no longer be needed. But although there

was no rain inside the arch, there were drips, random drips and
occasional water spouts implying pressure from without, barely
held in check.

What she should have done, she realized as the sparse daylight faded away, was provide herself with something warm.
The air trapped inside was cold, and though it must circulate
through the vents and through the openings at either end, it
felt as if it never did, as if this cold air was a dead medium un-
touched by sunlight for a million years. As a schoolgirl, Sally
had once worked at a mushroom farm which grew its crops in
underground vaults kept at a constant, low temperature. She
had hated the mushroom farm, and the man who ran it—who
would touch all the girls in a casually offensive way—and she
had buried the memory, but now it came to her as a crumb of
comfort. After all, the tunnel was only a long mushroom farm.

Sally steered as near as she could to the middle of the channel, going deeper and deeper into darkness, the headlight of the
Number One barely showing up the dark and dirty brickwork
on either side, while a light ahead was too faint for her to tell if
it was the tunnel end or an oncoming boat. She glanced round
from time to time to see the diminishing circle of light behind
them, but this swiftly shrank and began to change shape as the
slight variations in the tunnel's path half obscured it.

Arthur was standing on the rear deck with her; Eve was on
the top step of the stairs down to the cabin, head and shoulders
framed by the lockers on either side of the tiller. Arthur held his
hand out from time to time, to catch a drip or judge the distance
from the wall, or just for the feel of the cold air beyond the
boat's side. The ridiculous orange poncho, leached of its color
in the dark, looked like a sheet he had draped over himself. No

one spoke. The throb of the engine, the *Number One*'s light bouncing back off the ridges of water, the walls narrowing to an invisible point in the distance, the familiar smell of diesel, now stiflingly manifest: Sally began to feel she might do something silly. She might scream, or cry, or stop the engine or drive into a wall, or simply take her hand off the tiller and sit down facing the way they had come. And just as this feeling became unbearable, Arthur took his harmonica out of his pocket and began to play a soft, melancholy tune that filled the space they were traveling through and made it, all at once, stable, three-dimensional. Eve came up the last step onto the deck and said:

"Do you want me to take a turn?"

"Do you want to?"

"Frankly? No. I'm trying to pretend this is a ghost train at the fairground being operated by someone else. I don't want to be in control. But I will take over if you want me to."

"I'm all right," said Sally. "I was trying to pretend I was walking to school in the dark, but I've accepted I'm driving a boat through a tunnel, so I'll carry on doing that."

Arthur's playing became livelier, faster. Eve took a step down, giving Sally a clearer view ahead. The light she had seen was closer now.

"Is that the end?" she asked.

Arthur stopped playing and turned his head. "No," he said. "It's another boat coming toward you. There's room to pass, but only just, so you'll have to hug the wall on your right."

"Shall I slow down?"

"No. You're going slow enough. It'll become sluggish if you drop the revs further. At the point you go past the other boat, throttle right back so you are drifting past each other. And don't worry about the paintwork. The wall is covered in slime and it won't do any damage—or none that Anastasia is going to notice."

Eve had gone down yet another step and her voice was muffled. "Hug something slimy, Sally. I'm sure it wouldn't be the first time."

"Oh, I think it would."

"What have you been doing all your life?" asked Eve.

The sound of the approaching boat's engine was filling the void between them and its dazzling headlamp, and the outline of its bow was close and then closer, then both boats put their engines into a speed just above idling and they slid past each other.

"How do," said the man at the stern as he passed them, as if they had met at a stile and Sally had stood aside to let him step over first. Then they were facing darkness again, outside the reach of the *Number One*'s beam of light, with another light farther off, beyond the vaulted blackness in between. This, too, was another boat, which went by with more noise and less control, and then the circle of light that marked the end became more than a hint, became a fact, then another archway to steer through, and at last they were out in the daylight, in a deep cutting with a church perched on top and a village reaching away up a hill. Eve came up the steps and gave Sally a hug, causing the *Number One* to veer toward a row of moored boats.

"Steady on," said Arthur.

"Look," said Eve, "just remember. A couple of weeks ago our biggest challenge would have been navigating our trolleys down the fruit-and-veg aisle in Sainsbury's on a Saturday morning. That's a whole new experience Sally's coped with."

"I only meant, mind the other boats," said Arthur, at his meekest.

"Thank you for the music," Sally said. "It helped."

"It frightens the ghosts," he said. "Keeps them at arm's length, as it were."

"What ghosts?" Sally asked.

"Have you met Billy?"

"We have."

Arthur nodded as if this was just as he expected. "Ask him. He tells a better story than I do."

Then he smiled at her and she smiled back and wondered how she could so recently have feared the arm that was lurking inside a tent ready to reach out and grab her.

AFTER THE TUNNEL, THEY REACHED a junction where a branch of the canal turned off to the right.

"Now, you see, you could have gone the wrong way here, if I hadn't been with you," Arthur said.

"Hardly," Sally said. "We can understand the Guide better than that."

"There again," said Arthur, "this arm goes to Northampton, which would be perfect for me. Per-fect. I don't suppose you've got time to take me there, though, do you?"

"It's seventeen locks and five miles," said Sally, consulting the book. "According to the formula—miles plus locks divided by three—that's seven hours there and seven hours back. You could walk it in an hour and a half."

"The feet," murmured Arthur. "The feet."

They chugged on through open farmland, Arthur asleep in

the cabin, Sally driving, Eve going up and down the gunwale tidying ropes, wiping water off the rail.

"You're fidgeting," Sally said.

"I know. Do you mind dropping me off at the next bridge? I could cycle down to the next village and buy something for lunch."

"Why would I mind?"

Eve cocked her head in the direction of the cabin.

"Don't worry," Sally said. "I can cope."

Although the rain had stopped it was dull and breezy. Sally, wearing a fleece, felt a different kind of contentment to the sense she'd had the previous day, before Arthur and the tunnel, of eating a particularly long, tasty, fulfilling but not filling meal. Now, she was happy to be traveling, to be moving forward, and it was less dreamy, more risky, but more satisfying.

Arthur came out of the cabin looking tousled and sleepy and asked when they would reach Norton Junction.

"You tell me," Sally said. "You're the expert." Though she realized she had no reason to suppose him one. All she knew about him was that he knew Anastasia; that he was an accountant living in Uttoxeter who took frequent breaks. This much she had heard through the open hatch the night before. And she did not know whether any or all of this was true. "Actually," she said, "how much time have you spent on a canal boat?"

"You're great ones for questions, the two of you," said Arthur. He lay down on the rear deck and trailed his fingers in the water. Sally could think of nothing further to say. She pondered whether they did ask too many questions and came to the conclusion Arthur was wrong; they were normally rather circumspect, finding out about each other bit by bit. What had happened here, Sally concluded, was that Arthur had arrived as a mystery and had made no effort to demystify himself; quite the opposite. Apart from the possibly-not-true Uttoxeter and accountant facts, he had avoided revealing anything at all about himself. She said so.

"You know I want to win," he said. "I'm not sure I know anything as significant about you."

Sally thought about 42 Beech Grove and the way she had behaved in those impossibly different days, and from that perspective she recognized that Arthur had a perfect right to tell them nothing and they had no right to probe. So she looked at the Guide, calculated where they were and said: "We should reach the locks before Norton Junction about teatime. We can decide then whether to carry on tonight as far as the wharf where we'll be meeting Anastasia, or leave it until tomorrow morning."

Arthur became upright by some sequence of movements she missed and dried his hand on his trouser leg.

"I'm being of no use to you, look. I'm doing nothing at all to earn my passage in this boat, so I will make a cup of tea."

As the day wore on, winding round bends, acknowledging passing boats, mooring for a lunch of bread, cheese, pâté, pork pie, Scotch eggs and ham ("Well, I didn't know what Arthur liked," Eve said; it turned out he liked all of it and ate a considerable amount), Arthur became restless. He kept checking the Guide, then his watch. They passed over an aqueduct and reached a point where the railway and the motorway and the A5 all ran more or less parallel to, even alongside, the canal. Eve was excited by all these engineering feats: most impressed by the ability of the Romans to cut a straight road going in the right direction, least impressed by the ability of modern civil engineers to create a six-lane highway on stilts. The canal came in above the railway, in Eve's hierarchy, because it involved water.

"Fluids," she said. "So hard to manage. In contrast to rock and iron and steel and concrete, which can be counted on not to change shape even if they change position."

Arthur recovered briefly from his self-absorption and argued that the skill required was less relevant than the social impact of the various ways of facilitating movement. On this basis, he said, the railway would be in first place, followed by the canal, then the motorway, leaving the Roman road in last place. After all, it had just been about helping a conquering army to conquer, then maintaining control of the conquered. Eve, pleased to be challenged, began to construct an argument that the Roman road still came out on top because the whole pattern of modern Britain was imprinted with the legacy of that conquest.

"In what way?" said Arthur, and Eve had to admit that she had no idea, but she was certain it was a truth she would be able to prove if she ever bothered to research it. Sally felt absurdly fond of both of them.

When they reached the first of the seven locks they needed to go through to reach Norton Junction, Arthur proposed they stop for the night. It was four o'clock.

"I thought we could keep going to Norton Junction," Eve said. "There's a pub there. And we wouldn't be sandwiched between the railway and the motorway, like we are here."

The lock gates ahead of them opened and a boat came through.

"Maybe some of the locks, then," said Arthur, and Eve gestured to the oncoming boat crew to leave the gates open.

Eve drove and Sally and Arthur worked the locks, as they had done the previous day, with Arthur climbing aboard between each one and Sally walking on. Only, yesterday she had been trying to avoid being close to Arthur and today she was simply pleased to be walking, to feel the breeze on her face, to contemplate the varying rates of forward propulsion of the cars on the motorway, the occasional train, the *Number One* and herself. She was walking faster than the *Number One*; the trains were traveling faster than the cars. But to say that the cars were therefore going faster than she was walking was like comparing a pea to a pumpkin, or a mouse to an elephant; the same broad categories (vegetable, mammal), but in no other way to be placed in the same box charted on the same scale.

They went through six locks, passed under a railway as a train, obscenely loud, went over it. There was a quiet stretch before the final lock, yet within reach of the road where, according to the Guide, the bus from Long Buckby station would pass.

"Let's stop here," said Arthur, climbing back on board. "Look, a hedge, a tree—perfect for a man with a tent."

As soon as they had banged in the stakes, tightened the ropes and Arthur had, with a flick of the wrist, erected his tent, he insisted they go to the pub. It was half a mile down the towpath, but Arthur was perky now, naming the wild flowers they passed, pointing out a butterfly, spotting a heron hidden by trees. Eve and Sally would have walked straight past it without noticing. He would buy them supper, he said, when they reached the pub.

"Aren't we supposed to pay you, for working the locks?" said Eve. "Isn't that how it works?"

"When I've spent the best part of a day idling in your cabin, drinking your tea, eating your biscuits, your pies and your bread? No, no. This is how it works: I treat you. What will it be?"

There were people in the pub who knew Arthur. Twice someone came over to say hello—two men, then a man and a woman—and at least three more times Sally was conscious of a slight nod exchanged with someone she could not pick out from the crowd, for the pub was crowded. Arthur appeared to want to talk to no one but them. He concentrated on Sally and Eve, no matter what the distractions. The people who spoke to him, he responded to with a smile, but without breaking off from what he was saying. Sally had the impression he was exerting a force field to keep everyone who might otherwise have tried to engage him in conversation at a distance.

He told them stories about hitching lifts from boats on the canal, working the locks in exchange for sleeping on board, if there was room, or in exchange for meals if there was no room and he had to sleep on the towpath. He had been doing this, he said, for fifty years. He knew the waterways as well as anyone, having learned about them on foot, on boats, from buses and trains, traveling to and from Uttoxeter. It was rare, nowadays, for him to have to appeal to strangers for a lift. He knew so many of the people who spent their lives, or much of their lives, on the canal. When the weather was fine he would walk for days without hailing a boat, knowing an acquaintance would turn up soon and he would be spared the necessity of making himself known to someone new.

"Like us," Eve said.

"Except you haven't," said Sally. "Made yourself known to us. You've behaved as if we already knew you."

Arthur put down the pint glass of lemonade he had been

raising to his lips and touched her hand. Sally was aware she had not touched him, or been touched by him, before—she'd been careful to avoid it—and she was surprised at how firm, warm and dry was the sensation of his fingers upon hers.

"But you're on the *Number One*," he said. "How could I treat as strangers those who are living and working the *Number One*?" He drank some lemonade. "And, of course," he said, with a look at once sheepish and sly, "I have to be careful because you will tell Anastasia you have met me. She will want a report. You will give her one. It has been on my mind."

"You talk as if you won't see her yourself," said Sally. "But you will, if you wait around."

"If I see her," said Arthur, "she will plunge in and uncover everything I keep hidden, things I keep hidden even from myself. I am like a cupboard, to Anastasia. She gets in there and inspects the contents, makes judgments, throws things out, rearranges what's left, cleans all the crumbs and dust out of the corners and lays down fresh sheets of lining paper to keep in peak condition those things she has newly sorted. There are times when I need Anastasia, when I need my shelves emptied, cleaned and reorganized. But at this moment, I'm not sure."

"I know what you mean," said Eve. "That's the feeling I get, too. That she has somehow spotted what you were trying to ignore. And she makes you challenge what you never thought to challenge, because it suddenly seems obvious that you should have been."

Sally wasn't sure she knew what they were talking about. She wondered whether Arthur and Eve—who were both, in different ways, so sure of themselves—found Anastasia a challenge to that sure-ness and were perked up by it. Perhaps she was immune because she was so inchoate, so unformed, so lacking in certainties to be challenged, without surfaces for a challenge to bounce off.

"So what are you saying?" said Eve. "You're going to run away before Anastasia gets here?"

"That's about it," Arthur whispered, as if Anastasia might hear him and thwart his plan if he spoke aloud. "I'm planning to escape."

Now that he was suggesting it, Sally regretted he was going but still wanted him gone. She had traveled from wishing he had never turned up to finding his company soothing, but she wanted him gone so she could coalesce her ideas of who he was without the constant distraction of his actual presence. It had always been one of the things she had waited for: for someone to go, for an experience to be over, because only then would she be able to make sense of it. When she was alone. But there was a risk Arthur was going too soon, before all his complexities had revealed themselves, and she would find, when she tried to re-call the memory of him, that she was missing parts of the story; he would be like a TV serial where some of the episodes had not been shown even though the end had been reached.

"You've used the word 'escape' before," Sally said. "I over-heard you talking to Eve about it. She said she was escaping to avoid making a decision, but you didn't say what you were escaping from."

"Yes," said Arthur. He looked not at Sally but at Eve. "I would say, having known you now for so many hours"—he held his hands out to indicate a stretch of time bigger than the empty plate in front of him, smaller than the width of the table—"that it isn't decisions you're running away from. It's the pressure of having to win."

"Would you?" Eve said. "Well, I have no idea what you're running away from because, having known you for this long"—she held out her hands to indicate an area the width of her wine glass—"I don't know you at all."

"I will tell you," said Arthur, "but first I want to say"—he turned to Sally—"that I don't believe you know what you are running away from. But whatever it is, you have to escape from your fear of failure first."

"She's escaping from tedium," Eve said. "From mediocrity, sameness."

Sally felt closer, in that moment, to Arthur than to Eve. "Now you," she said to him.

"Responsibility," Arthur said. "Pity me, dear ladies, because you know, and I know, there is no escape from that. Once taken up, the burden of it never leaves you, even if you walk away, let fall whatever may fall when you no longer stand and hold it. Still, it is inescapable. Take it or reject it, what follows? Toil or guilt. The only thing to do is choose between them."

The towpath was too narrow for them to walk three abreast between the junction and the *Number One*. On the way to the pub, Arthur had gone ahead. On the way back, Eve did. She had the torch, so Sally and Arthur fell into place alongside each other, following the beam partially obscured by Eve's legs. As the noise of the pub died away behind them, all the other noises of the night became audible once more: a rumble from the steady but reduced flow of traffic on the A5; the sound of voices or laughter from moored boats; the cough of a smoker sent out

to perch on a bollard for his late-night cigarette; the screech of
an owl and the harsh, insistent barking of a fox.

"In *Midsomer Murders*," Sally said, "a fox barking always
means a murder is about to be committed."

"And so it may," said Arthur.

"Will we see you again," Sally asked, "before we get back to
Uxbridge?"

"It is possible, my lovely lady. It is possible."

The next morning, he was gone.

NOAH WOKE EVE WHEN THE sun was still low in the sky to the
east. She knew by the way it lit up the ceiling above her that it
was nowhere near time to get up, but Noah was waiting by the
cabin door, expressing his urgent need to leave, with a sniffle
and a scrabble and an anxious cock of his head which she found
harder to resist than his howls. These she had become accustomed to and knew were merely a form of teenage overacting.

She went through to the galley and opened the door for him,
watched from the window as he explored the patch of ground
where Arthur's tent had been, analyzed its every vestige of
scent. Then sat and looked the way they had come the previous
day, toward the bridge where the road to Long Buckby crossed
the canal, where the bus stopped. Eve watched Noah and the
empty patch of ground, which looked both surprisingly empty
and just as she expected it to be.

A man from a boat moored on the towpath in the direction
Noah was looking had come out half dressed and was peeing
on the weeds by the hedge. It would be the only good thing

about being born a man, Eve thought. Otherwise, she felt sorry for those who had been born male. She had realized, when she started work, the burden of having expectations to live up to, a position within a masculine society to maintain, that the men carried and she didn't. Expectations of her were so low as to be easy to exceed.

And now, when the idea of diversity, the constant challenges to the notion that being a man required and even mandated certain patterns of behavior, they were, instead of being liberated, cast into a darkness where the rules were not yet clear enough for them to be sure they had read and interpreted them correctly.

Sally came through from her cabin.

"Has Arthur gone?"

"So it seems. Noah woke me. I can't tell if he's sorry to see Arthur go or keen to make sure he's really gone."

"I know how he feels," said Sally. "Now we need to prepare ourselves for Anastasia."

Eve looked round the cabin, trying to see it as Anastasia would see it. It was clean, as Anastasia would have it, and neat, but not quite neat enough. There was a fleece discarded by Sally on the bench; someone had left the coffee jar on the worktop instead of putting it away, at once, in its space in the cupboard; a book was lying on the table. Eve put the coffee jar away. Sally picked up the fleece and put it on. They were left with the book. It had a plain, red, scuffed cloth cover and discoloration on the page edges; it did not look like a book that had been read once and placed on a shelf. It looked like a book that had been read again and again and carried about and left lying in the sun. Eve bent sideways to read the spine.

"*Mr. Lucton's Freedom*," she read. "Yours?"

Sally shook her head. "I've never heard of it."

Eve opened the front cover and found a note tucked inside. It was written on the back of a piece of scrap paper used to score a Scrabble game—E: 329, S: 387, Eve noted, before she unfolded it. It read:

> *Ladies,*
> *Speaking of escape, as we did, or nearly did, I invite you to read this book which has been with me for many years. I trust you not to lose it or destroy it. I will reclaim it when next I visit the* Number One. *If you should have gone before I return, please leave it in Anastasia's keeping.*

It was signed: *The Hitchhiker.*

Eve picked the book up and looked for clues about the story and the author, as she would do with any other book she was thinking about reading. But there were none. It was a book-club edition of a novel by Francis Brett Young, and told her nothing except that he had written a number of other titles, all of them unfamiliar, and this edition had been published in 1941. It was in three parts, titled *North Bromwich*, *The Country of Strange Adventures* and *Quietest Under the Sun*.

She closed it up and held it out to Sally, who took it and tucked it into the pocket of her fleece. She turned away and started to leave the cabin, then came back.

"Is it all right if I read it first?" she said.

"Of course," said Eve. "You can let me know if it's worth reading."

"I don't think Arthur would have left it if it wasn't," Sally said.

Eve and Sally waited for Anastasia and she did not come. They occupied themselves with wiping and mopping and rearranging until every corner of every object was square with the object beside it, and anything identical with its neighbor was lined, facing the same way, with no gaps between, or evenly spaced gaps where gaps were necessary. All the time, they were watching the bridge, noting the arrival and departure of buses, pausing in their work as one departed, to wait for the sturdy figure of Anastasia to come stumping down the steps to the towpath.

After lunch, Eve set off on her bicycle to the station to look at the timetable, and to see how far away the station was—or so she said. Sally noted that Eve's impatience for Anastasia's arrival was greater than hers. She remembered all the times when someone was expected at 42 Beech Grove, how she would have finished preparing for their arrival long before they could be expected to appear, and then had been unable to do anything except wait until the doorbell rang. Then, once whoever it was had finally come, after a moment or two of relief that they had turned up, more or less at the time expected, she would be looking forward, anxiously and eagerly, to the moment they left. Now it was Eve behaving as she had behaved in the past, while she had adapted so readily to canal time, where nothing is accomplished quickly, and times of arrival may be agreed in terms of a given week rather than a given hour.

She made herself a cup of tea and sat in the well at the front of the boat, sheltered from the slight breeze, with an eye-level view of the short grass on the edge of the towpath and, if she lifted her eyes higher, of a section of bricks on the bridge with, above that, a tangle of clouds lit up by the sun. She opened *Mr. Lucton's Freedom* and began to read.

Eve was subject to a number of annoyances as she cycled to Long Buckby. First, the wind, which was inconsistent enough to be irritating and steady enough to make pedalling hard work. Then there was the traffic. It was not a wide enough road for the vehicles coming up behind her to overtake safely if there was something coming the other way or if the driver could not be sure there was nothing coming. Hardly one of them got it right, as far as Eve was concerned. Some of them dawdled along behind her far too long, making her anxious, when there was ample room to pass. Others came past at speed when there was a risk they would meet something equally speedy at just the moment when they were occupying the middle of the road. There were gratings and potholes along the shoulder which Eve was forced to bump into and over by drivers too careless or too nervous to pull out far enough. On the other hand, she felt patronized by those who made a point of going as far as the opposite shoulder to be sure of giving her sufficient space to wobble, weave or fall off. And finally there were the other cyclists. She met one group coming toward her and another overtook her. They were all wearing Lycra. They were moving at a speed she thought quite unnecessary but secretly aspired to; they made it plain they felt themselves to be a species apart by not acknowledging her nod of recognition, one cyclist to another.

She reached the station tired and irritable and realized she had no idea what she was doing there. She had imagined something like the stations she used in London, with a café and a shop or two, but this was just two platforms, a tunnel between them, a Portakabin (closed) for ticket sales. A train arrived, from the south, and people climbed out. None of them was Anastasia, who, even in this abundance of variety, would have stood out as fitting into a category of one. Eve was disappointed. She must be fonder of the old lady than she had imagined. Or maybe, after the weeks of nothing happening, she was suddenly desperate for something to happen.

She cycled on into Long Buckby and found a café, bought herself a hot chocolate and a slice of carrot cake. She sat in a corner and phoned Jacob from the flat upstairs. He did something that involved computers—she had been told, she could not remember who by, that he was a games designer, but she refused to believe this; it sounded exactly the sort of thing a chirpy little toerag like Jacob would tell people. She imagined he designed websites for small businesses. He lived with his partner, a large, silent man called Vic, who worked irregular hours and was often away. Eve assumed it must be Vic's high-powered job that had funded the purchase of the flat and kept Jacob in a style which suited him without the need for much effort in the pursuit of money. They were unobjectionable neighbors, but she had limited her contact with them to collecting the parcel deliveries that Jacob, at home all day, took in for her, in exchange for which she gave them a bottle of gin at Christmas. She had his number in her phone, though, as the delivery of parcels had meant occasional contact needed to be made.

Jacob answered on the second ring.

"Ho, there, Eve! Quelle surprise. I thought you were off boating in the back of beyond."

"I am, but there is a phone signal in this particular part of the further side of beyond. Anastasia tells me you've been helping her organize a trip to visit us."

"I have, I have. What a woman that is! Can you imagine having her for a grandmother? Or a mother, even? You'd be well sorted out, wouldn't you? Properly buffed up by the time you were ten."

"Do you know what train she was planning to catch? I'm keen to have her boat looking the way she'd want it to, before she arrives."

"I should think you are! Right, the plan is, she goes with Vic tomorrow morning to Euston, when he goes to work. He has to be in in time to take the ten forty to Edinburgh, so she should be able to get a train to Long Buckby mid-morning."

"That's very kind of Vic."

"Well, it is, actually. He's terrified of her. I might have to tag along with them to make sure he doesn't have conniptions before they get there. There again, she'll only assume I'm coming along to make sure she gets the train safely, and that'll wind her up. She's a bit on the independent side, isn't she?"

"Yes, but she's not well. Perhaps Vic can make sure she's OK at your end, and if you let me know when she's arriving at this end, we can meet her."

"Vic's got his colleagues all lined up to keep a surreptitious eye on her, don't you worry. The whole station staff will be looking out for her."

"What does Vic do, then?" she asked.

"He's a train driver. Did you honestly not know that? My dear, we have not got to know each other as well as neighbors ought. You must come round when you get back and we'll have a good old gossip, find out everything there is to know about each other. How does that sound?"

"Terrible," said Eve, and Jacob laughed and hung up.

She did not enjoy the hot chocolate or the carrot cake as much as she had planned she would when she decided to indulge herself. She was cross with herself for having fallen into misconceptions about Jacob and Vic; entirely through her own laziness, she had adopted a cliché as if it were fact and now found that, as so often, the fact was more interesting than the cliché. But as well as this shameful feeling, she was unsettled by the suggestion that there was a point in the not-too-distant future when she would go back to her flat, would be around to take time for a cozy little chat over coffee or wine with Jacob. It was like the moment when she realized, rather more than halfway through her time in the sixth form, that at some point the day of the first exam would arrive. She had always known it would, but at some impossibly remote date by which time some mystical dust would have transformed her into the sort of person with the sort of knowledge that made exams easy. It was not today, or tomorrow, so what did it matter if the dust had not yet blown in? Or so she had thought until she allowed herself to recognize that day would follow day to the dread day and there was no hope, no dust on the horizon. It was entirely down to the person she now was and would ever be. So she had better take steps to make the day, when it came, as painless as possible. She had fallen into the same sense of timelessness, of expecting something to happen before the buffers at the end of the track (in this case, she was thinking, Chester) were reached that would make everything easy, everything obvious.

She bought another piece of carrot cake for Sally and cycled

back with the wind behind her. Sally was sitting idle, reading a
book, and accepted both the carrot cake and the news that Anastasia would not be arriving until the next day so calmly that
Eve had to walk Noah a couple of miles along the towpath and
back to re-establish the rhythm of living on the canal.

EVE AND SALLY CAME CLOSE to falling out over breakfast. The
subject of their disagreement was Anastasia, but even as they
were failing to agree on whether one of them or both of them
should go to meet her at the station, in preference to both of
them waiting with the *Number One*, they were aware that the
real reason they were arguing was elsewhere, buried. Sally
thought they should watch the bus stop until a bus arrived, then
go up to the bridge if they spotted Anastasia alighting to carry
her bag down to the boat. No, no, said Eve. She'll need help
with her bag at the station. But then, Sally said, it will look as if
we are escorting her to the *Number One*, as if it is our boat, not
hers. So we will, countered Eve, if we meet her by the bus stop.
No, said Sally, we can hang back, let her approach by herself.
We can do that if we're *on* the bus *with* her, said Eve. We could
be hanging around Long Buckby station all day, said Sally. We
could go to the café in the village, said Eve, and wait there.
Even though it's half a mile away, said Sally.

They occupied themselves at different ends of the boat, waiting for their normal harmony to be restored. At least, that was
what Sally was waiting for until she remembered the conversations with Arthur about winning and losing, and she began to
suspect that what Eve was waiting for was a capitulation that
would mean victory for her side of the argument. Or, to put it

another way, for Sally to lose. She stopped folding her pajamas and sat down on the bunk, thinking this through. She thought back to all the previous times when they had not both come to the same conclusion—where to moor, whether to eat in or go out, when to stop for lunch, for water, for a pump-out, for fuel. There was no pattern, she realized. Sometimes, Eve fell in with her alternative, sometimes she fell in with Eve's. Between them, there had never been the tension that comes from one of two people always wanting to be right. No matter how trivial the matter in hand was, no matter how much stronger the arguments for the other solution might be.

Sally put her pajamas away and went to find Eve, who was polishing the kettle.

"It doesn't honestly matter, does it?" she said.

"No," said Eve. "Of course it doesn't." She gave Sally a hug.

"I think we're both just nervous of Anastasia turning up. Which is pretty ridiculous. What's the worst that could happen?"

"She could throw us off the *Number One*," said Eve.

"Oh, no," said Sally. "I don't think we'd allow her to do that."

Eve's phone announced an incoming text message. It was Jacob, telling them which train Anastasia would be on, what time she would arrive.

"That's settled, then," said Sally. "Let's go and meet her."

They caught a bus to the station. Moving fast, away from the canal. They reached the station early and sat on a bench on the platform, waiting for the train to arrive. Eve stuck her legs out in front of her and asked Sally why they never seemed to tan at the same rate as the rest of her. There was a wide, white strip on her arm when she took off her watch, and a tideline where her T-shirt sleeves ended, but her legs remained as white as ever.

"You probably need to lie down in the sun," Sally said. "Stretch out on the roof and rotate yourself every half hour. If you're that bothered, that is."

"I'm not," admitted Eve, tucking her heels back under the bench. "Just idly wondering. Your legs look brown enough without you having to behave like a spit-roasted chicken."

"Perhaps I sit still more than you do," said Sally. "I'm not as restless. Also, I tan more easily."

"Am I restless? I always thought I was a bit of a lump. Inert to the point of idleness."

"Maybe you were when you had whatever people do in an office to occupy yourself with. But you skip about a lot now."

"I have lost weight. Look." Eve pulled the waistband of her shorts away from her middle. "Time was, there wasn't any room for a flea to fit in there."

The train arrived. They stood up. A handful of people alighted briskly onto the platform and dispersed. Another two or three emerged more sedately and began to walk away from the train. At the last moment, the figure of Anastasia appeared in the doorway of the quiet coach and slowly descended. A man in a hi-vis jacket waiting to wave the train off, Eve, Sally and another passenger who was still strolling past, rushed to help her.

"What is so difficult," she said, "about getting off a train? I may be old but I'm not helpless."

They all backed away and waited at a distance until Anastasia's feet were firmly planted on the platform, a soft, zip-up bag that Eve recognized as one of hers, sitting beside her.

"Anastasia," said Sally. "It's so lovely to see you."

Anastasia looked at her fiercely, probing for insincerity and, apparently finding none, nodded.

"Good to be here," she said, and the wrinkles on her face (surely deeper now?) produced a smile. "It's been an adventure."

Eve picked up the bag and they set off for the steps down to the tunnel under the track, setting a pace that was designed to be slow enough without being insulting. By the time they had negotiated the steps, tunnel and more steps and reached the bus stop, Anastasia was breathing a little heavily, but there again, she was wearing too many clothes for what had turned out to be a warm day. The bus arrived and they were on it and then off it, at the bridge, with Eve and Sally hanging back to let Anastasia reach the parapet first, to let her take her first look at the neatly moored, sparkling clean *Number One* without them.

As the noise of the bus faded away, they became aware of another, horribly familiar sound. On the *Number One*, Noah was howling. Eve and Sally rushed over the road to join Anastasia at the parapet. A woman had come out of the hire boat moored ahead of them. A couple walking past had stopped in their tracks. All three were transfixed, looking at the boat and at one another. The male half of the couple took a step toward the *Number One* and crouched down to peer through the windows. The woman from the hire boat took out her mobile phone.

"Well, get a move on," said Anastasia. "Get down there."

"I'll go," said Sally, and sprinted down the steps, along the towpath.

"Sorry, sorry," she called, as she ran. "It's only the dog showing off. He's all right."

"He doesn't sound it," said the man.

"No," said Sally. "But he is. I'll show you."

She unlocked the rear doors and Noah barreled past her, reaching Anastasia as she neared the bottom of the steps. Anastasia sat down, or Noah knocked her over, it was hard to tell. One moment she was upright and Noah was moving forward, the next, both woman and dog were in a heap on the steps.

"Is that dog safe?" asked the woman from the boat, still holding her phone.

"That dog," said Sally, "is ecstatic." She walked back to where Eve was still standing, holding the bag, watching the reunion. She could hear the baritone rumble of Anastasia's voice as she approached, heaping abuse on Noah without disguising that she was as delighted to see him as he was to see her.

At last they made it onto the boat, with Noah keeping some part of his anatomy in contact with some part of Anastasia's anatomy all the way. She looked round. Then she laughed her rumbling, disconcerting laugh.

"I have never seen this boat so clean," she said. "What were you thinking? One dull surface and I'd demand my boat back? What a pair of idiots. Now make me a cup of tea." She shed a layer and sat down. "And what have you done to yourself?" she asked, looking at Sally.

"We've been exploring the Yasmin-ness of Sally," said Eve. "Introducing a bit of color, a bit of freedom."

Anastasia picked up her mug and sucked noisily at the contents.

"Superficially," said Sally.

"Yes," said Anastasia, putting the mug down, but not before Sally had noticed the ring of hazy moisture it had left behind, which she had to prevent herself from wiping up, given this conversation—any conversation with Anastasia—was more important than a mark on the table. "Doesn't suit you."

"It doesn't suit the person she was," said Eve. "Mrs. Sally Allsop of 42 Beech Grove."

"But I can't leave that person behind simply by not looking like her," said Sally. "I agree with Anastasia. It doesn't suit me."

"I thought you liked it," said Eve. "Didn't you say how liberating it was?"

"Yes, and that was true, but it was like my daughter's punk phase, before she'd grown up enough to work out it wasn't all about the way she looked. It was about the person she was, and wanted to be."

"Until she'd grown up," repeated Anastasia.

"Yes," said Sally. "Am I grown up, do you think?"

"Yes," said Anastasia.

"But what does that mean?" asked Eve. "Does being grown up mean we are all doomed to be ordinary?"

"No," said Anastasia. "It means accepting we are all extraordinary in ordinary ways." Then she sat up a little straighter and said: "I see you've met Arthur."

They followed Anastasia's eyes to where the book Sally was reading lay on the shelf.

"We were going to tell you," said Sally, as if they had been caught out in some sort of deceit.

"Tell me now. How was he?"

"Worried about you."

Anastasia said nothing, carried on looking at the dull, scuffed spine of *Mr. Lucton's Freedom*. "Apart from that?"

"Well, he seemed very odd," said Sally.

"Oh, yes," said Anastasia. "Always and ever."

"And mysterious," said Eve. "We were hoping you would tell us a bit more about him."

"I could," said Anastasia. "I could tell you his story and it wouldn't make him seem any less odd, but it would explain a thing or two. But I'm not sure I will. I'll think about it."

"If we're not going to talk about Arthur, we should talk about you," said Sally. "Tell us exactly what the doctors said. What happens next."

"I knew you didn't need the silly hair and the ridiculous clothes," said Anastasia. But she didn't answer the question.

They stayed at the mooring overnight. Anastasia was happy to drink tea and read the log, sitting under the shade of the hedge with the business of the canal going past in front of her. One of the boats passing tooted its horn and the people on board waved at her. A couple on a boat moored farther up toward the junction walked past and stopped to remind her she had helped them out of a tricky situation the summer before last, on the Llangollen Canal.

"Pure selfishness, I expect," said Anastasia. "You were probably going to cause me a problem if I didn't help."

"No, no," said the woman. She was younger than Eve and Sally and was wearing a T-shirt with writing on it: at the top, "True Belief," below that, "Angie," below that "Lechlade." Sally, observing the meeting from the roof of the *Number One*, assumed these were the names of the boat, then the name of the woman, and then either her surname or the place where the boat was registered. It was too much information, Sally thought. The man with her was wearing a sleeveless jerkin over his T-shirt, so if he was also carrying his name across his nipples he was keeping it under wraps.

"Don't you remember?" said Angie. "We'd just about run out of diesel. The engine was beginning to cough a bit, you know, and we realized what was happening, so we pulled into the bank and turned the engine off, to make sure it didn't actually run dry. We knew better than to let it do that! Of course, we were complete novices back then."

"Oh, yes," said Anastasia. "I remember the boat now. All painted up and pretty. I wouldn't have recognized you, though. Not because you've changed but because I don't find people vary enough, one from another, to stick in my mind."

"Well, you were the only person who stopped to help, so we remember you," said the man. "We asked everyone passing if they had a spare can and none of them did, and they said so and went on their way. But you gave us a lift down to the boatyard and you persuaded someone you knew at the yard to lend us a can and run us back to the *True Belief*."

"We're old hands, now," said Angie. "We're spending at least six months of the year on the canal."

"What's the boat looking like now?" asked Anastasia. "A little less perfect?"

"Oh, no! We're looking after it. Come down and see."

Sally thought Anastasia would refuse this invitation, but she levered herself out of the chair and jerked her head at Sally, who slid off the roof and walked along with them.

The *True Belief* was perfect. It was the sort of boat that those advertising the canals would use on posters or in brochures. It was painted green, with a broad red line around the sides, and in between each of the porthole windows was a picture, densely packed with stylized roses and leaves, with a roundel in the middle showing something unconnected with the *True Belief* or indeed with the canal, such as a dog's head in profile, or a castle with a winding road leading up to it. Sally had been interested in the first examples of this type of painting when she first noticed it, in the shops they went into or on pots and jugs on the roofs of other boats, but she had found it impossible to understand or analyze and now it felt like the canal equivalent of scented candles—a ubiquitous example of something once relevant but now purely ornamental. The *True Belief*, as well as the paintings on the side, had the same motifs on a bucket on the roof, full of geraniums in a color slightly less bright than that which the painter had used for the representation of flowers on their container. The ropes were in coils; the brass cowl on the chimney was polished to a shine Sally did not believe they could ever dream of achieving on the *Number One*. There were some scores in the paint on the bow, and the fenders, traditionally woven from plaited rope, were scuffed and dirty. Otherwise, the *True Belief* could have been run off that moment by a 3D printer programmed to produce the perfect narrowboat.

"Congratulations," said Anastasia. "You've maintained it to an appropriate standard."

The couple both looked smug.

"Would your daughter like to see inside?" asked Angie.

Sally took a second to realize this meant her, and she would have rejected the description—she did not know how old Anastasia was and though it might be mathematically possible, she felt unworthy of the distinction. If Anastasia had a daughter, which was after all possible, she would have to be a much stronger and more significant person than she, Sally Allsop, was. But she had no chance to speak before Anastasia, without correcting the error, accepted the invitation on her behalf.

Inside, the *True Belief* immediately struck Sally as cluttered. The windows were festooned with bits of wispy lace and patterned curtains made with far more cloth than was necessary to do the job they were intended to do, and thus had to be held back from the portholes with brass hooks. There were metal oval plaques commemorating the various canals that Angie and, it turned out, Brian had been along or intended to go along, screwed to the fronts of shelves designed to hold the knick-knacks that Anastasia would never have on her boat, just as she would not have contemplated the quantity of cushions and pictures, which ought to make the place look cozy, but that was not the word Sally was searching for to be able to say something positive to the owners. Nor was it charming, though it might have been; it might have been elegant but, again, it wasn't. In the end she picked a word she thought was true and which the True Believers would like.

"It's very authentic," she said.

After she had been shown the toilet and shower (which were rather more inviting than those on the *Number One*) and the front cabin (too soft) and they had refused refreshment, Sally was released from the ordeal and allowed to catch up Anastasia, who had set off without her.

"It isn't, you know," Anastasia said, as she came alongside.

"Sorry—isn't what?"

"Authentic. The history of the canals is one of reinvention; often of simultaneous reinventions which coexisted alongside each other. Whoever found a use for a canal created a tradition of using it in a way that suited their purposes. Any tradition can only be authentic in that one context."

"I'm not sure I know what you mean."

"I mean, it's a place where everyone has the choice as to what it is going to be for them. No one can tell you that you are out of step. That's the joy of it. Being able to be out of step."

"But the True Believers think they are authentic. They think there is a tradition of canal-boat painting and hardware and so on. Are you saying this never existed?"

"Look, the canals were made to transport goods, by men with money for other men with money. They created employment and prosperity, like factories did. They had a purpose, which was to create wealth, and they did—for the men who owned the companies and, albeit at a lower level, for the men who worked for the companies. Then the railways came and the canals weren't as important, so the commercial activity scaled down and it was smaller companies making less money, but still enough, and individuals, working for themselves."

They had arrived back at the *Number One* and Anastasia, who had begun to breathe heavily with the effort of walking and talking, sat down on the chair in the shade of the hedge. She pointed at her boat. "They were proud of their boats, the Number Ones, and they decorated them. At the same time, other people looking for a way to use the canals to make money began to offer pleasure-boat trips. As the commercial prospects faded, the idea of using the canals for leisure took hold, and some of the features of the working boats were carried across to the boats being used for the sheer fun of it. Just as the developers converting redundant factories to flats and offices keep a few of the features from the industrial past—the pipes, a hoist or two, a clocking-in machine. And now, of course"—she gestured right and left along the towpath—"anyone can use the canal, for holidays, for living, for plying a trade. They've always been a bit alternative. An alternative to a horse and cart, then an alternative to a railway, then an alternative to a caravan holiday, an alternative to a house. I like that. I like that it's not fixed. No one owns it. And I like that it is slow, which is exactly what made the search for alternatives essential. The canals were wide enough to cope with a boat moving at the walking pace of a horse. Any faster, and they break apart. That's the only thing that needs to be preserved: the banks, the locks, the bridges. And what would destroy them is speed. I like that."

"Eve is fascinated by the engineering brilliance of their design."

"Right! Quite right. That's her canal, an almost unbelievable triumph of engineering and human ingenuity. Think about that, next time you see roses painted on the side of a boat, and consider the scale of achievement of the one against the other."

5

To Solihull

EVE MADE AN EFFORT with the meal that night. She had been through the battered copy of the *Good Housekeeping* cookbook that was the only one Sally had brought on board. It had not occurred to her to bring one at all, but now she was becoming interested in the business of cooking, she was wondering if there wasn't more adventure to be had from the world of recipe books. But since she was restricted to the one, she picked out something that felt as close to exotic as possible: a lamb tagine with apricots. She prepared couscous to go with it and an Eton mess to follow, though she was unhappy with this. It felt too easy and there was a lack of harmony between the two courses. She amazed herself by thinking this, and felt rather smug for having thought it.

She worked methodically, laying out the ingredients before she started each step and completing that step before going on to the next, cleaning up as she went along. It made her feel empowered and in control—those magic concepts she had heard bandied about at work, and had bandied about herself, as the secret to a successful outcome and a satisfied workforce. At the time, the word "feel" had a whiff of the weasel about it: we want to *feel* empowered and in control, or, more often, we want you/ them to feel, etc. As if it did not matter whether any power was actually delegated, only that those doing the work should be under the illusion that it had been. Eve, as she grated nutmeg and whisked cream, knew that she genuinely did feel that way, and also, that she had rarely, if ever, felt as she did now back when she was at work.

"I might reinvent myself as a chef," she told Sally and Anastasia when they got back from their visit to the *True Belief.*

"Is it going to be that good?" asked Sally.

"Not necessarily, but it's been such fun cooking it."

"There's fun and there's hard work," said Anastasia. "Cooking, now, that's hard work. You'd have to be sure there was enough fun involved to make the hard work worth it."

"I'm not sure I was being serious," said Eve.

The food was good and the glow sustained Eve through a Scrabble game where Sally came very close to beating Anastasia and she was a poor third. When it came to bedtime, Anastasia rejected their offer to sleep together on the double bed conversion in the middle cabin.

"I wouldn't do that for anyone," she said. "Climb in with either of you. So I don't see why I should expect you to."

"You're not just anyone," said Eve.

"Don't be so wet," said Anastasia.

So Sally moved her things back into the rear cabin and Eve joined her. It was still a disturbed night. Although Eve knew she was a noisy sleeper, Anastasia was noisier still, her coughs, wheezes and snores little diminished by the two doors and the bathroom between the cabins. Eve had been delighted when Noah decided to join them, in preference to staying with Anastasia, until Anastasia pointed out she had never let him into a room where she was sleeping and never would. Although Eve was used to his whiffles and grunts, they contributed to a restlessness, not helped by the realization that, whenever she dropped off, she was probably helping keep Sally awake. She fell asleep finally and woke up to find Sally was already dressed; had taken the dog out; had made the tea. Eve felt a bit like the junior partner of the three of them; it was only then she realized she had previously thought of Sally as occupying that position. She needed, she thought, to get a grip on her ego. Not the first time she'd thought that, but maybe the first time she'd meant it.

After breakfast, they moved. Eve and Sally unhitched the ropes and Anastasia steered until they were through the last lock and past Norton Junction, when she handed the tiller over to Eve.

"Are you sure?" Eve said.

"Perhaps I've got used to doing nothing," said Anastasia, and went down to the front to join Sally. The cover was folded back and all the doors were open. When they spoke to each other, their voices lifted in the still, warm air and carried back to Eve, the words sometimes audible, sometimes not. But they spoke little, and most of what was said was questions from Sally about where the other arm of the canal went off to at Norton Junction, about the names of wild flowers, of trees, and Anastasia's brief, barked responses.

Within half an hour they reached another tunnel. This one—Eve consulted the book—was only two-thirds as long as the Blisworth Tunnel had been, but still over a mile. Sally came out of the cabin and handed Eve a coat.

"It's hard to believe we need a coat," said Eve, but she put it on, and switched the headlamp on, as the dark entrance came closer and closer. She'd hoped Sally wouldn't offer to drive again; she was worried she might agree and then hate herself for failing to take up the challenge of getting through the darkness, but instead, Sally said: "I'm glad it's your turn," and she was able to admit she was not looking forward to it.

The darkness filled up the space around them as the *Number One* nosed into the tunnel's mouth. The air temperature dropped and the throb of the engine was amplified, echoing from the walls, the roof, the water, only feet away from where Eve stood. She found it hard to know what to fix her eyes on, how to keep the boat on a straight course. The tunnel was not entirely straight, and the bright spot of light at the end was not at first visible, but when it appeared and she concentrated on this far-off beacon, heading for the point where it would all be over, it was almost impossible to keep the nose straight, parallel to the bricks on either side. When she forced herself to focus on the farthest point on the wall to her right where the boat's headlamp beam reached, she became almost mesmerized by the interplay of the light on the bricks and the water, both sliding toward her then vanishing again, over and over in a repeated but not identical pattern, as the bricks were variously colored, or discolored. In the previous tunnel, when she had not been driving, she had looked at the tunnel roof, the curve of its sides, and thought about the construction, the techniques and tools used, the problems that must have needed to be overcome. Now, with the responsibility for keeping the *Number One* safe in the center of the available space, she was forced to look at the interface of the two elements—brick and water—and it struck her how unreal the water appeared, in this setting. Logic told her it was no harder to create a mile-long trough to hold a given quantity of water under the arch of a tunnel roof than it was to do the same thing out in the open, but something about the feeling of being indoors, inside a man-made structure, turned the water from being something understood to something mysterious, displaced.

"We could do with Arthur," Sally said. "And his harmonica."

When they finally emerged into the heat of the day, the so-distant circle enlarging, almost in the last few yards, to something wide enough and high enough to allow the *Number One* to pass through, Eve found her arm was aching from the tension of holding the tiller steady. Anastasia, who had stayed in the front, only moving to fetch a blanket to wrap herself in, came back to the rear deck and took over driving, as there was a flight of five locks, she pointed out, between them and Braunston, and she saw no reason to exert herself when she had a handy crew aboard. Eve took this as some acknowledgment that she had navigated the tunnel without too many errors; though, when she was standing by the paddles on the first lock watching the *Number One* drop down as the water flowed out, she noticed a collection of debris on the sill, near where Anastasia had been sitting: a coating of brick flakes and dust dislodged when she had allowed the *Number One* to scrape along it rather than keeping to a center path. She looked up and saw Anastasia was noticing she had noticed it.

"I seem to have brought some of the tunnel out with me," Eve said.

"No more than most people," said Anastasia.

At Braunston they bought lunch and carried on down the Grand Union, ignoring the turn to the North Oxford Canal.

"You could take it," said Anastasia as they cruised toward the turn. "It would bypass Birmingham and it's a canal I'm particularly fond of." Sally, who had taken over the tiller, reached for the throttle to slow them down, waiting for a decision. "What are you doing?" asked Anastasia. "I only said you could take that route, not that you were actually going to take it."

They moored for the night at Napton Junction. When they had calculated that morning, as they did every morning, where they thought they should aim to be at the end of the day, Eve and Sally had assumed they would go farther, but when they set off after lunch, Anastasia asked them what the rush was, though Sally was keeping below the 4mph maximum. So she slowed even further, which meant other boats came up behind them, and Sally pulled in to the bank a few times to let the faster boat go first through one of the many narrow bridges. It was a long, featureless stretch, but lovely in a way that Sally had come to recognize any stretch of countryside with a canal running through it was transformed into a frame of tranquility.

Anastasia sat in the front, with the logbook in her hands. It was a thick, black journal with narrow-ruled pages. Each day, a line was drawn across the page to mark the end of the previous day and the new day's entry started with the time at which the boat moved (if it did). Anything involving maintenance on the boat—fuel and water taken on board, toilet and bilge pumped out—was recorded as it happened. Then, once the day was over, a note of the place and time of the final mooring and any observations were added: damage seen on the banks, sightings of unusual or rare wildlife or plants, incidents involving other boats, other people. The book Sally and Eve were using, that Anastasia held in her hands, had been started over two years before and was still not quite half full. Anastasia's observations were curt and crisp: "Tree fallen across canal. Maintenance crew making a mess, slowly. Moored for night at 2:30 p.m." And the next day: "Did not move. Crew finished clearing tree at 4:30, slowed down by cups of tea, passersby and incompetence." Her writing was small and neat. Sally's was small but messy, Eve's large but clear, so they had been taking it in turns to fill in the log on the basis that neither of them came close to meeting Anastasia's standard. To begin with, they had tried to be as brisk as she was, but as time went on they had begun to include what she would undoubtedly regard as irrelevant detail, turning the book from a straightforward record into a fuller diary of the trip. They both enjoyed doing this and they enjoyed reading what the other had written. They had even begun to squeeze in additional observations in the margin of each other's daily accounts: "Octogenarian on bank called Sally *my lovely* and she *did* look lovely, in pink." "Eve and Noah covered the floor in mud. Eve helped clean it up; Noah hindered."

Now they both stayed at the rear waiting for Anastasia's criticism of what Sally remembered as prolix whimsy in comparison to her economy. Eve went down to make tea and when she brought Sally's out to her, she whispered that Anastasia seemed to be reading the book from start to finish but, so far as she could tell, there were no storm clouds looming.

When they moored, Anastasia went off on her own down the towpath with Noah, who had remained inches from her feet, wherever they happened to be, all day. She refused Eve's offer of company.

"I can't go far," she said. "You have my permission to come and look for me if I'm not back in an hour. But not before."

She was back within half an hour, and sat in a chair in the front cabin watching Sally cook, while Eve wrote up the log, constraining herself to Anastasia's laconic style, even though their exuberance had not been mentioned. The boat rocked and Trompette, in a tweed peaked cap and a pair of overalls worn without a shirt, came down the steps into the cabin. She looked, as ever, immaculate.

"Whoa, Anastasia," she said, scratching Noah behind his ear as he wriggled his coarse-furred little body in delight. "I thought you were in Uxbridge."

"So I was," said Anastasia. "And so I will be again. But for now, I am here."

Trompette went back to the *Grimm*, moored a few boat lengths behind them, and returned with Billy. He hung about in the doorway, looking unkempt as usual, but unusually sheepish. He had a bottle of wine in each hand and waited for Anastasia to nod before he advanced into the cabin. He fetched the squat Duralex tumblers that were the nearest thing to a wine glass that Anastasia allowed on the *Number One* and proposed a toast: "To canals!"

Eve could think of plenty of other toasts they might have made, but on balance, this seemed to be the best one available.

SALLY ADDED MORE RICE, PEAS and ham to her risotto and invited Trompette and Billy to share it. There wasn't enough room for them all to sit comfortably inside and it was a warm, still, overcast evening, so Anastasia and Sally carried their bowls of food to the front deck, Eve took hers up onto the roof, and Trompette and Billy sat on the towpath. Little was said while the food was eaten and the wine was drunk, but when it was finished, Sally said to Billy, "Arthur told us you had stories about the Blisworth Tunnel."

Billy wiped his fingers on the grass and rose to his feet, jogged down the towpath toward the *Grimm*.

"Was that the wrong thing to say?" asked Sally. Trompette shook her head.

"He can't tell a story without something in his hands to make a noise with," she said.

Billy came jogging back with a guitar in his hands and resumed his former position on the towpath. He struck a chord, then began to speak:

Imagine, as you listen to my story, imagine you are in darkness so deep you would not know, were you to stretch out your hand, whether you would touch something soft or something hard, something wet or something dry, something hot or cold, living or dead. Or nothing at all. Hear water, in the darkness: water that drips, splashes. Be aware that you are in the presence of water, of walls. Imagine you are in a tunnel. Now, I will begin.

Sally had heard stories being told in the classroom by teachers or volunteers, and she herself had taken a turn. While some children fidgeted or fell asleep, most of them would listen, interested. But occasionally someone with a gift for telling stories would turn up; when that happened, every child, every adult, fell into the place the teller created for them. For as long as the storyteller was speaking, they forgot to do anything except breathe in and out. So she recognized Billy's skill. As he spoke, she found herself back in Blisworth Tunnel, in the dark, with the roof dripping.

He told them the story of a disaster that occurred as the tunnel was being dug. Fourteen men were killed when the shaft they were digging collapsed and buried them alive:

The lucky ones die at once, killed by a prop falling as the roof comes down. The rest of you—who knows? Who knows how long you lie, suffocating as the earth settles on your bodies, pressing the air from your lungs, filling your eyes and your mouths and pinning your limbs to the ground, robbing you of the small comfort of wiping your face clean as all the life you might have had is reduced to one last desperate effort to draw breath.

Sally studied his face. Under that absurd thatch of wiry hair, he looked angry. There was no anger in his voice, but the words he was using led the listener to understand the buried men had been let down, sacrificed to those people who chose the shortest route through the hill that stood in their way, in order to save money. As he finished, he looked at his audience, which had grown from the four of them to a dozen or more as people passing on the towpath paused, drawn toward Billy, this version of Billy with his guitar and his softly spoken words.

Eve stretched her legs, ready to slide down off the roof to fetch more drink, more food, but Billy struck another chord and started again:

If you think that is all the life the tunnel has taken, you would be wrong.

Sixty years later, he said, one of the first steam-powered boats went through the tunnel when the wind was in the wrong direction, with the boiler pushing out smoke that blinded and then rendered them insensible; killed two of them. Because there was only one ventilation shaft, and that was partially blocked. The chairman of the company responsible for the tunnel, which also employed the victims, assured the inquest jury that more shafts had been sunk, and the families of the poor men who had died (though whether he was using the word "poor" to indicate poverty or misfortune cannot be known) would be provided for. At the end of this story, too, Billy left the audience with the thought that the men had been sacrificed to profit.

There were as many as twenty people on the towpath now, listening to Billy. He stood up, took off his hat and bowed to them before dropping it, upside down on the ground in front of him. He sat down and teased a melancholy tune out of his guitar as the group dispersed, some of them tossing an offering into the hat.

"Was that all true?" asked an earnest young woman.

Billy did not stop strumming. "It is a version of the truth," he said. "A storyteller's version."

Eve watched them all go, listened to the chat—as much about the discomfort of having been sitting on the damp grass as about the story they had heard—and when she next looked over the edge of the roof into the front well, she found both Anastasia and Sally had gone to bed. Trompette, too, had scooped up the hat and returned to the *Grimm*. The towpath was empty except for her and Billy, who had stopped playing and was smiling up at her.

"What are you doing here, anyway?" he said. "A grown woman like you should have responsibilities, something serious to do, a proper job. So why are you idling away on the canal?"

"As it happens," said Eve, "I don't have any responsibilities or a proper job, or indeed anything to do. I don't think of myself as a 'grown woman.' So where better for me to be?"

"Well, one of us has got you wrong," said Billy, slinging his guitar over his shoulder and heading down the path.

THE NEXT DAY THEY WORKED twenty locks, close together. Sally and Eve felt as if they'd spent most of the morning turning paddles and opening and closing gates. The locks took two boats, side by side, and Trompette cast off *Grimm* as soon as she saw the *Number One* starting to move, entering the first one with them, leaning against the tiller as the water flowed out. Of Billy, there was no sign.

The *Grimm* went on ahead of them when they stopped at a pub for lunch, Trompette lifting a hand as she cruised on. Anastasia told them as they ate their sandwiches that Billy was only one of a number of entertainers to be found on the canals. Musicians, drama groups and storytellers.

"Is he better or worse than the average?" asked Eve. He had enthralled her, both times he had told a story, and she didn't know how much of this was the darkness, the atmosphere of the towpath, the unfamiliarity of the experience, and how much was because he was, in fact, good.

"He's a good showman," said Anastasia. "And he's no romantic. I'd always pause to listen."

They cruised on to the outskirts of Leamington Spa where Anastasia was due to catch a train back to London the next day. Since they would have time in the morning to do the last few locks and find a mooring close to the station, they stopped on a rural stretch and Eve set about making mushroom omelettes. She knew there was supposed to be some magic or mystery about making omelettes, but she had no idea what it was. Sally said her omelette was fine—and she must be much more practiced in the art of making them than Eve was—and Anastasia said it was an omelette, which was praise of a sort.

"Tell us," said Sally, after they had eaten, "about the operation."

It seemed to Sally that Anastasia had come to behave around them as if they weren't there, and it was this that gave her the courage to ask the question. Anastasia's former vigilance, her air of being ready to pounce, had softened into what could have been indifference but which Sally interpreted as acceptance.

"It's something called a lobectomy," Anastasia said. "There are cancer cells in my lungs. They know this because they knocked me out and put something down my neck and scraped a bit off and tested it. So what they do is, they go in and lop off the part that has these cells in it, then follow up with a bit of chemotherapy in the hope that will see me right for a few more years. I've only listened to the parts of all this that seemed to matter, so I may be misunderstanding the detail. I think I have the overall picture right, though."

No one would know, she said, how good were her chances of survival until they had done the operation. It all depended on what they found.

"My mother died of lung cancer," Eve said.

"When?" Anastasia asked.

"Twenty years ago."

"They're learning all the time," said Sally. "Finding more successful forms of treatment."

"I know. I wasn't actually thinking about outcomes," Eve said. "I was comparing attitude. My mother was pretty emotional, from the first hint something might be wrong to the last bitter breath."

"Why wouldn't you be," Anastasia said, "if you have a home and a family and you're relatively young, which I suppose she must have been, twenty years ago. She must have been looking forward to other phases of life yet to come. Hard to think about losing all that. It's different for me."

"Yes," said Eve. "That's exactly what she felt. But you have a good life, too. Don't you feel angry at the thought of losing it? Don't you still hope for good things to come?"

"I've never had many hopes or expectations," said Anastasia. "If good things happen, I enjoy them. If they don't, I'm not surprised. Anyway, it's not over yet. Another installment or two to come. Could be ones you'd rather skip, but some sort of experience nevertheless."

"I know," Sally said. "My father dropped dead from an aneurysm between putting down his book and picking up his coffee cup, and I remember thinking how furious I would be, not to have had time to contemplate and consider and understand that the end might be coming. Is there anyone you want us to tell— about the operation? Arthur, for instance?"

Anastasia sucked her teeth. Sally used to think this was a phrase used in novels to avoid saying "looked thoughtful." But

Anastasia never did look thoughtful, and was definitely making a sucking sound.

"Perhaps," she said at length. "And Owen."

"Who is Owen?" asked Sally.

Anastasia glared at her. "Owen!" she shouted. "Do concentrate. You're due to deliver the *Number One* to him in a month or so—or a year or more, the way you two are going—and now you tell me you don't know who he is! How am I meant to trust you?"

Sally had been thinking of their destination as a place, not a person, but faced with this return to aggressive form by Anastasia, she didn't like to say so. She glanced at Eve for support.

Eve said: "His name and the address of the boatyard are written in the front of the log. We knew that. I just don't think we'd bothered to remember them."

"Well, you should," said Anastasia. Then she made a sound that might have been the word "flaky" or might have been a cough.

"We can let them know, of course," said Sally. "Although we don't have an address for Arthur."

Anastasia closed her eyes. "Tell Owen to tell Arthur," she said. "If you must. Just tell them the date of the op. That's all."

"And the name of the hospital?"

"I've told you already. Fuss. Can't abide it."

"Well, they need to know. Then they can ring for a bulletin from the nurses. Set their minds at rest."

"Very well. Date. Hospital. No detail. Now get out of my way. I'm going to bed."

As they cruised toward Leamington the next day, Eve had a text from Jacob.

Arriving in Leamington in 10. Where will I find you?

Not there yet, Eve texted back. *Suggest you find the towpath and start walking south toward Stockton and Long Itchington away from Warwick.*

She didn't tell Anastasia. It was obviously too late to stop this possibly unwanted escort from coming and Eve could only hope Anastasia would be pleased to see him, or pretend to be pleased to see him, when he arrived. It would not have occurred to her to suspect Anastasia of pretending, before these last couple of days, but now she wondered if there wasn't quite a lot of, if not pretense, at least suppression and omission in the way Anastasia behaved.

They met Jacob as they approached a railway bridge. He had paused to contemplate some swans, crouching down to peer at them, fumbling with his phone. He was wearing ripped jeans and his hair was a mass of coarse spikes with yellow tips. He would make a better photo than the swans, Eve thought. A cyclist came past, ringing his bell to alert Jacob, who looked up and saw Eve waving at him. He did a little dance on the towpath, impeding a jogger, who kept jogging on the spot waiting for Jacob to move out of the way.

"Better slow down at the bridge," Anastasia said to Sally. "I suppose we'll have to pick him up."

"Who on earth is it?" asked Sally.

"Someone who doesn't think I'm capable of traveling from Leamington to London on my own."

But once Jacob was on board, it was hard to imagine he had made this trip for any reason other than his own pleasure. He loved the way the canal was at once pretty and functional, the way the town was audible but mostly invisible, the way the architecture had molded itself round the needs of the canal, the way it fitted into the landscape. Most of all, he loved the boat. If either of them had squealed and exclaimed as much as Jacob did, Eve was sure Anastasia would have lost patience with them. Perhaps, she thought, keeping an eye on Anastasia's wrinkles, she was suppressing her impatience with Jacob, allowing him to be the person he was, however irritating that might be. In the end, Anastasia said, "If you're that excited about it, why don't you move onto a boat on the Regent's Canal? There are moorings available."

"Oh, I would love that!" said Jacob. "But I don't think I'd ever get Vic to agree. He spends his days cramped up in a little cab and he needs his space when he gets home. And I'd rather live anywhere with Vic than live in a dream house without him."

"How touching," said Anastasia.

"You're very lucky," said Sally.

"I am, I am, I admit it," said Jacob.

Then he went through the cupboards and the fridge and put together a salad for lunch. It was a delicious combination of flavors and textures which Eve would never have attempted to try out together unless she had a recipe and had procured all the ingredients in advance.

"How can I learn to cook like you?" she asked. "I want to be able to do what you've just done. Throw things together and make it work."

"You don't want to talk to me about cooking," Jacob said. "I've served a bit of a painful apprenticeship. You know how some people have eating disorders? Well, I used to have a cooking disorder. It was all my mother's fault. And she learned from her mother. She believed, because her mother did, that the way to a man's heart was through his stomach, and because she believed it, I did. I was such a needy little arse, desperate for whoever was the man of the moment to love me and stay with me, so I used to get into the kitchen and try harder and harder to make more and more exciting food until whoever it was left. Then I would go out and find someone else to take me on, me with my spices and sauces and my mandoline and stick blender. And the next time, I'd try even harder. Until I met Vic. I was an expert by then. Could turn an onion and two potatoes into something delicious at the first hint I might be about to be abandoned. It took me a while to realize that Vic couldn't give a fart about food—he'd live on pasties and chips if I wasn't there keeping up his fresh-fruit-and-fiber intake. And since he loves me as much as I love him, it would take more than an underdone steak to drive him away. He couldn't understand why I felt the need to spend so much time in the kitchen, why I had to be putting all this effort into cooking a meal instead of chilling out with him on the sofa, and do you know what he said when I told him this story? He said: 'But your dad left when you were eleven. You must have known it didn't work.'" When Jacob laughed it involved his whole body and was a pleasure to watch. "You need to start with a decent recipe book," he said, when he'd stopped. "I'll find you one. And then, when you're back home, we'll have a few sessions in the kitchen. That'll be fun."

They all walked up to the station, slowly to allow for Anastasia. They took Noah with them for fear he would start howling as soon as they shut the door behind them. He started howling anyway, the moment Anastasia walked through the turnstile and was beyond his reach.

"Is your dog sick?" a passing child asked them.

"No, just forlorn," said Sally.

"I feel a bit forlorn myself," said Eve. "I don't feel as if I've got a grip, or a good enough grip."

"Keep practicing," Sally said.

BEFORE THEY LEFT LEAMINGTON, EVE went in search of a charity shop to buy a recipe book. She could have found a bookshop selling new books but was afraid the choice would be too daunting, so she decided to buy one in the first shop she found. It felt like an adventure and she remembered her grandmother, who had lived to a great, idle cantankerous age. She had always insisted that the jigsaws on which she depended to keep herself amused must come from charity shops. It was the thrill of never knowing until the end whether all the pieces were there. Much better to do a puzzle with a picture she loathed, she argued, than to be secure in the knowledge that every time she searched for a certain piece—a certain shape with a bit of green on the left-hand edge—it would always turn out to be there. On occasion, the puzzles were found to have too many pieces. Her grandmother loved it when that happened. As she pushed through the door of an animal charity shop, Eve knew how her grandmother must have felt, anticipating the joy of carrying home something that might be completely marvelous or positively useless. Looking forward to the challenge of making a masterpiece out of faulty materials.

There were only five cookery books on the five shelves of randomly stocked secondhand books. Any customer deciding to buy the first book that a hand fell upon was as likely to carry off a Booker Prize winner as the self-published memoirs of a railway enthusiast. Eve's grandmother would have loved it, and so did Eve.

Dogged persistence in reading the spines, not all of them the right way up, eventually revealed that her choice was between Delia Smith's *Winter Cookery, 1001 Things to Cook in Your Slow Cooker, Italian Classics, Gluten-Free Cooking for One* and Claudia Roden's *Mediterranean Cookery*. Delia seemed the safe choice. The aunt in whose house she had spent so much of her childhood had been fond of saying, when serving up anything more challenging than casseroles and pasta sauces, "You can always trust Delia." But it wasn't winter, and Eve didn't feel like playing safe. She was surprised to find, on consulting the index of Italian classics, that much of the bland slop her aunt had served up—indeed much of the slop she had prepared for herself and friends, was classic Italian, albeit executed with fewer ingredients and omitting all the processes which presumably made the food as tasty as an Italian would expect. There was no slow cooker on the boat. She might have bought it anyway, for the outlay of £1:50, to force herself to be creative in adapting the recipes for any old saucepan with a lid, but when she looked inside, there were no recipes she could not have found in the battered *Good Housekeeping* that was already on the boat. The gluten-free book had dull recipes featuring alternative ingredients that Eve could not believe were either freely available in canal-side shops or at all nice. So that left Claudia Roden. She picked the book up and it fell open at a page with a recipe for Imam Bayildi, also known, so it said, as "The Imam Fainted." On the facing page was a line drawing of a pair of hands shaping a vine leaf into a parcel over a spoonful of stuffing. She riffled through the pages and found she could learn how to make

Mr. Hiély's Rabbit with Onions. She felt the presence of the Imam and Mr. Hiély as she read. At the front were pages of pictures of vegetables she knew (cucumber, Florence fennel), but looking so much fuller of possibility than the same vegetables on a supermarket rack, and also vegetables she had hardly heard of and never seen (colocasia, kohlrabi). Throughout the book—accompanied by line drawings which made preparing an artichoke, for example, look like something within her grasp— were sumptuous pictures of food, on plates or in markets. She wanted to be, right now, within reach of it all.

She was so enthralled, felt so emotionally connected to the book in her hand, that when another customer, trying to read the random spines beside her, noticed what she was holding and said: "Oh, that's good. If you haven't already got it, you should definitely buy it," she immediately hated the woman for implying that she was more familiar than Eve with the loved object. She snapped it shut and carried it to the till, where a lady with as many wrinkles as Anastasia but the softest skin, so that they fell in gentle pleats and made her face look sad, caring and lovable, pointed out a multitude of blobs and stains on the pages, wondering if one pound fifty wasn't too much—might a pound be more appropriate, or even fifty pence? To Eve, these stains were like the missing or misplaced jigsaw pieces, evidence that this book had had a life before.

"You must take two pounds for it," she said. "I insist."

The next set of locks was the Hatton flight, which went up in a daunting hill of gates ahead of them. They moored behind the *Grimm*. There was no sign of either Trompette or Billy, but since these were double locks, Sally was sure Trompette would want to set off when they did so whichever of them was not driving could work the locks for her. Billy, Sally assumed, would be asleep or otherwise engaged out of sight until the last lock had been negotiated. In this, she was wrong. It was Billy who came and rapped on the door as they ate breakfast next morning.

"Going up?" he asked, jerking his head toward the flight stretched out above them. "Want a buddy through the locks?"

Billy and Trompette worked as a team through the whole twenty-one locks in the flight, one driving in, one preparing and filling the lock, then, as the *Grimm* reached the top level and the gates were ready to be opened, whoever had been driving would step off and the one doing the work would step on and take the tiller. They were like butterflies, constantly moving, changing position, coming to rest for a short moment then off again. It was impossible to have a conversation and Sally wanted to have a conversation. They had become familiar to her without being known.

Eve drove the *Number One* through the first ten locks and Sally thought that, when she took over, there would be time to talk in the dripping gloom of an empty lock while they waited for it to fill up. This, however, proved impossible. It was necessary to keep the boat steady in the lock, avoid it drifting too far forward, where the nose could become trapped on a beam of the gate, or too far back, where the sill could foul the rudder, and the concentration needed, plus the noise, the engines and the roar of the water coming into the lock, meant that nothing could be said that needed consideration, until the last, calm moments as the lock filled right to the top, when the *Grimm*'s crew swapped over.

It felt like a purposeful morning because there was a purpose to their journey. When they passed hire boats coming down, full of families or parties of friends flaunting quite a bit of burned, red flesh and laughter, demonstrating what even after a relatively short time on the canal Sally knew was clumsy incompetence, she wondered what their purpose was. Why spend so many hours filling and emptying locks and moving a boat through them, only to have (echoes of those family walks with Duncan and the children) the task of doing it all again before the end of the holiday.

By lunchtime they were through the locks and moored one behind the other. Sally and Eve made sandwiches for the four of them, Billy brought some cold beers, and there was a lolling laziness to the afternoon that contrasted to the morning's activity. Sally listened to the idle remarks Trompette and Billy and Eve were bandying back and forth, sitting in the sunshine with no work to do, full of food and drink and talking about nothing in particular. In the past, she would always have been the one who stood up first to go and do something, anything. Like clearing away a plate of food from in front of a dinner guest when, as it turned out, he had not finished eating it.

They went through a short, dripping and slimy tunnel with the *Number One* in the lead. When Sally and Eve agreed they would moor for the night in a rural spot, out of sight and earshot of the motorway and the railway line, fields on either side, Sally expected *Grimm* to stop, too, but it went cruising past, Billy leaning down to blast the horn in farewell. Eve announced she was going to take Noah for a walk, with a map. She was planning to use the footpaths marked as well as the towpath, to be able to do a circuit and avoid walking the same path twice.

"We've become too linear, don't you think?" she said to Sally. "A bit one-way."

"Can I come?" Sally said.

It took them two hours, and would have taken Eve longer had Sally not been with her. After Eve had paused to consult the map at every point where a decision had to be made on which path to take, Sally took it away from her.

"It's a guide, not a recipe," she said. It was hot and standing still made her legs ache. "Look, you can tell where we are because of what we can see—that hill, that spire, that farmhouse—and because we know where we are in relation to the motorway. There's only one place on this map we can be. It doesn't matter if there are three tracks instead of two. Tracks are created or get overgrown; hills, houses, churches and motorways don't tend to move about."

"Oh, no," said Eve. "I've delved into the detail and missed the big picture. I hate people who do that."

"You just don't like fuzziness. I'm never well enough informed to expect anything else."

When they had been walking for about half an hour, Sally began to wonder why she had offered to come, remembering again the family walks and how relieved she had been when they stopped. She had promised herself then that she would never again tramp up and down hills without the satisfaction of arriving somewhere that was an actual destination.

"Why are we doing this?" she asked Eve. "When we could be back at the boat reading a book and drinking wine."

"Because," said Eve, then laughed. "Because Noah enjoys it."

Noah was certainly exhibiting signs of enjoyment, like a child unexpectedly and unusually finding itself in an adventure playground.

"But he's only a dog," said Sally. "And in case you've forgotten,

I don't care for dogs, so why should I be putting myself out to entertain him?"

"All right," said Eve. "Now you've asked the question, let's create a list of all the reasons why marching up hill and down dale is something we might choose to do. Number one, we get to see the countryside."

"We can do that from the *Number One*."

"No, we can't. We can look at the hills but we can't get in among them, see the view from the top, find out what the scenery is like on the other side. We can't walk right up to this tree, for example, and marvel at the pattern of the bark."

They both stopped walking and looked at the tree Eve had selected, which had deeply fissured and lined bark—not unlike, Sally thought, Anastasia's face.

"It is worth looking at," she admitted, "but is it worth the effort?"

"All right, then: number two—it's good for us. It helps us lose weight."

"I don't want to lose weight."

"No, but I do. I always have, for as long as I can remember. It is my most consistent fantasy, that one day, I will wake up and be slim. I will unfold myself from my bed and my legs and arms and stomach will be firm and sleek. Nothing will quiver or droop. I know, I know, it's a ridiculous fantasy, and I know that being slim doesn't equal being happy and that being slim doesn't necessarily mean having firm flesh either. I know all that, and I also know that in the overall scheme of things, being slim is a goal which is well within my capabilities—unlike, for example, playing hockey for England or winning *X Factor* or having a novel published or becoming CEO of a Footsie 100 company. Not that those aren't fantasies worth dreaming about—except winning *X Factor*. I can't imagine what I would wear on TV that wouldn't make me look fat."

"For goodness' sake," said Sally. "You're not fat."

They walked on for a while in silence. Noah emerged from the undergrowth with a dead rabbit in his jaws. Whether it had been dead when he came across it or not, he looked like a dog who expected admiration and reward. Eve urged him to put the rabbit down; Sally grabbed his jaws and eased them apart till it fell on the path, then kicked it into the long grass.

"What's number three?" she asked.

"Keeping fit?"

"In principle, I suppose. In practice, working the locks is doing it for me."

"And me."

A bramble shoot trailing over the path caught Eve's leg as she pushed past it. She stopped, licked a finger and wiped away the beads of blood that welled up from the scratch. The slightness of the hurt and the ease with which Eve dealt with it made Sally think of Anastasia.

"We should be counting ourselves lucky to be able to do this. To walk and talk and be free of pain."

"You're thinking of Anastasia," said Eve. "And you're right. Here we are, in the sunshine, in the middle of the countryside, with Noah thrown in. So is that reason number four: because we can?"

"No. That's a reason to be thankful, but not a reason for getting hot and scratched and lost."

"I've a feeling you're going to say this doesn't count, but number four is the pleasure of the book and the wine when you finally get back to it, which I contend is deeper and sweeter than the book and the wine without the five-mile hike beforehand."

"That's about the best reason you've come up with."

"Oh, is it? Good. It must be your turn now."

So Sally told her about the walks she had done with her family, and how, now that she looked back on it, she could see that the advantages were time to think and the chance to say, in a casual way, things that there never seemed to be a right time to say over the business of breakfast, supper, household maintenance and childcare, which occupied most of their time and their conversation when they were at home.

"I think number four, feeling happy to be back home, was the greatest pleasure, but the other two were five and six, if you like."

"But I don't know if I accept those," said Eve, "in our current way of life. The joy of moving all the time, so slowly and without physical effort—leaving aside the locks—is that there is endless time for the mind to wander. Whenever I think of something I want to say, however random, I don't feel I have to wait for the right moment to say it."

"True. We have thinking time and we can talk about anything, whenever it occurs to us. I've never been in that position before. Are you going to tell me it's always been like that for you?"

"No, no it hasn't. Is it because we are in suspense? Between our serious past and an unknown but probably serious future? So, at this moment, anything is possible, nothing is prohibited?"

"I told my hairdresser," said Sally, "the day after I told Duncan

I was leaving, that I was going to have a gap year. I think that's what we're in. A gap."

"A good gap," said Eve. "Just look at that view!"

IT WAS THE MIDDLE OF the afternoon when they came across *Grimm* again. It was moored in a surprisingly rural stretch just before they began the long trek through Birmingham's industrial outposts, suburbs, center, and industrial hinterland. Trompette was sitting on the roof facing the canal, knitting.

"You need to moor here," Trompette said. "There be dragons." She pointed in the direction they were traveling.

Sally steered into the bank, as directed, but left the engine idling.

"We have to go past the dragons sometime," she said. "And it's early to stop."

"Yes," said Trompette, who had hopped off onto the towpath still holding her knitting, "but there's nowhere safe to moor after this until you're right in the middle, and it's too late to start."

As soon as they'd secured the boat, Eve cycled off to the nearest shops to look for the ingredients for the recipes she wanted to try from her new, much-used cookbook. Sally climbed onto the roof of *Grimm*, shifting a bag of potting compost, an umbrella, a spare fender wrapped up in an old anorak and a watering can to make enough space to sit down, close enough to Trompette to be able to see what she was doing. The knitting was in several colors, all somewhere in the green spectrum with splashes of scarlet. Trompette was wearing a smock with two deep pockets that extended the width of the garment, side seam to side seam. The balls of wool were in these pockets, presumably stashed in some order Trompette understood because she hardly seemed to look before plunging in a hand to pull up another strand, severing one she had been using with her teeth as she did so. The worked piece hanging below the needles, apart from being dazzlingly beautiful in its range of colors, was not identifiable as fitting any particular purpose. Scarf, jumper, wall-hanging—it could be any of those. Sally, moving the watering can again to be able to stretch her legs out, asked what it was.

Trompette held it up, stretching the knitted fabric out across the needles so the sun caught and flashed on the brilliant scarlet, and illuminated the pale fern greens so that they stood out against the deep, almost inky emerald shade that reminded Sally of the head of a male teal duck.

"What do you think?" Trompette asked. It was a rhomboid, Sally saw now: wider at the base with a bit of a taper toward the top. If she had knitted it—supposing she was capable of producing something that combined random colors so skillfully— the narrowing would have been a mistake, the result of stitches inadvertently dropped in a moment of inattentiveness. But for all she appeared to be completely indifferent to what her hands were doing, Trompette's knitting looked crafted, carefully done.

"It could be anything," Sally said. "Do you know what it's going to be?"

"Not yet," Trompette said. "Waistcoat probably."

At once Sally could see it, the drape of the garment hanging from Trompette's shoulders, its colors separating and merging as it swung with her movements.

"That'll be lovely," she said. "It'll suit you."

"Oh, not for me," said Trompette, never pausing in her work. "To sell."

"Well, I'd buy it," said Sally.

Trompette turned toward her and held the knitting up against her. "Yes," she said. "That will work. I'll knit it for you, then."

"Do you do much of this?" Sally asked. "Knitting things to sell?"

"When I can get the wool. I've a friend lives over there"— she indicated a direction somewhere northwest of them—"who collects it for me and I pick it up when we pass."

"You're very creative," Sally said, mesmerized by the action of Trompette's neat little fingers, the way the strands came up out of her pockets and combined into the fabric. Trompette shrugged.

"I don't have a choice," she said, "if I want clothes."

"You mean, you make the things you wear?" Sally was aware that the tone of this was too close to the patronizing exclamations of adults to the children selling cupcakes for Red Nose Day. "Sorry, I don't mean to sound as if I'm congratulating a performing monkey. I am genuinely amazed and impressed. Everything you wear is so perfect."

Trompette smiled, leaned sideways and rested her head briefly on Sally's shoulder.

"You're so sweet. I can spot a bullshitter, no problem. You're not it."

Billy came out of the *Grimm* carrying his guitar. He set it on the grass, hitched up his jeans, scratched his belly through his T-shirt, then sat down and began to replace one of the strings. There were bees busy among the wild flowers, an occasional plane flying over, a distant rumble of traffic, the sound of voices approaching then fading away as cyclists and walkers came along the towpath. The thrum of a boat's engine and a greeting as it passed.

"How did you two meet?" Sally asked.

"Ah," Billy said. "Shall I tell you a story?"

"Go on, then."

"We met on the water, but the water we met on was frozen. Frozen hard. So hard, you could skate on it—and that's what we were doing, the day we met: skating. This was in Canada, and we were both, in a way, on the run. Trompette had been sent to stay with friends of her mother's—perhaps too late—because her stepfather had begun to show an unhealthy interest. So there was Trompette, exiled to a small Canadian town where nothing she did or said or wore, none of her opinions, her habits or her attitudes fitted in. She was on the run from her stepfather and was contemplating where to run to next. I was on the run from a criminal past. Not from any actual criminal charges but from the pressure to commit crime, which was the result of the family I was brought up in. Three of my four brothers, all older than me, had been in jail. It was only a matter of time before I would be the one the police caught in an alley with too many drugs and an incriminating phone. So I stole a bit of money, or siphoned off a bit of money someone else had stolen, placed a few clever bets, and left the country.

"I was traveling through Canada, finding jobs to do, keeping out of trouble, but I was homeless and rootless. I was beginning to think, maybe I should give in, go back to the house I used to live in where I was never alone, to escape from this life where I was always on the outside. There you have it: two refugees who have escaped one fate, or the threat of a fate, only to find themselves doomed to isolation in a place they never should have been.

"Still, we might never have found each other but for the lake that was frozen and the weather pattern, which was bringing a warm front in from the west. The sun was shining, the day was warm enough to lift your spirits however far into the depths of your boots they had sunk, and we had both strapped on borrowed skates and gone out on the ice, along with the entire population of the town—or at least those who were physically capable of skating.

"And then, in the midst of this throng of expert skaters, among whom I was the only one knowing nothing about anyone else, knowing no one's name, how did I manage to find Trompette? The warm front—remember that? The sun got us all out there in the sparkle and the freshness, but this was not the first hint of warmth; there had been other warm days. The season was changing and the ice was growing thinner and thinner, starting from the middle where the deepest water was.

"The other people on the lake, the Canadians, were alert to the signs that the ice was about to crack; they knew where it was thinnest; all the variations in color, in the sound it made as a set of skates sped over it; they knew what it meant, and there came a moment when these signs, to them, became inescapable and they turned and skated toward the edge. Trompette went with them. She was in company with the family she was living with and did not want to do anything that might make them scoff at her. Anything more than the hundreds of things she did, unwittingly, every day. But I carried on skating away from the pack, going out into the middle, facing the open, so that I didn't even see them go. No one called out and I only knew I was in danger when the ice in front of me cracked. I heard it and I saw it and, even as a child from Croydon, I knew what that meant and I was terrified.

"I turned back toward the shore and saw the population of the town either skating away from me or already in a place of safety. My skates slid sideways; my knees started to give; behind me, the crack was widening, the edge beginning to crumble. I was seconds away from falling into the water, which—I didn't know this at the time but was told later—was so cold I would have lived for no more than three minutes had I gone in.

"But one figure was ready to save me. Someone was skating back toward me, holding out a hand for me to grasp, to steady myself, set my feet back square on the ice and begin to skate away, away from the hole getting larger and larger behind us, but not fast enough to catch us, me and my savior. The only person who came to help me. Trompette.

"After that, we ran away together. And if you're wondering why she bothers to stay with someone as unsavory to be with as I am sure you think I am—and I wouldn't disagree with you—well, that is why. She saved my life and so we are bound together for eternity. I cannot leave her because I owe her too much; she cannot leave me because she has taken to herself the responsibility for my well-being.

"We met, my dear Sally, when the ice cracked."

Sally turned toward Trompette, who put down her knitting with a sigh and stretched her arms above her head.

"We were at school together," she said.

Sally looked back at Billy, who shrugged.

"Metaphorical ice, metaphorical crack," he said. "Still, a version of the truth."

*

Eve came back and went into the galley on the *Number One* and began to make cooking sounds. Sally looked up from the book she was reading and saw Billy setting off down the towpath on Eve's bike, which she had left leaning against the hedge. He looked unsteady and Sally was cross with him for borrowing it without asking, so she put her book down and went after him. He wobbled past a few other boats on the mooring and reached a bend. He was out of sight when Sally, walking briskly, heard a splash. She speeded up and ran round the corner to see the bike's front wheel, still spinning, sticking up above the bank, the rest of the machine submerged. Billy was in the water beside it, upright but waving his arms about and stationary. Sally's first thought was to rescue the bike, and she ran toward it, reaching out to grasp the wheel, but before her hand came close to the bike, it was grabbed by another hand, Billy's hand—perhaps that was what she had intended to do in the first place: rescue the human not the machine, and maybe she pulled back against his grip with the intention of heaving him up onto the towpath. However it happened, one moment she was trying to help and the next, her feet were slipping on the grassy edge and she tumbled into the canal. It was surprisingly warm and she missed the bike, or at least those parts of it which might have bruised or cut her, but then it proved difficult to right herself. She seemed to be held in the silky, silt-filled water, rolling over too quickly to close her mouth in time. There was a moment of panic before she broke the surface and found herself wrapped in Billy's arms, being hoisted back onto the path. He climbed out after her, then sat beside her, squeezing the water from his hair with his hands.

"What happened?" she asked.

"I fell in, the bike fell in, you fell in. Now you and I are out again. And look . . ." He stood up and pulled the bike from the canal, lifting it clear of Sally and dumping it on the path behind them. "The bike is out, too."

"I don't know what you thought you were doing," Sally said. She meant, what was he doing borrowing Eve's bike, but the murkier question of what he was doing when he gripped her hand—pulling her in or trying to haul himself out—was uppermost in her mind.

"I never think," Billy said. "I just do."

He stood the bike upright and looked as if he might be about to get on it, so Sally, moving awkwardly in her saturated clothing and beginning to feel chilly despite the sunshine, took it from him.

"I'll take it," she said.

"You know the old canal joke?" Billy said, as they walked back. "What do you shout if there's a man overboard?" Sally shook her head. "Stand up!"

He was telling her there was no risk of drowning in the canal, she understood that. Though clearly it wasn't true, because had she been trapped beneath the bike, injured, she might not have been able to reach the surface in time.

"I'll remember that," she said, "next time I see you thrashing about in the water."

He laughed and put his arm round her, pulled her against him, the boniness of his young, thin frame pressing against her ribs.

She climbed into the front well of the *Number One* and dried herself, changed into dry clothes before going through to the galley.

"Billy borrowed your bike," she told Eve, "and fell into the canal with it. I've brought it back, but I haven't checked it's all right."

"It had better be," Eve said, concentrating on peeling an eggplant. "I'll skin the little bastard if he's wrecked it. I don't know, feckless or what? No respect for property." She looked up. "Hang on, why's your hair wet?"

"I fell in, too, trying to get them out."

"Them?"

"Billy and the bike."

"Oh, I'd have left Billy. Are you all right?"

"Of course. The canal's not deep, you know, just rather dirty."

But when Eve insisted on opening a bottle of wine, although it was too early to start drinking, or would have been at 42 Beech Grove, she found she felt better for having drunk a glass.

⌇

SALLY HAD FINISHED *Mr. Lucton's Freedom* and passed it on to Eve.

"You should read it," she said.

Eve had always felt books were important to her. She read more than most of her acquaintances, and she read what she considered to be an admirably wide range: biographies, history and fiction. But having spent a few weeks in company with Sally, who seemed to read at least two books a week and was treating the charity shops like lending libraries—buying a supply, reading them and dropping them off at the next source of new titles—she had downgraded herself from "keen reader" to "a bit of a reader." Sally chose books Eve had never heard of— title, author, genre—and would not have thought to choose.

Sometimes, Sally said, she picked them simply because she knew nothing about the author or the book, in the spirit of experimentation, which pleased Eve. She liked to think Sally was loosening up, letting go.

The gulf between Sally's understanding of the world of books and Eve's was too great for Eve to bridge, so she told herself she didn't need to try. Instead, she settled into a diet of canal history and contemporary crime, which was perfectly satisfying and adequately filled the moments when there seemed to be nothing else to look at or think about or talk about or do. So she was not looking forward to reading the book Arthur had left them. It was a bit old and tatty, for a start. Not tatty like a secondhand paperback that she could imagine some casual reader enjoying while drinking coffee or waiting at a Tube stop. Arthur's book had the look of something that had been through many hands, been held by many different types of people in different circumstances over years and years. The rough fabric of the cover seemed designed to trap the moisture and flakes of skin in a way a smooth, slippery paperback would not. She had noticed Sally fondling it as if it were an object giving more tactile pleasure than the other books she read, and this was exactly what made Eve reluctant to pick it up. Some of this may have been down to its association with Arthur. In the time he had been aboard, Eve had gone from seeing him as pathetic, gray and insignificant, to finding him challenging, almost powerful. But if she had recognized that her first impression, based on his appearance, was superficial and wrong, she could not rid herself of that physical perception of Arthur as someone not quite wholesome, not quite clean and fragrant.

Still, she knew Sally wanted her to read the book and, however boring, irritating or impenetrable it was, in addition to being a health hazard, read it she would. And she would form an
opinion, because that was what Sally would expect.

It was the story of Owen Lucton, a successful, middle-aged
accountant in the 1930s, who finds himself out of step with
those closest to him. His son and his wife both have ambitions
to be modern, to be up-to-date, to strive for material things,
while Lucton values simplicity and tradition, but lacks the certainty to defy the people he has spent his life working to support. He goes out on a drive, in a new car—cars are one aspect
of the twentieth century he appreciates—and makes a mistake,
as a result of which the car sinks into a river, out of sight, and
Lucton sees his chance for escape. Over the next few months,
he tries out different ways of life, living incognito and hand to
mouth to avoid being found by his family and the worthies of
the town, who have put out a hue and cry to discover him or his
body. He walks, he sleeps in barns, he labors on a farm, he plays
cricket, and finally he washes up in a village where he finds he
can be useful to a pair of elderly spinsters. He is needed and
accepted. He lives simply, as he always wanted to do. But the
women need money, urgently, and he has it, but can only access
it by walking back out of his new life into his old. So this is what
he decides he must do, sacrificing the happiness he has found
for the well-being of the community he is living in.

When he goes through the doors of his house and his office,
though, having slipped back into the life he knew, it is with a
new-found confidence and a degree of satisfaction that here,
he truly is someone. He has a position. Is respected. The book

concludes on an optimistic note: it was good to leave, but there is pleasure in going back. The chains Mr. Lucton puts back on are not, after all, as onerous as he thought them before he left.

Eve would not have gone more than two or three pages into this book; would have thrown it aside as dealing with small, mannered people in a small, provincial world and one, more-over, long gone. But she had committed to reading it, so she worked her way through, wondering what it was that Arthur understood it to mean, respecting his own life. That it was good to escape but important to go back? Or that it would have been better if the escape had been forever, that Mr. Lucton had shaken off entirely the person he was for the first fifty years of his life and lived on into happy old age doing manual but satisfying jobs, playing a part in the life of the narrow community where he found himself, becoming an altogether more relaxed, more sociable, more contented, if poorer, man?

And then, Sally, what would she have thought of it? The position Mr. Lucton escaped from was very different from Sally's own, yet similar at a domestic level. Although Duncan was clearly— Sally had been at pains to make this clear—a thoroughly nice man, a caring person who would never intentionally stand in the way of his wife's happiness, he shared, in Eve's opinion, something with Mr. Lucton's family: a lack of imagination, of the ability to dream dreams beyond his workaday world. It was beyond him to understand what it was that Sally needed from life in addition to what she had (in fairness, Sally herself would admit she did not know either) and he therefore assumed she must be happy. He sat, Sally had told her, in the very center of his life, seeing everything as it radiated out from himself, while she felt perpetually on the edge, craning for a glimpse of what lay beyond. The ending of the book, Eve thought, must have made Sally contemplate her own circumstances. It must have made her wonder whether, if she were to decide on reaching the end of the journey that her next move should be back to Uxbridge, that would turn out to be as satisfying as Mr. Lucton's return to North Bromwich had been.

Once she had thought all this through, Eve felt ready to discuss the book with Sally.

"What did you think?" she asked, and Sally began by saying everything Eve had thought about the dated, mannered tone of the book, its narrow and stereotyped range of characters and situations. "So what's good about it, then?" she asked. "Why is Arthur so keen on it?"

"What's good about it is that it makes you think," Sally said. "And it offers you a moral dilemma and the author leaves space for the reader to decide how to judge. 'This is good,' he seems to be saying, when Lucton escapes. 'This is fun and mind-opening, it's turning our hero into a better person.' Then he says, 'But look, going back to where he started—that has its compensations, too.'"

"I don't think I've ever looked at a book in those sorts of terms," Eve said. "How do you do it?"

"Reading a lot," Sally said. "And taking an Open University degree in English literature. That helped."

"I didn't know you'd done that."

"It was something I did for me. And it taught me how to make judgments. But I don't know what the book's appeal is to Arthur, to answer your other question. I'd have to know his story but I suspect he may see it as a sort of allegory, a story embodying a universal truth in a stylized way."

"If you say so," said Eve. "And what about you, what do you feel about it? Do you think of yourself as in the idyll for the moment but expecting to find there are compensations in being back where you started at the end? Or are you looking for ways to make the escape permanent? Have you found your equivalent of the idyllic village, or are you still looking?"

Sally laughed. "When I read it," she said, "I was thinking of you. It seemed to fit your situation better than mine. You had a position and a responsible job and a reputation. You could be more use to the world if you went back and did what you were doing before. So I was wondering, all the time I was reading, whether you would read into it that that was the right thing to do."

Eve stared at her. "But I thought it was about you!" she said. "You have a family, you're settled, with people who need you and want you to be with them. I don't. I don't even have a job to go back to."

"You could find another."

"Well, if I'm honest, I know I could. But no one will miss me if I never go back. If I invest my redundancy money in a boat and spend the rest of my life turning into Anastasia."

They were both silent for a moment, then Sally said:

"It's odd, isn't it, that we each see the other's situation as so different from our own. I wonder whether we're right. I mean, I'm saying to you, 'Look, you can do something significant and play a part in achieving things beyond the simply domestic and day-to-day.'"

"The next generation of hydraulic pumps, you mean."

"Well, yes, but more than that. In helping create employment, prosperity. You could be part of something more complex and challenging than I have ever been. And in comparison, I think of myself as quite insignificant. Then you say to me, 'You're not insignificant because there are individuals who rely on you.'"

"That's right. Real people, not pumps. You were central to your world, I was only a cog in mine."

"Well," said Sally. She picked the book up and stroked its nubbly cloth cover. "So now we've worked all that out, what *does* it mean to you?"

"It's a story," said Eve. "It's a made-up piece of whimsy. It doesn't mean anything."

"I don't see it like that."

"Go on, then, what does it mean to you if you find it so full of meaning?"

"There's no need to get cross," Sally said. Eve thought both the phrase and the tone of voice were what Sally would have used to her children, to her husband, but she didn't say so, and she was pleased rather than irritated by the thought. "It says to me that there has to be a very good reason for going back. And I haven't found one."

MALE VOICE: Owen Engineering.

EVE: Is that Owen?

MALE VOICE: No. Who is it?

EVE: He won't know me. My name's Eve Warburton and I'm phoning about a friend of his.

MALE VOICE: I'll get him.

OWEN: Owen here. What friend?

EVE: Anastasia.

OWEN: Right. So you're one of the women bringing me the *Number One*, is that it?

EVE: Yes.

OWEN: Where are you?

EVE: You sound like . . . never mind. We're near Birmingham, at Bridge 78 on the Grand Union.

OWEN: Bridge 78? Let me see . . . what have you been doing? You should be closer than that by now.

EVE: Well, I'm sorry if you think we're just drifting along as if tomorrow would do, but Anastasia said we had to be with you by August, and we will be.

OWEN: OK. Is that what you phoned to say? Anything wrong with the boat I need to know about? Any parts I ought to be ordering?

EVE: Not that I know of and no, it wasn't why I was phoning. Anastasia asked us to let you know when she was going in for her operation.

OWEN: Hold on, hold on. This isn't right. Anastasia *asked* you to tell me she was going into hospital? That doesn't sound likely. And what operation is this?

EVE: No, all right, we asked her who we should tell, and she agreed we could tell you. She's having an operation to remove a tumor from her lung. It's next Thursday. Are you still there?

OWEN: Yes. I'm absorbing the information, is all.

EVE: Did you know she was ill?

OWEN: Well, of course I did. Why else would she ask a couple of amateurs to bring the *Number One* up here?

I just didn't imagine it would be serious. I'm used to
her overcoming obstacles.

EVE: She may overcome this one.

OWEN: Did she say so?

EVE: No. She's treating it as an experience, I would say.
She is neither hopeful nor despairing.

OWEN: I can see that.

EVE: She agreed we could tell Arthur, too. She said
you'd know how to get hold of him.

OWEN: Now I'm worried. She agreed to let Arthur
know she's going into hospital to get part of her lung
removed next Thursday? Which hospital, are we allowed to know that?

EVE: Yes, it's Hillingdon Hospital in Uxbridge.

OWEN: And what did she tell you to tell me and Arthur,
exactly?

EVE: The date, the hospital, the fact that she was having
an operation.

OWEN: But not what operation?

EVE: I don't know. I'm not sure if that was prohibited.

OWEN (MUFFLED): Keep the fucking noise down, guys.
I'm on the phone.

EVE: Is there anything more you want to know?

OWEN: Lots, but nothing you can tell me. Thank you for
ringing, and for the information. I'm sorry if I sounded
cross. I do want you to keep me up to date with anything you find out. Can I rely on you to do that?

EVE: Yes, you can. By the way, she did say no fuss, no
grapes.

OWEN: I've known her a lot longer than you have and I
can't imagine what universe I would be living in if I
thought she wanted either of those.
EVE: Goodbye, then.

Click.

6

Birmingham

THE *NUMBER ONE* AND *Grimm* traveled the length of the Birmingham suburbs, *Grimm* taking the lead. It was surprisingly peaceful. It would have been possible, Eve noted, to moor almost anywhere in this stretch, but she was pleased that they had stopped at Trompette's command the previous afternoon. She had enjoyed the shopping and the cooking and the eating. She had made Sultan Reshat Pilavi, a pilaf with lamb meatballs that, Claudia told her, was on record in the archives of the Topkapi Palace. There was enough for Billy and Trompette but Sally had asked her not to invite them. So she hadn't. After all, Sally had fallen into the canal trying to rescue her bike so it was the least she could do. The leftovers would keep for a couple of days, Sally said. Which was probably true but they managed to eat most of it, with a bottle of Turkish wine Eve had found for next to nothing in Aldi.

While Sally drove, Eve contemplated the Guide. The options available for traveling through Birmingham on the canals and out the other side in the direction they wanted to go were

almost too complicated to grasp. For one thing, they had to use
a different Guide, and it had taken them most of the trip so far
to become used to the way the Guide they had used since Uxbridge moved from page to page—never in a logical direction
and not always to a contiguous page. Trying to reconcile where
they were with where they needed to end up (which was in a
third Guide), avoiding taking the wrong turn at the multiple
junctions they would pass, was going to be enough of a challenge
without the added problem of having to choose beyond the city
center (if they left it on the right canal) between the straight,
newer canal and the older, more rambling one. Eve was lost in
admiration for the men (they were all men—she had failed to
uncover a hint of a feminine brain being engaged in the work)
who had not only planned and executed this civil-engineering
miracle in the first place but had then decided to create something better—straighter, shorter—going between the same two
points. How was it that, when they could plan all this and carry
it out, she seemed incapable of following the routes they had
chosen on a perfectly reproduced, accurate, annotated, scaled
map? It was because, she comforted herself, she did not have it
all on a single sheet of paper. She had always liked plans on a
page. She could see the big picture when the north, south, east
and west of it were all apparent at once. On each of these pages
(they joined the next Guide on page 63, left it to go to page 195,
then exited to the next Guide from page 39) there was so much
detail she was continually distracted. It was like the experience
on the walk a few days ago. She had gone down and down and
down until she was lost to sight at a single point on the map and
Sally had lifted her head up and made sense of the whole thing.
Eve wondered if there was a lesson here she might carry back

into the way she approached her job, before remembering she no longer had a job. Might never have a job again, or not one where the ability to understand how to manipulate both the overall concept and the detail buried within it might be a requirement.

"Here," she said to Sally. "You look at the wretched Guide. I'll drive."

There was a subterranean feel to the canal through Birmingham. High brick walls and a flight of locks that were submerged beneath railway bridges. In between there were stretches with trees, modern or modernized buildings, but Sally was left with the impression that the casual phrase for visiting a town—"going into"—was entirely accurate. As if the city was at a lower level than the one they had left and they were going down into it.

Trompette, at the tiller of *Grimm* ahead of them, was a strange contrast to the surroundings of graffiti, litter and abandonment, standing still and straight in one of her triangular-shaped dresses with her hair in a neat little scarf tied in a knot on top. The floating debris included balloons, bottles, cans, plastic bags and a dead duck. Trompette glanced aside at none of them. They came to a narrow bridge where a group of young people, children, turned from their studied idleness to call and point as *Grimm* nosed through the arch. One of them reached out a hand to grab the rail and pull himself aboard. Trompette, without appearing to notice, picked up a lock key with the hand not holding the tiller and swung it round slowly, like a ratchet. The youth stepped back. The level of noise—Sally was too far back to hear the words—increased, but apart from rude gestures they let *Grimm* pass.

Eve was standing on the rear deck with Sally. Though the group chose to ignore them, she could feel Eve's tension as the arch of brick trapped their voices.

"I didn't enjoy that," she said. "Do you think they were dealing drugs?"

"No," Sally said. "I think they were waiting to grow up and become perfectly ordinary."

"Oh, really?" said Eve. "They looked unlikely to stay out of jail to me."

"That's because you've never had anything to do with teenagers," Sally said. "If you had, you'd be able to recognize the difference between the drug dealers and the embryo adults."

"I'd better stick close to you, then, while we're in Birmingham," Eve said. "So you can tell me when it's time to panic."

It was evening before they reached Aston Junction, where *Grimm* pulled in to a mooring. Sally steered the *Number One* in behind it.

Eve went to the post office to collect their post. She had had very little, until now, but she was hoping Jacob would have remembered his promise to send a cookery book, although she told herself he probably would not have done so. Sally was always pleased to receive her post because none of it was related to the boring business of operating bank accounts and household affairs. She had walked out of her life and left her husband to sort all that out. Eve did not know whether to be scornful or impressed.

The post office had a porch decorated with a miniature version of the dome of St. Paul's Cathedral, a folly that Eve contrasted with the purposeful beauty of all aspects of the architecture of the canals. Inside, she was irritated to discover she was not allowed to carry Sally's post away with her, having nothing that identified her as a person with responsibility for doing so, but pleased to find her own bundle included a padded envelope, book-shaped. She wanted to go at once to a café she had noted on the way past, to sit surrounded by other people spending time with their friends, laptops, books, papers and phones.

But it would not be fair to Sally to give in to the impulse. They had agreed they could not leave Noah alone on the boat in the center of Birmingham. And Sally would be preparing lunch, slicing the bread, unwrapping the cheese, finding the pickle in the cupboard. She was planning an outing of her own later, with Trompette, to a wool shop, and would be relying on Eve to come straight back from her errand. So, much as she wanted to linger, Eve had to return. Maybe this, she thought, was what it would be like to be married. Knowing that every time you left the house, you had to run a check on the well-being of someone else before going, before deciding to stay out.

It was ridiculous to regret the loss of the chance to divert into a coffee shop for half an hour, and Eve did not regret it. But she looked out, on the rest of the walk back to the moorings, for other reasons she might have wanted to pause. She had never been into the art gallery, with its sizeable collection of Pre-Raphaelite paintings, and she had always liked the bold, bright assertiveness of the style. She passed a particularly good busker playing a violin with feeling and verve, but could not loiter and listen. There was a table laden with leaflets opposing some outrage or other; she enjoyed a bit of outrage and it was possible she would have found this cause worth discussing, or arguing about.

Still, there was Jacob's parcel to look forward to. And the bread and cheese. And the peace of the *Number One* when Sally had gone out with Trompette and she was left by herself, with Noah, and the possibilities of the city beyond the porthole, for later.

SALLY HAD LIVED ALL HER life in towns and yet she felt oppressed. The *Number One* was too flimsy a protection from the pressures of a city: the noise, the people, the dirt and litter. She was too exposed. She was not physically afraid; it was more the feeling of having too few clothes on in a public place, of having no walls to keep herself separate. Also, Noah was not happy. She was less concerned about Noah's well-being than Eve would have been—he was only a dog, after all—but his restlessness contributed to her uneasiness, on her own behalf and on his.

She was relieved when Eve came back, and so, it seemed, was Noah. She left him, after lunch, curled up behind Eve's legs as she sat in a chair reading the cookery book Jacob had sent her.

"You're not supposed to read cookery books," Sally said. "You refer to them."

"Not this one," said Eve. "Jacob says it's worth reading for its own sake and not just for the recipes."

"He's probably wrong," Sally said.

Trompette appeared in her dungarees and they set off for a shop that was farther away than Sally expected, although that might have been because they had to go by way of the post office. She collected a couple of letters from her children, who were communicating with her more formally and, in fact, more regularly now. They had not grasped, because she had not told them, that she could pick up emails and messages on her phone; instead they were treating her as if she had embarked on a long and hazardous navigation of some remote country. There was also a bulky envelope from Duncan. To begin with, he had written long letters she hardly read, so full of illogical circularity they made her feel giddy. Was it his fault? he asked. Why didn't she say so, before, if it was? Had she ever loved him? Could he be blamed if she had married him without loving him? How was he supposed to know how she felt? Did she want him to apologize? Was it his fault? She had communicated with him briefly and calmly. She had told him where she was, what she was doing. She had described aspects of the view from a narrowboat. She had, every time, apologized for hurting him and stressed it was not his fault. Eventually he had begun to respond in kind: telling her what was going on in his life, letting her know the news from the piece of territory he still occupied. She began to remind him of the things she would have done if she still lived at 42 Beech Grove. She stuffed all her letters into her rucksack.

Trompette was an object of attention as they walked through the streets. Sally noticed people passing by noticing her, both men and women, young and old, following her with their eyes. Trompette, with her blue dungarees, her bare, brown arms, her head wrapped in a bright red-and-blue scarf tied in a bow on top of her head, with a huge tote bag over one shoulder in blocks of red, yellow, blue and black fabric, would have been interesting on the canal, but unsurprisingly so, as the canal was peopled and decorated with a range of the picturesque, the not-quite-normal and the colorful. Here, on the pavements of Birmingham, she was a rare enough creature to be watched and stared after. To which she was, or appeared to be, oblivious. Sally wondered if all these people thought she was Trompette's mother and, if so, whether they thought she was failing to live up to so splendid a creature.

They reached the shop and the woman behind the counter, who was wearing a hand-knitted cardigan woollier than the temperature would suggest was necessary, came out and hugged Trompette. She submitted to being hugged, then introduced the woman as Misty, which Sally misheard as Miss Tee, but realized her mistake when she noticed the shop was called Misty's Cave. At the back was a table covered in knitting-pattern books that Misty swept onto a chair with a wave of her stocking-stitched arm, to allow Trompette to empty her tote, which turned out to be full of pieces manufactured from wool: some toys, some clothes, some creations—flowers, cupcakes, random (but beautiful) shapes—which Sally would have thought had no connection with wool whatever. The conversation between the two women became technical.

"I can't see any seams on this."

"That's because there aren't any. I knitted it in one piece, with steeks."

"I can't tell. And this shawl?"

"Knitted from the top down with short row shaping."

"Good stitch definition. The yarn is partly yak, if I remember right."

Sally wandered round the racks and racks of different weights and colors and textures of wool, reaching out to touch the ones that looked particularly worth touching, picking up stray balls from the floor or counters and slotting them back in their place.

The effect of what were no more than bookcases with diagonal dividers splitting each cell into four, packed with wools, was both exciting and soothing. It was a display of missed opportunities. Because, like everything else in her life, she had thought knitting was something that needed to be done rather than something she wanted to do, she had stopped when she realized it was cheaper to buy the children sweaters than to knit them. She had only ever knitted with wool that was cheap, in colors and shapes suitable for school, it had been no hardship to stop. But here, in Misty's Cave, she was transfixed by the beauty of the unknitted, and the knitted, as displayed in finished pieces and on the covers of pattern books. From this, she thought, putting a finger on an iridescent skein of fine russet yarn, to this, and she felt the edge of a lacy shawl. It had to be possible that the work to go from the one to the other was within her grasp and that she would enjoy doing it.

When Misty and Trompette had finished talking and some of the work in Trompette's tote had been carried off and replaced by more wool, she expressed this "Could I? Should I?" thought to them both. From that moment she was never going to leave the shop without a pattern and some yarn—which might well have been her intention in accompanying Trompette in the first place. It was not the shawl pattern or the russet yarn; one was too complicated and the other too expensive, Misty declared. Instead she had everything she needed to knit a little cowl in an earthy ochre color, with a pattern she had been taken through from start to finish to make sure she understood it.

"Trompette will help me if I forget how to interpret it," she said.

"She might," said Misty. "But she doesn't hold with patterns. Trompette just creates, unfortunately."

"Isn't that better than copying someone else's idea?"

"Yes, but if the pattern you've created isn't written down once you've done it, you can't share it. You might not even be able to repeat it yourself."

"Who wants to repeat themselves?" said Trompette.

"I wish you'd learn pattern notation, though," said Misty. "And write up the instructions for the things you bring me to sell."

"It's too boring. Can't you work it out backward, as it were?"

Misty shrugged. "I can, up to a point. But I'd rather you did it, so you can make a living as a designer, or something approaching a living." She turned to Sally. "She's so talented."

On the way back to the boat they bought an ice cream from a kiosk near the canal and paused on a bench on the towpath to eat it.

"So what's stopping you taking designing more seriously?" Sally asked.

Trompette turned to look at her. "You think it's Billy, don't you?"

"Is it?"

"No."

"Then what is it?"

"I know I don't know enough. I know if I want to be any good, I have to learn, and practice, and experiment and be bold, and then go back from boldness to something bold enough but also strong and honest. Something I can put my hand up to and say 'That's me.' So, all of that, it needs time and money, and in the life I lead now, I don't have any money and I don't have the right sort of time. And I can't work out how to go from the life I lead now to one where I have the money and the right sort of time, and I'm not sure I want to have what I don't have as much as I want to keep what I do have."

"What a coherent person you are," Sally said.

"What a nice person you are," Trompette said. She picked up Sally's hand and licked a dribble of ice cream from her wrist.

SALLY AND EVE WERE PLAYING Scrabble in the cabin. It was a beautiful evening, the sky fading from its daytime blue through the softest range of pinks and reds and grays. But in the end there was no sky at all as the city suppressed whatever remained of dark and light with its nighttime brightness. They had not sat outside because the pressure of buildings and the affront of graffiti on the walls made the interior of the cabin seem much more appealing than it would normally be, as the sun set on a warm day.

Trompette arrived, rocking the boat as she stepped aboard, bringing with her the tinkling sound of two lengths of string with bells tied on to them at intervals. Little, brassy bells.

"You need to tie these to your mooring ropes," she said. "Come with me and I'll show you what knot to use."

"What not to use?" said Eve, who had had a glass or two of wine and was sure, before the interruption, that she had a seven-letter word within her grasp.

"Why?" said Sally.

"So you'll wake up if anyone tries to untie the ropes," said Trompette.

"Is that likely?" Sally asked.

Trompette shrugged. "It's Birmingham," she said. "Prepare for the worst."

"Noah would bark," said Eve.

"Possibly," said Trompette, "but only if they made a noise. And they might not. Are you coming or not?"

The towpath had taken on a different aspect now darkness had fallen, both more restful and more sinister. The area appeared to be deserted, but there were possibilities in the shadows, too. Apart from the *Number One* and *Grimm* there was only one other vessel, a couple of boat lengths ahead of *Grimm*. Someone was smoking on this boat, body inside, head and lighted tip thrust through the hatch on the side, smoke drifting away slowly in the still air. Eve found herself watching the glow and fade of the cigarette as the smoker breathed in, breathed out, instead of concentrating on the knots Trompette was demonstrating to Sally as necessary to foil the toerags, as she referred to these possibly mythical creatures of the night.

"Wouldn't they simply cut the rope?" Eve asked. "They could be gone, job done, before we had any idea they were there."

"No," said Trompette. "The rope's too thick."

"Rumor has it," Eve said (she was finding Trompette irritating and wanted to get back to the hunt for the elusive seven-letter word), "that they all carry knives capable of killing people."

"Flesh is easy to cut," said Trompette.

Noah leaped off the boat and trotted toward the smoker at the hatch, as if he knew just where he was going.

"No-ah!" called Eve. "You're meant to be guarding us against the urban hordes. Come back!" She was jogging after him, knowing he would ignore her.

He came to a stop where the head of a man was still visible, though the cigarette had gone.

"He's hoping I'm going to give him a biscuit, I expect," the man said. He was so deeply in shadow Eve could not have said what age he was, but he did not sound young.

"Have you moored here before?" Eve asked.

"Oh, yes."

"Is it safe, do you think?"

The man laughed and this brought on a cough, but when he had this under control he said: "You don't look like the kind of woman who goes round thinking every shadow is a rapist."

Eve realized that, while she couldn't see him, she was standing in a spill of light from a car park nearby, so he could see her. She wasn't sure what it was about her appearance that suggested a lack of nervousness—it might only be that she was large, un-flatteringly dressed and therefore, presumably, not a target, or it could be that he recognized her as someone who resisted seeing herself as a victim. She liked that.

"You're right, I'm not," she said.

"Anyway," he said. "You've got the Hound of the Baskervilles to protect you."

Eve looked round and saw Noah defecating on the edge of the path. She felt the pockets of her jeans, which were empty.

"I don't suppose you have a bag I can use to pick that up?" she said.

"Aah, forget it," he said. "Let the forces of darkness tread in it, if they come. Serve them right."

Back on the *Number One*, the Scrabble game conclusively won by Eve after she had detected that she could make the word "absolved" fit round the "b" of "bacon" with the "d" turning "ooze" into "oozed," they turned off all the lights and went to bed, neither of them quite believing that Trompette's precautions were necessary, neither of them feeling quite as safe as they would in the countryside.

"It's ridiculous, isn't it?" said Eve, as if they had voiced this thought to each other. "When we moor where there's no one about, we feel safer than when there are a million people living nearby. You'd think we'd be more worried in the middle of nowhere."

"Where no one can hear you scream," agreed Sally.

"Noah would."

"Yes, we're counting on you, Noah," Sally said.

Eve woke up to the sound of voices. She picked up her phone and checked the time: a little after midnight. She heard the thump of Noah's tail striking the floor; he, too, was awake, apparently waiting for her to make a suggestion. The voices were on the towpath, and not particularly close. She crept through to the rear deck, eased the hatch cover back and climbed the first couple of steps so she could see the length of the path without coming out into the open.

There was a group of people gathered around the front of *Grimm*. Eve could recognize Billy, sitting on the edge of the boat; apart from him, there were two men and a youth. The youth was holding two bicycles by the handlebars. The men had their heads down and were looking at something in their hands; Billy was watching them. Noah whimpered, below her in the cabin, wanting to come past her, but she pushed him back with her foot.

Trompette came out on to the rear deck of *Grimm*, still dressed as she had been earlier that evening. She turned her head toward the *Number One* and could not have missed Eve's head poking through the open hatch, but she gave no sign.

"Eve!" Sally called softly from the cabin. "What are you doing?"

Eve descended the steps. "Sorry. Trying not to wake you. I heard voices, but it looks to be friends of Billy's and Trompette's come to call."

"She told me they might," Sally said. "She said not to get involved."

"Get involved?" said Eve. "What did she mean?"

"Oh, Eve," said Sally. "I don't know, but Billy takes drugs, doesn't he? Don't we know that? So where does he get them from?"

Eve was still fuddled with wine, with the triumph of winning the game, with sleep. So far as she had thought anything, she had thought: "fishing."

"How come you thought of that and I didn't?" she said.

"I don't suppose there was much drug dealing in the corridors of power," said Sally. "I'll put the kettle on, shall I? Make a cup of tea."

"There may have been," Eve said. "I just didn't notice. I'm beginning to think I'm not a noticing sort of person."

"It's probably because you're strong-minded. You haven't needed to creep about keeping an eye out for what's going to bite you."

"Strong-minded or stupid."

From outside the boat came sudden, shocking loud noises—the sound of feet running, of shouting—and Noah started barking as loudly as it was possible for him to bark, almost drowning out the splash of something heavy falling in the water. Then Trompette screamed. It could only be Trompette; no other woman would be able to hit that note of command within a falsetto cry of alarm. When they reached the towpath, Noah, who had leaped out of the boat ahead of them, was chasing a group of figures who were running or, in the case of two of them, cycling away.

Trompette was standing on the roof of *Grimm* shouting Billy's name. A man was lying on the bank, face down, and it was only when Eve and Sally reached him, both expecting to find him dead or injured, that they realized he was neither. Rather, he was reaching out his hands to Billy, who was drifting in the murky water of the canal, not struggling, but rocking gently with the ripples caused by *Grimm* responding to Trompette's dance of rage or despair on the roof.

The man lying down was trying to coax Billy toward him and Eve recognized his voice as belonging to the smoker she had spoken to earlier in the boat moored ahead of them. She ran forward to where he lay, peering into the darkness where Billy was a paler shape against the blackness of the water. He was not responding to Trompette's shouts. Eve looked at the edge of the path in front of her bare feet and thought of all the things, organic and inorganic, that her toes would encounter if she slid into the water. She began to wade toward where Billy floated.

Then Sally, who had run back to the *Number One*, turned its headlight on and lit up the stretch of canal ahead of *Grimm*. Billy could be seen clearly, floating, his eyes shut and his mouth slightly open, tilting a little toward one side, looking to be at risk of ending up facedown.

The water came up to the top of Eve's thighs and she let the bottom of her T-shirt float as she held her arms out, ready to correct a stumble. It had become eerily quiet. Noah had stopped chasing the men, who had run away, and was sitting on the bank watching her. Trompette had stopped shouting. The stranger's breath was wheezing in and out as he lay still with his arms held out in a gesture of supplication.

Eve, after no more than a few steps, was within reach of one of Billy's floating arms. She made sure her feet were flat on the bottom, well spread, and then she touched his hand.

"Billy," she said. Like an echo, Trompette called "Billy!"

Billy gulped; took in a breath, let it out again noisily. Opened his eyes. Eve took hold of the hand nearest her, which curled round hers. She tugged.

"Come on," she said. "Time to get out of the water. Are you going to stand up or do I have to tow you to land?"

Billy struggled for a moment then stood up, and immediately staggered, beginning to fall backward, and Eve grabbed for the other hand to keep him upright. He had something clasped in his other hand, a package of some kind, and resisted Eve's efforts to wrap her fingers round his, so she took his wrist and they stood, both swaying slightly, inches apart in the bright beam of the *Number One*'s light. Eve could see Billy's face clearly. His eyes and now his mouth were open but she doubted if he was seeing her.

The water around them began to move, to lap and slap against them, and Eve had a moment of panic when she thought they were both certain to fall back into it; although Billy's right hand would not let go of the package to grip hers, his left was now clenched round her right hand and if he fell, she knew she would, too. She risked a look round to find the source of the commotion in the water and it was the stranger, wading slowly toward them. His head and neck declared him to be a thin man, a man in middle age with hair gone entirely from the front of his scalp but still flowing in lengthy wisps down to his collar at the back. His body, though, was fat.

He seized hold of the back of Billy's shirt, keeping him upright, while Eve pulled in the direction of the bank. Step by perilous step, the three of them moved to within reach of Trompette, down from the roof, and Sally, who dragged Billy onto the gritty path. The stranger rested, still standing in the canal, until Eve and Sally gave him a hand each and almost lifted the dead weight of him onto dry land.

Trompette was crouched over Billy. She seemed to be working on his clothing or his chest, but when she had time to look, Eve saw that all Trompette was doing was trying to force the fingers of Billy's right hand loose from round the package.

"Do we need an ambulance?" Sally asked.

"No," said Trompette. "Not for him, anyway." She poked Billy in the ribs and he groaned. "He'll come down soon enough. He hasn't overdosed. Not yet." She looked round. "I don't know about Thad, though. He looks to be in bad shape."

Eve thought she had referred to the stranger as "that," which struck her as unfriendly, in the circumstances. It was only later she found out his name.

"I'm all right," the man said, although his labored breathing suggested otherwise. "Just let me rest."

Trompette had finally loosened Billy's grip and had the package free. She stood up and walked away from him.

"What are you going to do with that?" asked the stranger.

Billy groaned and started to roll over; Eve stepped over him quickly to prevent him falling back into the canal.

"I haven't decided," Trompette said.

"Perhaps these nice ladies could look after it for you," said the stranger.

"No," said Trompette, and almost simultaneously Sally said: "No."

Trompette jumped onto *Grimm* and came back with two towels and without the package.

"Here," she said to Eve, who only now understood how wet, cold and slimy she was. With the other towel, Trompette began to pummel Billy's head, scrub at his chest, his arms and legs, while he howled from time to time, but otherwise put up with her attentions.

"Can you help me get him aboard?" she asked, when she'd finished. Between the three of them they wrestled him upright and this time, as if taking the package from him had returned him to some awareness of his surroundings, Billy managed to put one foot in front of the other without stumbling.

"Go to bed," said Trompette. "Keep the dog in."

Eve took a step toward the stranger, still hunched over on the towpath.

"Come on, you've done enough," said Sally. "Follow Trompette's orders."

Eve realized her legs had begun to wobble and she needed more than a towel to feel dry; she needed to take her T-shirt and leggings off. She needed to lie down in the dark. The kettle, which Sally had filled before the drama started, was put on the hob at last and Eve drank her tea in bed, barely keeping her eyes open long enough to finish it.

❦

THE BOAT ROCKED AND THE bells on the mooring ropes jingled merrily. Sally was already rising through the layers of sleep when Noah began to bark and someone banged on the doors at the rear of the boat. She opened her eyes to see lights moving and the slow, revolving, blue flash of an emergency services vehicle somewhere out of sight.

There were three people outside, two men and a woman, and by the time they had come down the steps in turn, warning her to control the dog, they filled the space. When Eve came through, the smallest of the three retreated up the steps to leave room for her inside. They were all wearing, as the police do nowadays, not just a uniform but power packs of equipment. Pockets and belts strapped to their bodies. The two men wore short-sleeved shirts and were altogether too large, too solid, too hairy to suit the sparse, unchallenging surroundings. Sally found she was holding her breath, keeping herself within the smallest scope possible to avoid actual physical contact.

They made a note of her name, Eve's name. Their dates of birth. Their addresses. As she named 42 Beech Grove, Sally had an urge to smile at how silly it sounded, and how unlikely it was she would ever have lived there.

"The dog's called Noah, if you want to make a note of that, too," said Eve, and Sally hoped she wasn't going to treat whatever was happening here as a joke, because she, Sally, knew it was not.

"There was an incident here, earlier," one of the men said. "Can you tell me what happened?"

"We heard something falling into the canal," Sally said

quickly. "We went out and found it was the young man from the boat in front, so Eve waded into the water and helped him on to the bank. Then we came back here and went to sleep."

"Do you know the young man?"

"We've met him," Sally said. "He knows the owner of this boat, so he and his girlfriend have been friendly to us since we met them along the way."

"This isn't your boat, then?" said the woman.

They were taking it to Chester, Sally explained, on behalf of the owner who was in hospital having an operation. The policeman doing most of the writing made a note of Anastasia's name, and lack of permanent address. No fixed abode, Sally thought.

"Mind if I have a walk through the boat?" said the first policeman, almost pleasantly, pushing past Eve even as he spoke.

"So what was this chap doing in the canal?" asked the second policeman, looking at Eve now.

"Well, floating?" said Eve.

"Did he fall in? Was he pushed?"

"I was asleep when it happened."

"There was someone else on the bank, am I right?" said the woman. "What do you know about him?"

"Oh, nothing," said Eve.

"Can you describe him, or his boat?"

"It was dark," Eve said. Sally knew they had both seen the man clearly in the *Number One*'s headlights and was relieved that Eve was awake enough and sober enough to know that it was better to say little until (and if) it became clear what the police were doing here, how this affected Billy and, more importantly, Trompette.

The first man came back into the cabin and said, "Did the young man go in to retrieve something, would you say?"

"We were asleep," Eve said, again.

"OK, but did he seem to be looking for anything? Was he holding anything when you pulled him out?"

"I didn't exactly pull him out," Eve said. "It was more a case of guiding him to the bank."

"We have no idea what he was doing," said Sally. "We went to help, as you'd expect, then we came back and went to sleep again."

"Briefly," said Eve, whose face looked rather doughy in the lights of the cabin which, after an evening playing Scrabble, were beginning to dim as the battery drained.

"Was he holding a knife?"

"A knife!" said Eve. "No, I hope not. I never saw one."

"Did you see anyone with a knife?"

Eve looked at Sally, who shook her head. "No one," she said.

"So remind me," said the second man. "What was the name of the boat at the front?"

They both shook their heads. "You could go and look," said Eve.

"We could," said the woman, "except it's not there anymore."

As suddenly as they had arrived, the police left.

"You must have an idea what was happening here," said the last man out, handing Sally a card with a name and a number on it. "I'd advise you to let us know if you remember anything else. It's a murky business"—the bristles on his arm, holding the door open, made Sally think of Rottweilers; she never had liked dogs—"and I appreciate you may not want to get the young couple into trouble, but you won't help by staying silent."

"What do you think?" asked Eve, when the door shut behind them and the boat had stopped rocking from their passage across the deck, the bells gradually falling silent.

When Eve was wading toward Billy, Sally had been overcome with dread, remembering her own encounter with Billy in the water. She had nearly called out to tell Eve to stop, now, turn back, but Eve was so sturdy, so solid, so sure, it would have been presumptuous to suggest she could not look after herself. But she had suspected that Trompette shared her concerns, that she was staying apart herself to see if Billy was not, after all, playing some game. But in the end, it had been all right. Billy did need rescuing and maybe Trompette knew that and had been shouting Billy's name to draw others to him rather than going in herself, weary perhaps of being the one to pull him, again and again, away from the crack in the ice.

Looking at Eve, bleary-eyed in the dim light, Sally wondered how much of what had happened either of them understood. "I think it's a good job we don't know anything and we should both go back to bed. And well done, by the way."

"What? Oh, just blundering on, you know. It's what I do," said Eve.

IN THE MORNING, A BREEZE was blowing, lifting and dropping the crisp packets, pieces of paper, the plastic and polythene debris. The same wind was creating patterns of shadow and light with the clouds overhead, and these patterns of light and dark were a comfort to Sally when she finally opened her eyes, unable to sleep any longer though still feeling the need for sleep. There was something tapping against the doors to the front deck; Sally

sat up and saw at once that there were no boats moored ahead of
them, just an empty stretch of ruffled water. In the space where,
during the hours of darkness, any horror had seemed possible, a
man was jogging, bright in lime-green Lycra, and a woman was
striding past with a baby in a sling across her front.

The tapping came from a carrier bag hooked on to the exte-
rior door handles. Inside it was a piece of card, folded over. On
the front was a line drawing of a kimono-style garment, and on
the reverse was a message: *Sorry. I will have knitted this by the
time I see you again*. It was unsigned.

Eve came through with a cup of tea.

"What's that?" she said.

"It's a goodbye note from Trompette," Sally said.

"Are we leaving, or has she?"

"She has."

They worked their way up the flight of thirteen locks to where
there were shops, bars, restaurants and other boats moored. They
were helped on the way by a couple of women following them
through. They introduced themselves as Jen and Chris and they
were reassuringly sturdy and wholesome in contrast to Trompette and Billy. Both Sally and Eve thought this, though Sally's
feelings toward the crew of *Grimm* had a sad flavor while Eve's
were seasoned with irritation.

They moored and found a café where there were chairs and
tables outside and a dog could sit with them, watching the flow
of people. Many of them, now that the day was well advanced,
dressed as befitted someone with an occupation and a place to
be, moving with a purpose that was nothing to do with taking
exercise or enjoying the sunshine, though they were able to do
both in the course of whatever business they were engaged in,

because of the happy contiguity of the canal and places to work. Eve pointed this out to Sally.

"Maybe for my next job I should be looking for an office near water," Eve said.

Sally was going through the bundle of post Duncan had sent. Their correspondence had become unemotional, which was still the tone of the letter she had in her hand in this café on the canal in Birmingham, but it set a different agenda. It talked about the future. He had been thinking, he said, that perhaps they should sort things out. To this end he had reduced their lives together to a series of financial transactions, though he didn't say that. He just said he was enclosing the information she might need to look through. It was all bank statements, mortgage statements, savings accounts statements and a spreadsheet showing their joint income and expenditure for the last ten years. Sally had no intention of looking at the figures, but when Eve spoke she had been deep in the meaning of it all. What Duncan meant her to feel and what she did feel. It took her a moment to process what Eve had said, then she looked, as Eve was looking, at the people walking past, and understood that for Eve they represented the world she had stepped away from, and was already thinking—Sally thought Eve was unaware of this but it came to her as a fact, in the moment—of how and when she would step back in.

"Perhaps I should buy a house by a canal," Sally said, for the sake of something to say, and because this was where the letter from Duncan was pushing her thoughts. But as she said it, it sounded true, so she added: "Not in Birmingham, though."

Eve went back to reading the paper supplied by the café. Sally sat on, pondering whether she could imagine going back to being some modified version of Mrs. Allsop of 42 Beech Grove, or whether that was no longer available to her.

They met Jen and Chris on the way back to the boat, carrying a reusable shopping bag, each holding one handle. Chris told Eve that Jen, in "real life," was a hairdresser. Eve said Sally's hair could do with a makeover as the pink highlights had reached the stage of looking accidental, as if she had dipped her head in a pot of tandoori paste and failed to wash it afterward. And without having agreed, or even being aware that she had a choice, Sally found herself on board the *Rainbow Flag* lying back in a chair, covered in towels, while Jen's thin, strong fingers massaged her scalp.

"I'll just do what I think you ought to want, whether you do want it or not," Jen said, when she had Sally upright again, a pair of scissors at the ready.

"I don't want any more highlights," Sally said.

"Maybe not," said Jen. "Not today, anyway. And definitely not pink."

There was no mirror, so she had no idea what Jen was doing. From force of habit, Sally attempted conversation but was immediately hushed.

"Shut up, I'm concentrating."

Jen put her scissors away and plugged in a hairdryer, but this part of the process, which Lynne from the Kut Above would spin out through several anecdotes about holidays and their respective children's love lives, took almost no time at all. Then Jen produced a mirror.

"I think I've got it," she said, looking rather stern and critical.

Sally turned her head, thinking, for a second, that the light was falling in such a way as to make her unknown to herself.

But it was not the light. Jen had turned Sally's hair into part of her appearance, which was an odd thought but nevertheless true. Her hands and feet, nose, mouth, breasts, ears and knees Sally had always accepted were what they were; together with the other parts of her body they made up the person she was, or the person she looked like. Her hair, though, had always been an adjunct. An extra, there to be tackled, yet never integral to the whole. Now it was.

"Oh," she said.

"I wanted to make it look natural," Jen said. "And I think I have."

"You have," said Sally. She looked past the mirror to the window that gave her a view of a bollard, a stretch of wall, a fleeting shadow as the clouds blew across the sun. "You've made a difference," she said. "Thank you."

"Look at you," Eve said, when Sally returned to the *Number One*. She kept looking at her for the rest of the afternoon, stealing glances when she thought Sally wouldn't notice.

"You can stop looking at me now," Sally said at last.

"Yes, but I feel I've sort of had you wrong, all these weeks," said Eve. "I don't know . . . the hair, the way you look and move—you've turned into someone else entirely."

"No, I haven't," Sally said. "You know that as well as I do."

"All right, then. You are the person you've always been, but that person is only now rising to the surface."

"What a lovely thing to say," said Sally, embarrassed at how tearful she felt.

They took Chris and Jen out for a meal. During the evening, as they waited to order, drank their wine, ate their food, drank their coffee, the two women were in touch with each other. Physically, a foot resting against a foot, a hand against a hand, but also in their enjoyment of the moment, passing forkfuls of food back and forth, sharing a pleasure in the tastes and textures. In the past, when Sally had seen other couples so much in accord, so together, it had depressed her and she had resented them. She had wished she could be the sort of person for whom this yielding of self in favor of coupledom came easily. She had believed that another couple's togetherness isolated her, excluded her. She did not feel that now. She still did not believe herself capable of such intimacy, such a close emotional connection with another person, but it no longer mattered.

They had finished the meal by the time a teenager from another moored boat, who had been given a tip to provide this service, arrived to tell them Noah was howling. They could hear him from the doorway to the restaurant, and could see the small crowd gathering in attendance, debating among itself which of the authorities to alert.

"Bless him," said Sally.

"New hairstyle, new tune," said Eve.

7

To Gnosall

EVE: Hello?

JACOB: It's me, lovely: Jacob. Updating you on Operation Anastasia.

EVE: Go on, then. Good news or bad?

JACOB: Well, not exactly falling neatly into either of those two categories—I mean, when did life ever? She went in as arranged—good, I suppose—and had the op, more or less on time, as I understand it. I rang this morning and all the nurse would tell me was that she'd spent a comfortable night. What on earth does that mean? That she hasn't died? She wouldn't tell me anything else—not related, you see. I pointed out that Anastasia hasn't got any relations and the nurse said that wasn't strictly true. They had a next of kin listed. Any idea who that is?

EVE: Not a clue. Like you, I thought there wasn't anyone. She might have a niece or nephew or a cousin or even a sibling. We wouldn't know, would we? She certainly didn't ask us to tell anyone about the op except a couple of canal friends.

JACOB: Well, anyway, I went in this afternoon to see for myself how she was doing.

EVE: You didn't take grapes, did you?

JACOB: Do you think I'm *mad*! She looked pretty rough when I finally found her. I'm thinking I could create a GPS-type app for hospitals. I might make a fortune. You could use your phone to navigate to the right building, the right floor and the right area and then, if they gave the beds numbers like postcodes, you could get to the person you're coming to see without ending up feeling you might as well just lie down on a passing gurney and let yourself be carted off for medical experiments.

EVE: Brilliant idea. Now get on with it. She looked rough, you said. She always looks rough. It's what I love about her.

JACOB: True, but she was gray and less . . . oh, come on, what do I want to say? . . . less sculpted.

EVE: Good word. A bit looser than normal.

JACOB: Exactly. And she was asleep. I've never seen her asleep. It didn't seem right. I had to go off and chat to the nurses while I waited for her to wake up. They told me the operation went well, no complications, but we have to wait for the consultant to find out what happens next, whether it's all good news or only partly good news.

EVE: Is there more?

JACOB: Don't be so impatient. Of course there is. She

woke up and asked what the fuck was I doing there—which was a relief; more normal, if you know what I mean. But then she said it was a good job I'd turned up, as it happened, because she needed some stuff. I've no idea what they told her to bring in with her, but either it wasn't a good list or she ignored it, because she hadn't got all sorts of things she needed, like a dressing gown and some lotions and potions—who knew Anastasia ever used lotions and potions, but it seems she does. So I nipped back to your flat and collected everything, and when I went back again I saw her before she saw me and, honestly, she looked sad. Then she noticed me and she looked Anastasia-ish again, all disapproving but tolerant. So that's what I thought I ought to tell you. She'll be in for at least two weeks, the nurses say, and I think she's hating it so much she might forgive us if we rally round. Any chance of a visit from you two ladies? That's about the sum of it.

EVE: Of course. Not both of us at once, naturally. We've got a boat and a dog to look after and both of those matter to Anastasia more than we do. We're making our way out of Birmingham at the moment, so we'll need to find somewhere safe to moor up for a few days, within reach of a bus or a station or a car-hire place. Whatever. We can sort it. I'll text you when I know what we're doing.

JACOB: Great. I won't tell her you're coming. She might tell me to tell you not to.

EVE: No doubt about it. She would. Oh, Jacob?

JACOB: What?

EVE: Thank you for the Keith Floyd book. I'm loving it.

JACOB: Yes, but are you cooking anything out of it?

EVE: Not yet, give us a chance. I'm busy absorbing it at the moment.

JACOB: Well, don't forget—he can be random with quantities. If he says use ten chillies when you think one will do, you're probably right.

EVE: I'll remember.

JACOB: Be seeing you, then.

WAITING BY THE BANK OR midstream, blipping the throttle forward, then into reverse, to keep the boat from drifting while the lock emptied or filled, or another boat came through or went ahead, allowed time for contemplation. Why, then, Eve wondered, as her shoulders began to ache with tension, was it so unthinkable to be forced to wait in a queue of cars?

It did not help that she had hired the cheapest car offered by the one hire company prepared to deliver canal-side. She felt too big for it as soon as she was in the driving seat, and amused herself for some miles remembering the last time she drove something this small, this downmarket, before her career had carried her into the ranks of those who justified more expensive products, which had happened while she was still in her twenties. Thirty years ago. Then the irritations of driving, and of driving this particular car, took her over. By the time she reached Uxbridge it was as if she had a piece of grit in her shoe, or an insect bite, or some other minor irritation that meant she was not happy even though there was nothing substantially wrong.

She went first to her flat. She collected a few things Jacob had said Anastasia still wanted but that he had been unable to find, identify or understand. The flat felt unexpectedly big. She had prepared herself for it to feel big after the boat but still it surprised her.

The other thing that struck her was what a long journey it had been, from outside, to reach the inside of the flat. A climb up into a place far detached from where there was weather, nature, other people. It had not occurred to her before how many doors, corridors, staircases lay between her living room and the street. All these obstacles to pass up or down or through before she, and Noah, could reach a patch of grass suitable for a dog's needs. The dog was not with her and she had no personal need to reach the outdoors in any particular hurry, but it no longer felt natural to be this isolated. She wondered how she could ever have believed it was.

She reached the hospital and found the ward by reference to a handy panel that told her in which wing, on which floor, she needed to be. She made a mental note to tell Jacob that no one who had the patience to stop and consult a board needed an app to navigate. She was directed to a room with two beds and a pleasant view. There was no one in the bed farthest from the window. A curtain shielded the bed next to it from the rest of the room and Eve tiptoed round this, suddenly frightened by what she might see.

She found Anastasia, asleep, colorless and small. Having prepared herself for worse, the fear turned at once to pity; not for the pallor, for Anastasia was never pink and rosy, nor the sleep, but for the smallness. The bulk of the woman, upright, awake, on the edge of outrage, should never be as diminished as the narrow bed, the taut sheets, the drip stand, even the lack of outdoor clothes made her.

Anastasia was not alone. In a chair by her bed, turning his head from the window as Eve entered the cave created by the drawn curtain, was a man in middle age. A stocky, sturdy man with hair cut so short it was hard to tell if it was mainly gray or mainly fair. He had an outdoor complexion. He was wearing baggy denims and a very old leather jacket. His hands, resting on his knees, were clean but not entirely free of the grease engrained in the creases and cracks.

"Are you Eve or Sally?" he asked quietly.

"Eve. Are you Owen?" When he nodded, she said, "I thought she didn't want anyone to visit."

"You're here," he said.

"Yes, but I've got"—she held up the bag—"things. And Jacob thought she might want visitors after all."

"Of course she does. Jacob was right."

There was nowhere else to sit except the bed. Eve leaned against the windowsill. Owen stayed where he was.

"How is she?" Eve asked.

"Doing well, apparently. Tell me, what is the state of the *Number One*?"

"We haven't done any damage, if that's what you mean. Or only cosmetic damage. Functionally, the batteries don't seem to be holding their charge very well; the fridge stops working in the middle of the night. And tickover seems a bit high, to me, but I don't know whether that's normal for a boat engine. Other than that, it's OK."

Anastasia groaned and opened her eyes. Then shut them again.

"Good lord," she said, her voice more of a croak, more of a whisper than when Eve had heard it last, "hordes of you."

"Only me, as before," said Owen. "And Eve has brought you . . . things."

"What things?"

"A couple of pairs of pajamas," Eve said. "Some face cream, lip salve, tissues."

"There's some point in you coming, then." Anastasia opened her eyes again. "Do you know where I was before your chatter interrupted me? I was in Audlem, before the last two locks in the flight. The sun was shining through the trees either side and I was sitting on the front deck, watching Noah finding every smell of piss left by every dog that had been along the towpath."

She closed her eyes again. Owen said nothing and, wanting to acknowledge that Anastasia had spoken, Eve said: "You'll be there again, soon enough."

Anastasia's eyes opened again and for a moment, in her fury, she looked much more normal, much more herself.

"For fuck's sake," she said. "Is that what you think I deserve, platitudes? If you think that, you'd better fuck off back to your suburban flat and forget me."

To her horror, Eve's eyes filled with tears.

"I could never forget you," she said.

"I heard," said Owen, shifting in the chair, making the legs squeak on the hard floor, "there was a boat caught in the top lock at Audlem. Week ago, it must be."

"Hire boat?" said Anastasia.

"Not what I heard. Couple from Wolverhampton, seemingly. Bought themselves a retirement present. Left all their fancy fenders out and got wedged as the water dropped. Had to be winched up to free the fenders then lowered back down again. Took hours."

Anastasia closed her eyes again.

"Well, off you go," she said. "Go away and talk to each other somewhere else. I'm about to turn up the Middlewich Branch and I don't want any distractions. It's a tricky turn."

"You're not coming to see me, then," said Owen.

"I am. I'm just in no hurry to finish the journey."

They went to the hospital café. Eve was hungry and wanted to avoid accepting an offer of coffee from Owen, which would prevent her reaching the counter and snaffling a sandwich, so she asked him what he was having before they were through the door. He didn't quibble. Not only that, he asked for a toasted cheese sandwich so she didn't have to feel greedy. When she joined him at the table he offered to pay for what she had ordered for him, which she refused.

"Do you think Anastasia's going to be all right?" she asked.

"I can't possibly tell," he said. "It's a stupid question."

When she thought about it, he was right. It had been a stupid question, just as her remark about Anastasia seeing the locks at Audlem again had been a stupid remark. That he had rebuked her so sharply meant either he was habitually blunt or was excessively fond of Anastasia. Or both.

"You're right. Sorry."

"I hate to see her so . . ." he breathed in and ran his work-man's fingers over the stubble of his hair, "so dependent."

"I admit, I expected her to look worse than she does."

"It's not how ill she looks, it's that she's lying there waiting for other people to decide when she eats, when she washes . . . when she pees, for Christ's sake."

Eve ate a mouthful of sandwich. Owen looked at his for a while, then picked up one half of it and managed to fit it all in his mouth, if not exactly in one go then with a staccato burst of bites that gave that impression and caused the sandwich to disappear without the need for him to lower his hands.

"She did say," said Eve, "that she was planning on treating the whole thing as an experience. Let's hope that's what she's doing: just observing it all."

Owen swallowed.

"That's probably crap, but better to think that than put my fist through a window in frustration. Now, where is the *Number One*?"

Eve told him.

"With the other one?"

"Sally, yes."

"I have a gap in two weeks' time. I need to get it to the yard by then."

"Anastasia said August."

"Yes, but I didn't know about the operation when I suggested that. You need to have time to get the boat back to Uxbridge for when she's well enough to live on board again."

Eve realized she had been concentrating so hard on reaching Chester, on delivering the *Number One* to Owen in time, in one piece, that this had begun to feel like the end of the journey. But they had agreed to take the boat to Chester *and back*. She had been worrying about the wrong deadline.

"Well," she said, "I suppose we did agree to bring the boat back."

He glared at her. "What do you mean, 'you *suppose* you agreed?' You were planning to dump her home three hundred miles away, at least six weeks' cruising away. What was she supposed to do? You'll want your flat back, obviously. So what about her? She'll have follow-up treatment, outpatient appointments—what's going to happen to all that? Transfer her to Chester Hospital? Great idea! The NHS is so good with systems and so long on capacity there should be no problem at all. Seamless. Is that what you think?"

"Oh, shut up," said Eve. If he could be abrupt, well, so could she. "I hadn't thought about the return journey and when we needed to get back. Give me a chance. We may not have known Anastasia for long, but it's quite long enough to be certain we would never, ever leave her in the lurch. Now, I need a cake."

"I'll go," said Owen, and pushed his chair back.

Eve watched him in the queue, which had lengthened. There had been a couple of invitations in the post she had collected in Birmingham, and she thought about these while she waited. One had been for a fiftieth birthday party in August and one was for a wedding in September. These had seemed like the sort of things she used to do. She would previously have thought about both of them, when they arrived, with a degree of interest or even excitement: what would she wear, who would be there, what would the venue, the weather, the entertainment be like? When she opened them in the cabin of the *Number One*, moored in Gas Street Basin, she had immediately formed the opinion that she couldn't go. As if she had committed to living like this for the foreseeable future; as if she had accepted that the woman who had had a car, a wardrobe full of clothes, an income that meant the cost of buying presents, of overnight accommodation and drinks was not a factor in deciding whether to accept or not, no longer existed. She resented the implication that she would be clear about what she was doing at the end of August, in September. But she knew that, if she accepted, she would begin to look forward to these two celebrations, to think about what to wear and so on. In which case, she would have acknowledged that the journey on the *Number One* was nearly over and had always been only an interlude. Not a step on a road which led up a hill toward some other point on the compass, but a circular trip, out and back, with the final destination close to if not exactly the same as the place she started.

Now Owen, still patiently queuing, holding the tray of the woman in front of him who was burdened with two sticks and a shaky hand, had reminded her that there was no need for the journey to end, at least until after the birthday party and possibly even the wedding had taken place. She couldn't work out whether that was entirely a relief. He had also reminded her that the journey was circular. It did not end in Chester but in Uxbridge, exactly where she had started out from.

Owen came back with a double-choc-chip muffin which was exactly what she would have chosen if he had bothered to ask.

She felt obliged to offer him her spare room overnight, but he had a train to catch. Only time enough to nip back to the ward and say goodbye to Anastasia.

"Let me know," he said, "when you can get to the yard.
You might want to work out how long it will take to get back
here, if you needed to travel more quickly than you have been
doing."

"I'll talk to Sally," Eve said, licking her finger to pick up the
last muffin crumbs on her plate.

꙰

EVE: It's me.

SALLY: Yes, I know. How is she?

EVE: I don't know.

SALLY: Haven't you seen her?

EVE: Yes, yes I have. It's just hard to tell. She's not as
bad as I feared she might be, but it still seems a vio-
lation of her human dignity to stick her in a hospital
with tubes and central heating and squeaky floors.

SALLY: What was her mood like?

EVE: Oh, she was grumpy.

SALLY: That's good news.

EVE: She was positively rude to me in a way she hasn't
been before. I felt thoroughly cut down to size.

SALLY: I expect you deserved it.

EVE: Well, I have to say I did. I came over all patronizing—
caught on the hop, you know.

SALLY: And she snapped? That's quite a relief. My
father-in-law had surgery at about her age and he
was never the same again, mentally. He was a horribly abrupt man before that and creepily docile after
it. The anesthetic knocked a few of his marbles out
of line.

EVE: God, yes. You never said. I didn't know that was a possibility.

SALLY: Well, as it turns out, it wasn't, so we can relax. Any news on what happens now?

EVE: Not yet but I must tell you—Owen was there.

SALLY: Owen?

EVE: The man from Chester.

SALLY: Was Anastasia pleased to see him?

EVE: Hard to tell. He was already there when I arrived. But listen, this is the important thing, and you're going to tell me you've had this in mind all along, but he pointed out that Anastasia is going to need the *Number One* back in Uxbridge when she recovers enough to live on board again. So he wants us to be at his workshop in two weeks and ready to set off back south as soon as he's finished, which means we need to get there as quickly as we can.

SALLY: I see.

EVE: You were ahead of me, weren't you?

SALLY: No. I hadn't thought past Chester, but obviously we have to take the boat back. We said we would, didn't we? And she'll want to move on board as soon as she can. I don't know, I've been thinking all along about Chester as the end of the journey and of course it isn't and never was and now I don't know whether to be relieved or distraught.

EVE: Oh, Sally, it's such a joy to be talking to you. I don't know either.

SALLY: Well, it's time you worked out one of your demon plans. When can you get back?

EVE: I'd come back tonight, but Jacob's cooking for me
      and I daren't turn him down.
SALLY: Tomorrow. See you here.

⌖

IT WAS A MORNING WHEN a mist over the canal clung on as the
sun rose, picking out the hedges, the raindrops on the leaves,
the spiderwebs between the branches, but leaving the water
in its gauzy veil. The last few days had shaken Eve out of the
easy rhythm of being in the boat, and she slept badly. So here
she was, out early in this mystical, silent landscape with Noah
questing for any scents left overnight by passing wildlife. As
she walked back toward the *Number One* she saw a man coming
toward it from the other direction, knee-deep in mist. As she
drew nearer, she recognized Arthur. They reached the rear of
the *Number One* together.

"I've come to find you," he said. "Owen told me where you
were. I've a message for you from Trompette."

"Wouldn't it have been easier to phone?" Eve said.

Arthur was looking neater and cleaner than he had when she
saw him last, consistent with having only just left the comforts
and conveniences of whatever home he had in Uttoxeter.

"I don't know any numbers."

"Owen does."

"I didn't think to ask. Or perhaps, dear lady, I wanted the
excuse to come. Oh, what deceptions we practice on ourselves.
Do you want me to confront mine, or are you kind enough to
let it pass? To accept that I am here, you are here, the *Number
One* is here and the sun is even as we speak beginning to warm
our hands and faces?"

"All right. Hello, Arthur, it's a pleasure to see you."

"And you, my lovely lady, and you."

"What is the message, then? From Trompette."

"Ah, she wants you to get in touch. She's somewhere on the Trent and Mersey. She's in trouble."

"What a surprise. Get in touch how?"

"By phone, of course." Arthur took his rucksack off and placed it on the cabin roof, then unzipped one of its many pockets and extracted an old envelope with a phone number on the back. He handed this to Eve as if bestowing the body of Christ. Eve turned it over, curious to see what the address was on the other side, but it was a window envelope; the address had been on the letter inside, long gone. She still did not know Arthur's surname. Why should that be important? And if it was, why didn't she just ask?

"I'll give it to Sally," she said instead. "She has a better relationship with Trompette than I do."

Arthur became brisk. He had a few days to spare, he said. He could help move the boat northward. After all, Owen wanted them at the yard as soon as possible. Eve went below and checked with Sally, then confirmed he could stay.

"Excellent," said Arthur. "Excellent!"

It was good to be moving. As long as she needed to think ahead only as far as the next tap, the next locks, the next mooring, Eve had no room to worry about the next month, the next year. They went through a lock, Eve driving, Arthur doing the work. Sally was trying to contact Trompette but either there was no signal, or no answer. Eve thought, but didn't say, that Sally had dropped into worried-parent mode as naturally as a ball, given a kick, will run downhill. Arthur filled the water tank and oversaw the pump-out in the first village they came to, while Eve found a shop and bought food. She didn't consult a recipe book beforehand and, if she had, the range of ingredients needed would probably have been beyond the village shop, so she bought what it did have that she thought she could combine in some simple but tasty way.

She had seen enough of Arthur's eating habits to know he would be happy with anything, up to and including a Fray Bentos steak and kidney pie in a tin, one of which she remembered traveling with them on every self-catering holiday as a child—no matter what country they were visiting—and was astonished to find was still available after deep freezes, freeze-drying, microwaves and ready meals had all become available. She did not remember ever eating one, but her mother, whom she had thought of at the time as an irritating fusspot but now realized was a master of risk analysis, had always taken it with them "just in case."

They cruised on. A still day, a sunny day, views expanding in all directions across farms and farmland.

"It's hard to believe, isn't it," said Eve, "that all this was part of the Industrial Revolution? That these embankments and bridges and all the business of digging and construction will have upset the owners of this land; will have seemed to them to be an outrage, obliterating centuries of tradition, despoiling the landscape."

"Some of them," Arthur said, "would have welcomed it. Both for getting their produce to market and because it brought within their grasp the cheap things that factories made and which it had been hard for them to lay hands on before. Can you imagine having one plate, one knife, one spoon, and if those got lost or broken, you would have to save up and pay a crafts-man to produce a replacement? Then along comes the canal, and plates and knives can be delivered in such quantities and at such a price you can afford to buy extras to put on your dresser or hang on your wall. For ornament, not for use. But you're right, the people who lived where the canals were being dug would have complained, the same way everyone who lives where a major road is being built complains now. These days it's motorways that deliver clothes at a price that means you don't have to wear the same thing twice, but we can't see the connection anymore. The grid has become too convoluted for us to understand."

"So we carry on hating motorways even after they're built," said Eve. "We think they're noisy, dirty blots on our beautiful countryside."

"And yet, come the day motorways are redundant, when we don't need them for transport anymore because we have found other means of travel or have squandered the means of travel and are left with two legs or a set of self-powered wheels, think how you would see the motorway then. All those lovely views as you travel slowly along them, the banks and verges rich in wildlife and wild flowers."

"Exactly like a canal, you mean," said Eve. "You're right. I'll remember that next time I go up the M40 through the Stoken-church Gap. I can't wait, I'll think, for the traffic to go so I can walk this motorway at peace with nature."

"Are you being sarcastic, my lovely lady?"

"No. I'm agreeing with you."

Arthur took his mouth organ out of his pocket and played a little tune.

"How's Anastasia?" he asked, putting it away again. "In your opinion."

"What did Owen say?"

"Not much. He never does."

"I don't know, is the answer. Better than I feared, but ill nevertheless. You could go and see her yourself, you know. I think she has lifted the embargo on visitors, or accepted that it's unenforceable. But not the embargo on grapes or fuss."

"I'm not brave enough," said Arthur. "I wish I was. I cannot look on her in the state she is in without contemplating she might die. And you see, if she dies, part of me will die too and it will be the best part. I will become less of a proper person than I am now. Even less."

"I feel that, too," said Eve, who had not thought of it before but recognized at once what he meant. There was about Anastasia a certainty and honesty that stiffened you up, raised your standards, held you accountable. And without her, it might be impossible to maintain. She considered saying all this to Arthur, but when she looked at him, face averted, hands stroking the pockets of his tweed jacket as if looking for some familiar comfort, she knew it wasn't necessary.

❧

SALLY: Trompette?

TROMPETTE: Yes.

SALLY: Where are you?

TROMPETTE: Bridge 119 on the Trent and Mersey Canal.

SALLY: Trompette, I don't have a map of the canals to

hand. Tell me where you are as if I were an ordinary person living in an ordinary house.

TROMPETTE: I'm in Stoke-on-Trent.

SALLY: All right. Now, tell me how you are and what's happening.

TROMPETTE: Billy's been arrested.

SALLY: So you're on your own.

TROMPETTE: Yes.

SALLY: Are you coping? *Silence.* Trompette?

TROMPETTE: Not as well as I want to.

SALLY: Is Billy coming back soon or is this serious?

TROMPETTE: They won't give him bail because he hasn't got a fixed abode.

SALLY: Literally.

TROMPETTE: *Giggle.* Literally.

SALLY: Have they charged him with anything?

TROMPETTE: He's been charged with possessing drugs with intent to supply, and they're still deciding whether to charge him with murder.

SALLY: Oh. I don't know what to ask first. Whose murder? And is he innocent?

TROMPETTE: He's not innocent, no. Of course he isn't. But he isn't that bad, either. He doesn't deal drugs, not hard drugs. He's just always around them.

SALLY: And the murder?

TROMPETTE: Thad died. You remember, Thad from Birmingham? He was Billy's supplier. There was all sorts of trouble going on—well, you know that. Different gangs, knives, whatever. I think Billy was there when it happened. Only there, you know? Not involved. But, this is Billy. Who's going to believe him?

SALLY: I understand. What sort of mooring are you on?

TROMPETTE: Forty-eight hour.

SALLY: How long have you been there?

TROMPETTE: Five days. No one has been along to check yet, but it won't be long before some snooty-pants reports me.

SALLY: Can you move the boat on your own? Work the locks and so on?

TROMPETTE: Of course I can. If I have to.

SALLY: So you could keep moving.

TROMPETTE: Yes, but . . . Sally, Sally, Sally . . . what's the point? Where would I go?

SALLY: Where do you want to be?

TROMPETTE: Nowhere, that's the point. Or anywhere I don't feel so lonely.

SALLY: Don't cry, Trompette. We can sort this out. Do you have any family at all?

TROMPETTE: Yes. Mum and Stepdad. They moved to Spain as soon as my useless little arse took itself out of the house to be with Billy.

SALLY: I understand. Where are they holding Billy?

TROMPETTE: He's on remand in Birmingham.

SALLY: Well, we'll be in Chester shortly. Do you know where Owen's yard is?

TROMPETTE: Yes.

SALLY: Can you get there? I mean, do you have enough money for diesel and so on?

TROMPETTE: Yes.

SALLY: Then set off. If we've turned round before you reach us, we can come back down south on the Trent and Mersey and meet you on the way. Then we can work out what you want to do longer term. Does that sound all right?

TROMPETTE: Yes.

SALLY: Is that what you'd hoped I'd say?

TROMPETTE: Yes. What will Eve say?

SALLY: Don't worry about her.

TROMPETTE: I do. I reckon she thinks I'm a useless little arse, too.

SALLY: But she's not an unkind person.

TROMPETTE: No.

SALLY: Is there anything we can do to help Billy?

TROMPETTE: He's got a lawyer.

SALLY: Good. We'll talk about it when we see you.

TROMPETTE: You're the best thing that's happened to me since I met Anastasia.

SALLY: Trompette, how old are you?

TROMPETTE: Nineteen.

SALLY: Oh, my dear. I'll see you soon.

SALLY TRAVELED TO UXBRIDGE BY bus and train and underground, carrying the key to Eve's flat, a change of underwear, a toothbrush and two books (in case she finished one) in a rucksack. She also took her knitting, which she found soothing at the same time as feeling awkward while she did it. She went straight to the hospital. There were uncanny echoes of Eve's

account of arriving at Anastasia's bedside in her own experience: the drawn curtain, the afternoon light, the slight dread
of what she would find when she was in sight of the bed. And
again in what she did find: Anastasia a little pale and smaller
under the covers, and a man sitting in the only chair beside
her. It was a man Sally had never seen before but she had been
alerted to his presence by the low rumble of his voice. He was
young and dark, and heavy, both in his build and in the way he
sat in the chair. He did not match Eve's description of Owen.
He leaped to his feet at once, holding a book in his hand with
one large finger marking the page.

"This is Sally," Anastasia said. "Sally, this is Vic, who turns
out to be the only person so far who is worth having as a visitor.
He is reading an anthology of dog stories to me, one story at a
time."

"My granny was in a home," he explained.

"Find another chair," ordered Anastasia, "and finish the
story. Then you can go home with the satisfying feeling of a
duty performed."

The story was about a yellow dog, which had been a menace
in the part of the story Sally had missed but was now a reformed
and lovable character. Anastasia listened to the end with her
eyes shut then opened them to say: "Sally doesn't like dogs."

"I don't like dogs in general," Sally said. "But I've grown to
appreciate Noah in particular." When Vic had left, she said:
"Jacob told us Vic was terrified of you."

"Oh, he still is," said Anastasia. "But he's developed a strategy for coping."

"Have you?" asked Sally. "Developed a strategy for coping.
With being ill."

"No," said Anastasia. "I've got one foot stuck in denial and the other hovering over a swamp of self-pity. Tell me about you."

"I've got both feet on the ground," Sally said. "But I don't know where they're leading me."

"No rush," said Anastasia.

They sat in silence for a while, Anastasia watching the clouds through the window, Sally looking at the place where the cannula had been inserted, like a blood-sucking stick insect, into the back of Anastasia's hand.

"Tell me," she said, "how do you manage to take the *Number One* through a lock when you're on your own?"

Anastasia smiled. "A good question, my dear. A good question. You will need to work out the best way for yourself, but to start with, tie the boat up at the bollards before the gates. Prepare the lock. Open the gates. Then you have a choice. You can haul the boat in with the bow rope or you can drive it in. Either way, take the center rope round a bollard on the lock side as soon as the boat is in, to hold it steady in the center of the lock. Do not tie it up—just let the slack out as the lock empties or take it up as the lock fills."

"Which approach do you favor?"

"I used to haul the boat. I liked the physical effort. Then it became harder to do that, so I began to use the ladder. Now, I don't have the strength or the stamina to do it alone. But you do. You have options."

"I know," said Sally.

Sally woke up in Eve's bed in Eve's flat and realized she had room to spread. She could enjoy the feel of the fresh, taut cotton sheets to the very extremity of her reach. It was an experience she could not recall having often enough in her life to make it seem ordinary. Duncan was rarely absent from the double bed at 42 Beech Grove; the bunk on the *Number One* was no wider than she was. But here, she had a full king-size to herself; a flat to herself; space to move around in and do as she wanted. To be as self-indulgent as she chose, as idle or as productive as the mood took her. What it must have been like, she thought, to be Eve.

But she was not Eve. She had responsibilities for others that Eve did not have. She had arranged to meet her daughter for lunch before going back to Staffordshire. It was a pleasure to see Amy, whose bounce and freshness always delighted her, though she knew the phrases "I don't understand . . ." and "But why?" would feature heavily in an hour without many thoughtful silences, and so it proved. Her father's daughter, Sally thought, smiling at Amy over the wooden table in a vegan café she had not known existed and would not choose to visit again.

"What are you smiling at?" asked Amy.

"I'm only thinking how much I love you," Sally said.

"Do you?"

"Of course. Have I not been in the habit of mentioning it?"

"Not really. I love you too. In fact," she paused, "I can see you are happier than you used to be, and I suppose that must mean that, if I love you, I should stop going on at you and be pleased you're doing what you're doing."

"I'd like you to be pleased," said Sally. "But I don't expect it."

Amy rolled her eyes. "Same old Mum," she said. "Don't you worry about me." She lifted her fingers to indicate the last sentence was a quotation.

"Well, don't," said Sally.

It was late when she finally reached the *Number One*, which Eve and Arthur had moored outside a village on a bus route from Stafford. It was called Gnosall, and Sally savored the name but found, when she inquired at Stafford train station for the bus stop, that she was mispronouncing it. She paused for a minute in the dusk, on the towpath, looking toward the *Number One*, which she began to feel she could recognize however dark it was, much as she would be able to recognize her children or her husband from the merest gesture or smallest body part. It felt more like home than 42 Beech Grove had ever been.

8

To Chester

THERE WAS SOME CONVERSATION after Sally's return about the next part of the journey. Eve had had a message that a member of the family she had lived with as a child had died. She still thought of the cousins and aunts and uncles and the place they lived as family and home. This did not mean they felt like Eve's home and Eve's family, precisely—these were things that other people had while she only had houses and parents—but their home and their family circle were places where she knew she was welcome and where she felt she had some right to be. It was Great-Aunt Esme who had died. She had lived nearby and had been part of this home-ness, this family-ness. No question, Eve had to go to the funeral in a couple of days' time.

But they also needed to get to Chester. They both looked at Arthur.

"I don't know, I don't know. Perhaps . . . Owen could send someone to help Sally?"

"I don't have to leave for another three days," Eve said. "We should be below the locks at Audlem by then, and we could ask Owen to send someone to help from there."

"Or I could take it myself," said Sally.

Eve had a moment when she imagined Sally and the *Number One* as a self-sufficient unit, as woman and boat together, and she experienced the sensation—part envy, part a feeling of personal failure—she had had at work when someone else received a promotion when she had not. But it was only a slight flicker of pain; there was a purpose to the days ahead. Things to do, places to be. That turned out to be something she had missed. And anyway, Owen, when consulted, agreed to help.

When they woke up the next morning, Arthur and his tent had gone. A note written in tiny handwriting on the back of a Pay and Display parking ticket was tucked into the rear door. *Lovely ladies*, it said, *forgive me my cowardice.*

"He's a sad one," Sally said.

"Do you know," Eve said, "I thought, when we started out, there was a brighter, sparkier Yasmin-flavored Sally that needed to be teased out. Now I realize I was wrong. There was a softer, kinder Sally lurking inside and it's broken through with no help from me."

Sally's hair was lighter than it had been when they started the journey, the result of weeks in the sun, tipped here and there with pink highlights, now faded to a pleasanter, muted hue. She was wearing a loose blue shirt and a pair of jeans she had shortened, cutting off the bottoms of the legs and hemming them, neatly, below the knee. She looked—Eve could think of no other word—gentle.

"As far as I'm concerned," she said, "you're a failed project. Here I was, trying to make you bright and shiny and hard-edged, and you've let me down."

"Would you have liked Yasmin better?"

"She'd probably have begun to annoy me by now."

"And I haven't?"

"Funnily enough, no. Have I begun to annoy you?"

"No," said Sally, "and I can't imagine you ever will."

The day was wet but they both put on their waterproofs and went out to watch the landscape of the canal passing, even though only one of them was needed at the tiller and there were no locks. But they both sensed a turning point in this adventure as they neared Chester. They would not be coming back this way, if they had to go down the Trent and Mersey to meet up with Trompette, and it felt important to taste each minute as if it were the last precious drop of honey when the jar is almost empty. And it was a strange stretch that neither of them would have wanted to miss, with deep cuttings and long embankments, so one moment they seemed trapped in an eerie atmosphere of dripping vegetation, looking out for plants and wildlife a few feet from the boat, and the next they were raised above the land around them, exposed to the rain, eyes lifted to the views of distant fields and farms crouched under the gray sky.

They moored up early below the first of two sets of five locks. The rain was heavy and everything they touched and everywhere they put a foot was slick, slimy, slippery. Eve had been reading Anastasia's collection of memoirs of the men (and some women) who had led working lives on the canals, and she felt this early descent into the dry, warm coziness of the cabin, the avoidance of a couple of hours of physical effort, was a little bit shameful.

"These people went on through half the night," she told Sally.

"They had a living to make," Sally said.

"We have a purpose, too," said Eve. "We need to get to Chester."

But it was raining, and it would be a chore to work the locks in these conditions, whereas tomorrow, so the forecast said, it would be sunny and warm. They both knew that it would not be long before their last lock was behind them, and how might they regret, then, not having taken time at every opportunity to stroll across lock gates, over bridges, watch the water level sinking, feel the moment when the gate responded to pressure on the beam and the next section of canal opened up ahead of the *Number One*'s prow. They said none of this to each other, but they both felt it. So they stopped for the night.

After the first, short day, it had been hard work to reach this point. There had been a narrow section cut through rock ("Imagine doing this by hand," said Eve), and they'd had to maneuver to allow a couple of boats coming south to pass. Then they'd had to queue for each of the ten locks. This meant the trip, which should only have taken five hours, took nearer to eight. And it had been hot.

Beside the first lock they came to was a set of buildings, all neatly restored.

"I could fancy living somewhere like this," Eve said, as they waited for the lock to fill again to take the next boat in the queue down.

"Abandon the town?" said Sally. "Could you?"

"Oh, Sally, I still don't know. Are you any closer to deciding what to do next?"

"I'm clear about what I don't want."

"Actually, I am too. That's progress, isn't it?"

"It's the one essential thing."

"You're right."

Between the two sets of locks was the town of Market Drayton and they gave in to the lure of a table under a parasol and a cold beer in the garden of a pub, to food brought to them on a plate.

"So what don't you want?" asked Sally.

"You first."

"That's easy. Going back to live with Duncan at 42 Beech Grove. Even if he wanted me back, which I can't assume he does. Now you."

"Going back to work for Rambusch—which isn't a possibility, of course, because they don't want me—or any company like Rambusch. I don't want a big, corporate job which fills hours and hours of every day with the housekeeping involved in a large organization—the staff meetings, the policies and procedures, the briefings, the conferences. Do you know, I can't believe I stuck it for so long. Never again. If I'm going back to work, I want to be doing the job, not talking about doing the job, discussing how the job is being done, proving I'm doing the job properly. Never again." She raised her glass and chinked it against Sally's. "Not now I know what it's like to have discretion over how to use my time. That probably means contract work. Let's face it, it's necessary to earn a living, but it would be good to have gaps in between. And something worth doing in the gaps."

"Define worth doing," said Sally.

"I can't," said Eve. "Do you know what's just come into my mind? A theory I came across once when we worried we weren't being innovative enough to stay competitive. I did a bit of work on innovation—what it is, where it comes from—and I found this theory about the border between chaos and order. If I had a pencil and some paper I'd draw a picture, but you'll just have to concentrate. On one side is everything we know and understand; everything that's been invented or thought up, and there are loads of little dots, all perfectly distinct and nicely lined up. On the other side is a soup of possibilities so far from the known order of things we can't possibly grasp them. This is a solid mass of overlapping dots. But where order meets chaos are the possibilities that are beginning to coalesce out of the soup, where we can just about recognize them, where we can begin to pick out patterns and certainties and there is a chance, in the right circumstances, with the right type of mind applied to them, that there can be a breakthrough. Another layer of order added to our known world."

"I like that," said Sally.

"So did I," said Eve. "Actually, one of our design engineers told me years later, after everyone else had forgotten I'd ever shared this with them, that he had applied this thinking to a problem he was working on and had come up with an innovative solution as a result. But I'd forgotten it myself until now. Do you think that's where we are? On the border between order and chaos?"

"I do. We've both rejected parts of what has been our world order, and we're trying to make sense of the margins of the soup of unknowns, where there's a crust forming."

"Exactly. So I don't think we should be in a rush to define what's worth doing, do you? We don't want to risk imposing some framework on the borders of chaos that might eliminate the possibilities and leave us with only the same answers as we had before. My word, I feel really pleased with myself for having thought all that through."

"Have you just argued that not having a clue what we're going to do when Anastasia wants her boat back is the perfect situation to be in?"

"Yes. Aren't I clever?"

"I can see you were an asset in your last job."

While Sally took the *Number One* on toward the next set of locks, Eve cycled round the town in search of ingredients for an evening meal. Once they'd finally moored up that evening, she cooked with the same care and attention to detail, Sally noticed, as if it were not late, they were not both tired and hungry. She herself, she knew, would have skipped a stage or thrown everything in at the same time, in order to get to the end quicker. In order to satisfy the appetite of whoever was waiting for the food. In order not to waste their time. And yet, when it was her appetite waiting to be satisfied, she recognized it didn't matter. All her rush to please people in the past—that had not been worth it.

They went to bed late and worn out, and now it was morning. The *Number One* was moored between two bridges, no roads or railways within earshot, and the sun was sparkling off the canal, creating dancing patterns of light on the cabin ceiling. Promising a warm day to look forward to being on the canal.

Except today would be different, might turn out to be less of a pleasure. Eve was getting ready to walk into the nearest village to meet the taxi she had ordered to take her to the station to go to a funeral. While Sally was left with the *Number One* and Noah and a wait for help to arrive from Owen's yard to take her up the next set of locks. She did not know how long the wait or who the helper would be. And she was in no hurry. When she had seen Eve off, she would move the boat up to just before the top lock in the flight, and enjoy the time she had to be idle before something else happened.

SALLY SAT WAITING ON THE rear deck. She began to study her hands, which, she had suddenly noticed, were not the hands she recognized. They were browner, decorated with small cuts and scratches healing and just healed; her nails were ragged; the little pleats of skin at the knuckles were deeper. They were the hands of someone whose life was not empty. She was pleased with them.

She looked up. A bonfire was burning on the other side of the hedge and the smoke was drifting over the towpath. There was someone walking toward her; the smoke made the figure insubstantial, and yet something about the way it moved was familiar. When the man walking toward her now had passed through the smoke and emerged into the sunlight, he was a complete stranger.

He stopped beside her. "Owen," he said.

Caught by surprise—she had been expecting him to walk on past—she repeated his name, then, recollecting herself, gave him hers.

"I guessed," he said. "Shall we go? The lock's set."

He put a hand on the rail and she moved aside to leave him room to come aboard and take possession of the tiller. She had assumed, without being conscious of having assumed it, that whoever came to help her would take charge and that she would be relegated to the position of crew. She would be operating the paddles; he would be driving the boat. But she was wrong: Owen was only steadying himself while he lifted the fender. As soon as he'd untied the ropes, he left her to start the engine and take the *Number One* through the lock. She concentrated on achieving this without touching the side, even though Owen, leaning against the beam of the gate, ready to shut it behind her, had his back to her.

Sally continued to watch him as he went from side to side, closing the gates, operating the paddles, as he leaned on the bottom gate watching the water level in the lock dropping, and she could not see what it was about him that had felt familiar. He was an unremarkable-looking man. But there was an ease and power about the way he moved and carried out the tasks which was pleasing and, in truth, comforting. Sally substituted the figure of Duncan (another unremarkable-looking man) for Owen's and knew at once what level of anxiety she would feel if it was her husband who was working his way around the lock sides above her. Even had he known what he was doing, she would be waiting for him to start talking to a passerby, forgetting some essential move, or taking some shortcut in the process, claiming as better or quicker something that would put one or both of them, or the boat, at risk.

Owen did talk to passersby, but briefly, never diverting his attention from the state of the lock. He did have ways of doing things that were different from the ways that Anastasia had taught Eve and Sally, but Sally felt safe. She relaxed; she drove the boat perfectly, in full control. If Owen was watching out for her, checking to make sure she did not need any help, it was not obvious. And she no longer had to be responsible for Noah. The dog had been ecstatic at Owen's arrival, which Owen reciprocated by informing him that he was an atrocious dog, possibly good for only one thing, but no one had worked out what that one thing was. After this, for as long as Owen was with them, Noah ignored Sally, much as he had done when Eve was on the boat. She'd been demoted to fourth place in his affections.

After the first eight of the flight of fifteen, they swapped over. Sally strode ahead and engaged in the usual conversations with other boaters—Where have you come from? Where are you headed? Have you heard there are problems on the Llangollen locks? Do you know where the next water point is? Isn't it a lovely day? . . . The inexperienced boaters were always keen to share their lack of experience. Listening to a woman from Wolverhampton explaining her total inability to grasp how a lock worked, Sally remembered that she had done this, too, that first week. Apologized for being useless. She had never felt less like apologizing or less useless in her life than now, working her way down the Audlem flight.

They tied up outside a pub ahead of the last two locks and sat at a table at the end of the terrace where there was shade from overhanging trees and less noise. This seemed to have been accomplished with an astonishing absence of words but no misunderstanding.

"Shall we?" Owen said, nodding toward the pub.

"Yes," said Sally.

They sat for a while in silence. Sally could think of a number of things she would have liked to ask but was in no hurry to ask them. Owen was in no hurry either, but he was the one who spoke first.

"Anastasia talked about this spot," he said. "In hospital."

Sally looked round, taking in the sheltering trees, the moored boats, a family with a toddler toddling down the towpath, the lock gates opening to let through a hire cruiser with too many people on board, all holding cans of beer, and a collie sniffing at the base of a tree.

"It has everything," she said.

"Precisely. She was imagining herself being here, rather than where she is."

"I remember now. Eve said."

Sally watched the clumsy maneuvering of the boat that had just left the lock. She became aware that Owen was watching her and turned back, caught his eye. He smiled. Like his gait, his smile had familiar echoes.

"It's a curious thing to have done," he said. "Leaving your home for a matter of months to take a complete stranger's boat to Chester and back. When you hadn't been on a boat before. Have I got that right?"

"Almost. I didn't leave my home to travel with the *Number One*. I left my home because I wanted to leave it. Actually, I wanted to leave my marriage. I think if my husband had moved out I might have stayed where I was. But I realize now I didn't want a life lived in Beech Grove."

"No beeches, I imagine."

"No beeches, no grove. There was never a precise moment when I recognized that everything about my life was wrong, and made up my mind to walk out on it, but one of the defining moments was about just that: beeches and groves. I work as a classroom assistant and we took the children for a day out in the country, with sheets of things for them to identify—birds and insects and plants and so on. They had to tick the box and color in the drawing. One of the things they had to find was an oak leaf, and they were all picking up leaves at random and shouting, 'Miss, Miss, is this an oak leaf?' One of the teachers was an expert—or she knew more than me, anyway—and she kept saying, 'No, that's a beech leaf, and that's another one. You're all looking in the wrong part of the wood.' I suddenly realized that I was in a beech wood, a not particularly big beech wood so, technically, a grove, and it was endlessly calm, even with the children in it, and beautiful and altogether natural. I imagined the view, standing at the kitchen sink in the house I lived in, in the capital B, capital G Beech Grove, where all I would be able to see would be the top of next door's whirligig washing line poking up above the fence panels between our garden and theirs."

"I can imagine," said Owen.

"Can you? For all I know, you may live in Cherry Tree Crescent and love every blade of grass in every lawn."

"I live on a narrowboat."

"Of course you do."

Owen laughed. "I've been temporarily living on a narrowboat for fifteen years. Before that I lived in Bingham Close, which was named after some local worthy. No one remembers who he was, but he is doomed to be remembered forever as a cul-de-sac. I moved out for the same reason you said you did. Not the lack of woods and trees, but because I did not want to be married anymore. I didn't feel quite myself, in my marriage."

"All of a sudden?"

"No, from the start. Growing up, I thought it was all I wanted: a house something like the one in Bingham Close, a wife who was reliably there every night, every morning. I wanted to be having the conversations I heard in the houses of other boys, about where to go on holiday, about whose turn it was to take the bins out, about whether to cut down this or that shrub in the garden. And then, when I had it, I couldn't see the point in it."

"I take it you didn't grow up in a house where those sorts of conversations happened?"

"I didn't grow up in a house at all, to begin with. When I was about ten, I think, we moved off the boat into a house, so I could go to the same school every term, but we were never like other families, my mother and I."

"You lived on a boat as a child?"

"I was born on one."

"Not," said Sally, suddenly understanding who it was that Owen called to mind, "the *Number One*?"

"No. Anastasia acquired that when living on the bank became too much for her."

"Anastasia is your mother."

"Yes."

Sally felt momentarily winded. She almost said: "But she can't be," so hard was it to imagine Anastasia as anyone's mother. But she stopped herself.

"Well. Have you met Jacob?"

"I have."

"He told us he wondered what it would be like to have Anastasia as a mother. He said he thought it would be terrifying but you would end up properly buffed up. That might not have been the word he used, but you can understand what he meant."

"I can, but he was wrong. It was only terrifying in its uncertainty. Where she was going to take us to next, what she would say to the people I thought of as normal people. And she didn't buff me up. I think she felt wary of having too much influence on me, so she erred on the side of having too little. None of this is an excuse for having turned out to be an unsatisfactory husband. I just misunderstood what I wanted."

"I did, too. I have no excuse. I grew up in exactly the household you describe, all certainty about what would happen on any day, at any hour. Talking about the bins or the drains or the Gower Peninsula. And I don't even think I thought about whether or not I wanted my life to be the same. It just seemed to be what there was. So I was an unsatisfactory wife. Actually, my husband may not have realized that yet; I'm hoping he will. But it's true what you say: I couldn't see the point of the life I was leading, after the children left."

"I didn't have any children, and my wife didn't think I was unsatisfactory, either, when I went. She recognizes it now."

"Well," said Sally. "So here we are, the happily unmarried."

Owen lifted his glass, chinked it against hers. "To us," he said.

They went down a couple of locks in a staircase, one emptying into the next. There was room for two boats in each, side by

side, and a couple of middle-aged men in hi-vis jackets working the gates and the paddles and maneuvering boats from side
to side so that the maximum capacity was reached, the minimum amount of water lost. Watching this from the vertiginous
heights of the top lock, keeping the *Number One* close to the
edge, central between the gates, Sally noticed the people on
the other boats taking photos of the old buildings alongside, of
the view from the top, of the bridge at the bottom over which
occasional cars passed, suspended for a moment above the boats
traveling at right angles beneath them. She and Eve had taken
no photos and it suddenly struck her as odd. On holidays and
days out and special occasions, she had never missed capturing
a moment or two: a landscape, a place where they had stayed,
smiling faces round a table. But taking photos as they traveled in the *Number One* was as unlikely as taking photos at her
kitchen sink. This was not a holiday. It was life, going on in
unrecorded moments.

Sally offered to take a picture of the couple on the boat beside
her in the lock, both of them smiling, leaning against the tiller
and one another. Before all this was over, she thought, she might
ask someone to take that same picture of her and Eve. Together
on the *Number One*. That one photo was all she would need.
Not endless snaps of one more stretch of water reaching toward
one more bend, one more black-and-white lock gate, one more
view of countryside and distant hills, another duck or swan or
moorhen paddling up, hoping to be fed. She would never lose
the image of those things, however many years passed without
further sight of them. But a picture of herself, as she was now,
and of Eve, with one hand on the tiller—she might need that as
a reminder of what this trip had been.

While Sally managed the boat down the staircase, Owen joined the men on the side, chatting, lending a hand. Another man strolled past and stopped, had a word or two. These were not random encounters with strangers, Sally realized. This was a community of people connected, in one way or another, with the canals. Known to each other, even if meetings such as this were occasional and occurred by chance. It was a community rooted in a geography that was defined by its distance end to end rather than by boundaries round a fixed center.

They moored for the night shortly after the staircase locks. Sally cooked sausages, onions, fried potatoes, tinned tomatoes. It was not what Eve, with her new-found commitment to ingredients and recipes, would have contemplated, but it was what was available, and Sally knew she could deliver it to an acceptable standard. She was also pretty sure that Owen would eat it, and would not mention it either during or after the eating, and she was right. He didn't. He ate everything she put on his plate then went outside and opened up the engine cover. She sat on the roof watching him unscrew a nut, pull off some component, inspect it, put it back. He started the engine and then made some adjustments that meant it ran slightly slower, with less noise than it had before. He did not tell her what he was doing and she did not ask.

What she wanted to ask him was about Anastasia, her life, before and after he was born, but even before he had taken himself off to work on the engine, she had decided she would not ask. She was already regretting that she knew something about Anastasia that Eve did not know. So she sat in silence, watching him work.

Before they went to bed—Sally in the front, Owen where Eve normally slept in the middle of the boat—she said:

"When Eve gets back, will you tell us about Anastasia's life?"

"If you want."

As Sally pulled up the covers and turned off the light, she was aware of his presence, just a flimsy partition or two away; a man sleeping, breathing in a space which had been hers and Eve's for so long. It was unnerving, but not unpleasant.

THE FUNERAL TOOK PLACE IN a village outside Newark and involved a weary business of trains and taxis and a night in a Travelodge. Eve felt, even more than when she had gone to visit Anastasia, as if she was stepping out of one world into another, as if she were landing in another country, one with different architecture, culture and dress codes. Esme, whose funeral this was, had lived all her life in one or another of several small villages within a few miles of each other. Her funeral was to be held in the church where she had been married, within sight of the house she had lived in for over sixty years, as wife, mother, widow, grandmother. Within sight of the village hall where she had met her husband at a dance and where, as the congregation filed in to the service, the ladies of the village were filling the urn and setting it to boil, ready for the funeral tea.

Eve, coming into the gloom of the building and pausing to pick a seat toward the back, was beckoned forward by her cousin's son, Adam, a man now, in his thirties or even, for goodness' sake, in his forties. She had no choice but to sit down where she was directed, leaned forward to look round him and exchanged greetings with the other people sharing the pew—his wife, his children, another adult whom she could not place, much as she could not quite remember how the other familiar faces in the other pews slotted into the familial cat's cradle. She only knew they did. A hunched figure played melancholy tunes on the organ, which transformed the notes, as they passed from the keys through the bellows and pipes and out into the air, from the trite and ordinary to the monumental dignity of church music.

Adam passed her a leaflet with photos of Esme on the front and the back. On the front she was a little dab of color in a flowery frock, both arms hanging on to the arms of the dining-room chair in which she was sitting, as if it took all the meager strength in her tiny, wrinkled frame to avoid sliding off it on to the floor. Taken, so the caption said, on her ninetieth birthday. On the back was a photo of a pretty young woman in a white frock framed in the doorway that Eve had just walked through. On her wedding day. In between the two photos was an order of service, mercifully short. Two hymns, a reading, a few prayers, an address by the vicar. Presumably none of Esme's family, now filling at least half the pews in the church, had wanted to stand up and talk. They wanted only to sing the hymns, throw a handful of soil in the grave and get down to the hall before the tea was stewed.

The coffin was carried in by somber-suited men and the service began. The first hymn, "All Things Bright And Beautiful," was played briskly by the organist and sung with enthusiasm by the congregation. Eve rarely had the chance to sing and enjoyed it, though she had to share the sheet with the words on it with Adam as the family had underestimated the number who would turn up for the occasion.

The prayers and the reading were in a language so long familiar to Eve it was like a tune heard too often ever to be forgotten, even if she had not listened to it for decades. Each word falling into place after the word before as each note of the hymn tune had been followed by exactly the note anticipated. Then the vicar rose up to talk about Esme. Eve steeled herself for the usual hyperbole in which a flawed individual's achievements and positive character traits were magnified and whatever was irritating or unfortunate, whatever mistakes they might have made, were ignored as if these were not also part of the person, who, after all, many of the people present will have loved better than they might have loved the polished paragon being described.

But it was not like that. The vicar recited the facts of Esme's life. He did not try to claim any special virtue in its narrow geographical reach; did not try to present her domestic routines, her involvement in the society of the village, her friendships and consistent good humor, the skills she demonstrated in the kitchen and the garden, as anything other than a life well lived, one that had given comfort and stability to her family and had, to the extent it was in her power to do so, helped others.

As they stood to sing the second hymn, Eve became aware of how full the church was. She had assumed that there would be few mourners for someone who had outlived so many contemporaries and had traveled through life on so narrow a track, but she was wrong. The rustle of the muted clothing of pews full of people as they stood, the scrape of the emergency chairs on the stone floor, were a rebuke. Esme, by Eve's standards, had done nothing and been nowhere. The talents she'd had—sewing, cooking, dancing, singing—she had been content to exercise up to a standard consistent with the expectations of her family and friends. She had had no ambition to be or do anything more. But on her death, the church was full. People had come because she mattered to them, and she mattered because they had mattered to her. She had been committed to bringing whatever she could—be it company, comfort, practical help—to the people she cared about. And perhaps to some she did not like.

Eve had no way of checking or wiping away the tears that began to roll down her face. One hand was holding the service sheet so that both she and Adam could read the words to "Abide With Me," and the other hand was holding on to the back of the pew in front: she did not think that, without its support, she could remain upright. The service sheet was shaking and she could not see what she was meant to be singing, so she stopped singing. Only then did she realize that Adam, too, had stopped singing and was holding himself like a man whose balance needed concentration. His shoulders were rising and falling as he fumbled in his pocket for something to dry his face. The family had not left it to the vicar to do the talking in order to speed things up. They had known that their sorrow in losing this sweet, kind woman would prevent them making a good job of it.

Eve put the service sheet down and wiped her face. She felt overwhelmed with self-disgust. She was crying for herself, not for Esme, and she was crying because she had suddenly realized, after all these years of skipping through life pleasing herself and being pleased with herself for having so arranged it, that she mattered to no one. She was crying, for fuck's sake, at the idea that there would be no one crying at her funeral. What worse manifestation of self-pity could there be? And how she hated, hated, hated self-pity.

She looked down at her feet. She was wearing a pair of sandals more elegant, less practical, less comfortable than the ones she had been wearing all summer on the boat, and she could see the pattern of light and dark where the sun had etched the outline of the straps of the other sandals into her skin. It was comforting. The *Number One*, the weeks on the canal, that was real. It was not a rural church, a ready-dug hole, sandwiches in a village hall, an organ thundering out a tune that a congregation reduced to tears by the contemplation of a woman's life were struggling to keep up with. But it was something. It had value.

In the hall the company cheered up. It had been no tragedy to die peacefully at ninety-five. All the love and emotion could be put back where it belonged: in a place of safekeeping, to be brought out and shared in the future with others who felt the same. All the stories told about Esme round the tea urn were humorous: when the neighbor's goat ate her washing; when she put on the wrong glasses while making cakes for the bazaar and used salt instead of sugar; the way she would call all men John and all women Susan when she couldn't remember their names, as she often couldn't.

The cousins, second and maybe even third cousins, and other members of the extended family who were possibly no relation at all, interrogated Eve about her life, as she'd known they would. Their attitude toward her had always been one of pride tinged with scorn—they liked that she had an important job high up in a big company; they liked her to talk about the cars she drove, the places she had been. But really, they could not help letting her know they thought, what sort of life is that for a grown woman? All their occupations had obvious tasks resulting in concrete outcomes—postman, builder, market gardener—and they could not imagine what she found to do in an office all day. "I wouldn't want it," she could hear them not saying out loud, at least to her. She had intended to be casual about her current situation, to present it as a planned break with exciting opportunities in the future that it was too soon to talk about. But she couldn't, when it came to it, her face still feeling tight from the tears she had shed in the church.

"I've been given the push," she said. "Booted out. So I'm helping a friend on a canal boat and trying to work out what to do next."

There was no scorn in their reaction, nor any shadow of the glee at her comeuppance she would have expected. Instead, they were interested, caring, and she felt they liked her better. Or maybe she just liked herself better.

She was desperate to get back to the *Number One* but she had agreed to stay in the area overnight. There was a family barbecue; wine and beer to drink; the story of every pregnancy and birth since she had last met them; the story of every child's progress toward and into adulthood. They were recognizing her as part of the family in telling her all this, and she realized they had always done so and she had never appreciated it before, but she only wanted to talk to Sally about what it was she had learned in the church. On the long journey next day, she could not frame the thoughts into words. She only knew she wanted to tell Sally that, whatever happened next, Sally mattered to her and she was ready to demonstrate that, she had no idea how, in whatever decisions she took about the future.

It was evening when she walked into Owen's yard. The way to it was short of coherent signage but had no shortage of pot-holed private roads, so the taxi driver had a problem finding it and was keen to make his distaste for the journey perfectly clear. At last Eve lugged her rucksack through a metal gate, slightly ajar, and walked round a sizeable shed, a collection of machinery, a couple of boats on cradles sitting on the ground, past a dry dock and finally, following the sound of voices, through another fence to a canal-side wharf. The *Number One* was moored tight to it and Sally and Owen were sitting beside it on a bench, facing away from her toward the sunset, a bottle of wine and two glasses on a table in front of them. Eve paused, wishing Owen was not there, wishing the two of them did not look so comfortable together, so self-contained. She put down her rucksack and, hearing the sound it made as it met the broken concrete, Sally turned, leaped up and came to her. Owen fetched another glass, brought a chair so she and Sally could sit together, on the bench.

"All right?" said Sally.

"I believe so," said Eve.

THE NEXT DAY, SALLY CLIMBED into the front of Owen's van and Eve climbed into the back where she bounced about among a number of hard-edged, heavy objects (an engine part, a box of tools) and a pile of cloths, tarpaulins and rugs, none of them clean. It was a mercifully short journey to Chester station, where they caught a train to London. Owen drove off without waiting to see if they achieved this, only leaving the cab for long enough to slam the rear doors shut as soon as Eve had managed to step out.

"He's not exactly warm and cuddly, is he?" Eve said, watching the van head off out of sight.

"He's Anastasia's son," Sally reminded her.

They had talked to him about Anastasia the previous evening, as they ate pizzas delivered by a youth on a motorbike who appeared to be an employee of Owen's rather than the pizza restaurant. However it happened, pizzas were what Owen proposed, he had made a phone call and pizzas turned up. When they started to ask about Anastasia's past, he told them they would be more usefully employed in talking about her present, or immediate future. Blacking the boat would take five days and he did not want them to stay on board while it was in his dry dock. So why didn't they go to Uxbridge and talk to Anastasia about how she was now, how she expected to be in the future, what arrangements she was prepared to accept and they were prepared to make to look after her?

Sally did not want to go. She felt, though she knew this to be stupid, slightly hurt that Owen should be so ready to eject them from his yard. Also, it would dislocate her too suddenly and for too long from the sheltering calm of the canal and the *Number One*. Eve did not appear happy, either, but unusually did not argue. They agreed to go.

"I don't know for how long, though," Eve said. "We might buy a tent and come back and pitch it on one of your patches of weeds, to keep an eye on you."

"Like Arthur," Sally said.

"Exactly. After you've told us Anastasia's story, you can tell us Arthur's."

"No," said Owen. "You'll have to ask Anastasia about him."

Anastasia, Owen told them, had a childhood about which he knew nothing, only that it had been full of abuse and she had escaped it while still a child in the eyes of the law.

"So the only thing you probably want to know—how she came to be living on the canals in the first place—I can't tell you. When I was a child, I assumed she'd been born and raised on a working boat, as I was. But I've seen her birth certificate and she was born in Edinburgh, so nowhere near a canal. I just couldn't imagine any other childhood. You know how it is, you think everyone is the same as you, then you hit a certain age—with me it was about nine or ten—when you begin to think it is only you who is different; everyone else is normal and you are the one out of step."

"Did you not ask her?" said Eve. "About where she came from, who your grandparents were, and how she ended up on the canal?"

"Of course I did. It's my earliest memory, snuggled up beside her in the cabin of the boat we lived on, while she told me stories. I can picture that cabin; I believe I would know it if I stepped into it again. But when I tried describing it to Anastasia, years ago now, she told me all my memories were distorted or false. It had a coal-fired engine where the galley is on the *Number One*, and we lived in the cabin beside it—ate, slept, played—all in this small space. Anastasia says I was so young when she converted the boat to a diesel engine I can't be remembering it, but it's stuck in my mind—the smell and the heat from the engine and the stories Anastasia told. She says I made them up, or misunderstood, and if she did actually tell me what I say she did, it was only a story. But I knew that. I heard them as stories. When I was older and asked for a version of the truth, she came up with a few sentences that were completely unconvincing. And she never said the same thing twice."

He threw a pizza crust to a collection of ducks and watched them squabble over it.

"What I do know," he went on, "is that she was sixteen when she last lived in a house, up until we moved off the canal when I went to secondary school. She told me that several times and I feel it is the truth. But I don't know if she moved onto the canal then, or lived rough. I can imagine her living rough."

They all thought about this.

"She would never have been a bag lady," Sally said. "More than one bag would be ridiculous self-indulgence."

"She'd have been a splendid rough sleeper," said Eve. "She'd be so full of dignity she'd make everyone walking past feel she was a criticism of their sloppy approach to life and they'd end up wondering if they might not dig out a sleeping bag and join her."

"So, before you moved off the canal," Sally said, "what was life like?"

"I remember being happy—until I went to school. We were very close then. She taught me to read and write and quite a bit more besides and we were moving all the time. We were collecting loads and delivering them and collecting another, and I realize now that Anastasia must have been on the edge of exhaustion the whole time. On the edge of bankruptcy, too. She owned the boat we lived on, but this was in the last days of the Number Ones operating as haulage contractors and she would have had to hustle to get loads. I remember going to sleep night after night with the engine throbbing away and the boat moving, so she must have traveled through the night to keep herself afloat. Literally.

"Then when I was seven, she decided I needed to go to school. It wasn't to free herself from looking after me twenty-four hours a day, I'm sure—though that's what I thought at the time. That she wanted rid of me. But it became even harder for her to make a living because she could only do local runs round the Birmingham area, to be there to pick me up. I suspect she thought that if she left it any longer there was a risk I would never learn how to be a child among other children and this might mean I would never learn to be properly at home in company as an adult. Still, at the time, I resented it.

"Try as she might, she couldn't always be there to collect me, so she made an arrangement with Ted's family—I can't remember anything about it except my classmate was called Ted and he lived in a house with a father in it, as well as a mother, and other children. I began to realize that this was more or less normal. That on a normal scale, my way of life was so far to one end as to be embarrassing, and I stopped being cross about going to school, because that put me in among normal people, but I began to build up a picture of an ideal life, and that was Ted's, not mine."

"Then you moved into a house," said Sally.

"Yes." Owen ran a grease-stained hand over his stubbly hair, down his face, then looked at his palm as if surprised to find it belonged to him. "What seems to be happening here," he said, "is that I'm telling you my life story rather than Anastasia's, and that is truly boring, believe me."

"Keep talking anyway," said Eve.

"Well. It was a pretty grim time. She sold the boat and got a job at a yard on the Shropshire Union, out in the countryside, and her employers provided the house. I was so angry with her. I wanted to live in a house in Birmingham, why couldn't she understand that? And go to school with my friends. Of course, she hated it, too, but she didn't point this out, and she didn't tell me why she'd done it, why she hadn't found a permanent mooring in Birmingham and taken whatever jobs were available on the bank. Or taken any other options that would have kept us living where we did. Later I found out that one of my teachers had alerted the authorities to what she thought was child neglect at best, abuse at worst. I was always hungry, but so were my friends, only I also had bruises. Never without them. Living on an unlit towpath has more hazards than the average house on the average street. Bingham Close," he said, turning to smile at Sally.

"Or Beech Grove," she said, and he nodded.

"Plus, there were more opportunities to have fun and I was an adventurous child. So the bruises were carelessness or stupidity, and I never thought about them, but to my teacher they looked sinister, and Anastasia had to cope with the Social Services inspecting the way she lived and looked after me. They concluded she was not in a position to care for me properly. So she stopped living the way she wanted to because she couldn't run the risk I would be taken into care. And she moved out of the reach of the social workers."

"I can't imagine a conversation between Anastasia and a social worker," said Eve.

"In fact, they were not unsympathetic, so she said, when she finally told me all this. But she would understand what you mean; she knew herself well enough to know that eventually she would lose patience and bark or even bite, and that would be that. Anyway, we niggled and snapped at one another for a couple of years, then I became a teenager, which I know is supposed to be the signal to start despising your parents, but I'd got that out of the way early and it was our best time. Anastasia bought the *Number One* from the yard where she worked. It was just a rusting hulk and we worked on it together, rebuilt the superstructure, kitted it out, bought, restored and fitted an engine. So when I left school and got an apprenticeship with British Waterways, as it was then, she could cast off and go back to being the person she wanted to be."

Sally wondered most, listening to this story, about how Anastasia, at the time and now in old age, saw Owen. As her greatest achievement, her greatest joy? Or as a source of compromise, when compromise was not in her nature. She hoped it was the joy and the achievement.

"What about your father?" Eve asked. "Was he not around when you were growing up?"

"I told you," Owen said. "You'll have to ask Anastasia about Arthur."

ANASTASIA LOOKED BETTER. SHE WAS sitting in a chair and was dressed. She had no cannulas in her hands, though she was still connected to something draining fluid from her lungs, she told them, anticipating their questions about how she was by giving them a full update before they had spoken. There was a woman in the other bed in the ward, this time. She was much younger than Anastasia and looked frightened. She kept her head turned in Anastasia's direction and tears occasionally rolled down her cheeks. Eve thought how strong Anastasia was, in comparison. She asked at once, before her courage deserted her, for Arthur's story, but, like Owen, Anastasia suggested they hold on to their desire to know about the past until they had properly sewn up the immediate future.

She was within a week of being discharged, she said. The two things holding it up were the drain, though she could leave with that in place, and her ability to do simple tasks—washing and dressing herself, moving from bed to chair, boiling a kettle. If there was someone at home to look after her, no hurdles remained and she could leave. Having explained this, Anastasia shut her eyes.

"You don't like the idea of being dependent on someone else," said Sally.

"No."

"But you don't like the idea of staying here, either, so you will accept that it's the way out of here," said Eve.

Anastasia opened her eyes. "Yes."

"Well then, we'll sort it out," said Eve.

"How? You two are supposed to be bringing my boat back to me. There is only so much of Jacob's time available, and even that is probably more time than I could bear to have him making a fuss."

"There are two of us," said Sally. "And Trompette. Billy is in jail."

"Is he?" For a moment she looked like the Anastasia they had first met. "Convicted? On remand?"

"On remand."

"I see. That might work. Yes, that might work. But what about *Grimm*?"

"There are too many unknowns," announced Eve. "So what we need to do is to fix a point, and then work out what we need to do to reach that fixed point and set about doing it."

"What the fuck does that mean?" said Anastasia.

"It means, we should say that you are leaving hospital in seven days' time. Then we have seven days to put everything in place to make it possible."

"What if it isn't possible?"

"I'm surprised at you, Anastasia," said Eve, "talking of failure. We of the Easy Team do not accept that failure is possible. Once we have made a decision to implement a plan, we go forward with confidence."

Anastasia began her barking, howling laugh but then stopped herself as, plainly, it hurt.

"What a ridiculous woman you are," she said.

"I know," said Eve.

Anastasia looked over at the other bed and raised her voice.

"I hope you realize I don't know what she's talking about either." Then she sent them away. "Come back later," she said. "I'm tired now."

On the way out, the other patient raised a hand and beckoned them over.

"She's what's keeping me going," she whispered.

When they came back, with more clothes and a collection of tubs with offerings of food from Jacob ("Don't worry," he said, "I have permission to send them!"), the other patient was surrounded by family who looked, if anything, more anxious than she did. Anastasia was in bed and they sat beside her, with the curtain half drawn and the lights of Hillingdon coming on as dusk fell, and she told them Arthur's story. She told it without drama, without emotion. As unlike Billy as possible.

Arthur had been, she said, and still was, a gifted musician. He had studied music and made a living out of music in one way or another. He tuned pianos, taught the piano, the flute and the clarinet. He sang folk songs with a group of friends and made enough money to live on or even, in the good months, more than enough. He was competitive, and there was always a chance he would have made a breakthrough, created a name for himself. He married his childhood sweetheart, a woman called Mimi, or whom Arthur called Mimi; Anastasia did not know if that was her real name. She was an artist in the same way Arthur was a musician; a woman of artistic talent, making a living by teaching, painting, working in a gallery, while waiting for fame and fortune to strike. They had a child, a boy named Godfrey, who made little difference to their freelance, creative lifestyle. One or other of them would be at home, and when that wasn't possible, Godfrey went with one or other of them to gigs or lessons or exhibitions or recording sessions.

A golden life, as Anastasia described it.

Then Godfrey died. He was six. He was ill one morning when both of them had somewhere they needed to be and they rearranged their day so that first one of them spent an hour or two at home, then the other one hurried back for a spell, and so on, through the day. By the time it became apparent that this was not a cold to be treated with love and cough mixture, but something much more serious, it was too late to save him and impossible to say which of them was most at fault.

It destroyed them. Individually and as a couple. The guilt pushed them apart and the creativity that was at the core of who they were was implicated in the neglect that had resulted in the boy's death, and they could find no comfort in it. They began to run out of money, having no reserves and not being able to go back to doing what had brought the money in. Arthur, hating failure, ran away. He packed a few belongings and hitched or caught buses or trains, traveling he had no idea where. He slept rough and busked for pennies to buy himself food. Until one day he came through a gap in a hedge onto the towpath of a canal and came face to face with Anastasia, moored up, trying to sort out a cargo of steel rods that had shifted and was making the boat hard to handle.

They spent the next year together, plying for trade, using Arthur's musical skills to supplement their income. When Anastasia became pregnant, she thought Arthur would run away again—and he did, but only for a day or two. He came back, prepared to try again, he told her, as a long-term partner and as a father. And so he might have done, had he not been recognized by an erstwhile neighbor from Uttoxeter. They were working their way through a lock at Stoke Bruerne when a woman eating an ice-cream cone, the ice cream sliding down the side as it melted in the heat, shouted his name and he looked up. Mimi, she told him, as he raised the paddles and opened the gates, had attempted suicide after he left. She had failed to kill herself but had succeeded in doing so much damage to her body and her brain that she was no longer able to look after herself.

She had been taken in by her sister, a woman both she and Arthur hated, and it was only lack of opportunity and capacity that had prevented her from having another, more successful go at putting an end to her life. By the time the *Number One* left the lock, Arthur was forever trapped back in the marriage he thought he had escaped.

Sally had murmured "Oh, no!" at the point in the story when the child died. Eve had recognized how unthinkable that would be, but she was not a mother. It was the fate of Mimi that moved her most, the idea of being utterly bereft and physically helpless. Anastasia paused at this point, too, as if she was relating the position of this woman none of them had met to her own future life.

Arthur, Anastasia said, might appear irresponsible, because he was always trying to evade responsibility. This, though, was because he knew that, if he once recognized it, he could not escape it. He could not help himself. He was responsible for Mimi and it was impossible for him to stay in the life he and Anastasia had planned together. He went back to Uttoxeter and rescued Mimi. He trained as an accountant to be sure of having a job and an income to support her. Anastasia knew nothing, because Arthur had said nothing, about how he and Mimi existed together, what her state of health and state of mind now was, but whenever he could, he left Uttoxeter and fled back to the canals. He would find Anastasia and Owen, wherever they were, and slot back into their lives for a week or two, sometimes a month or six weeks, when Mimi was in hospital. Anastasia made it clear that he was not responsible for them, too, because she scorned the idea that she was anyone's responsibility but her own.

"He was the nearest thing to a husband you ever had," said Eve, at the end.

"I sometimes think he was the nearest thing to a child I ever had," said Anastasia, and closed her eyes.

BY THE TIME SALLY GOT out of bed the next day, Eve had a list of what needed to be done, at the top of which was contacting the hospital and confirming Anastasia's release date, with any particular care needs they might recommend. Second on the list was buying a car, third was talking to Jacob, fourth was talking to Trompette. Sally, munching some stale muesli, reflected that though she had spent her life pottering about and Eve had spent hers sitting at a desk, it was Eve who was the doer. Eve might not be as ready as she was to wipe up a spill, collect dirty plates, load the washing machine, clean the windows, but when some activity that required determination was involved, Sally was the idle dreamer while Eve was the motivating force. In the past, Sally would have been irritated by Eve, but she had learned so much, about herself as well as Eve, that recognizing this only made her fonder of this large, forceful woman.

Sally offered to accomplish task number four, and rang Trompette, who had that morning arrived, it turned out, at Owen's yard.

"I thought you'd be here," Trompette said.

"Is there room for me on *Grimm*?"

"There is. Yes, there is."

"Then I'll come back."

Eve endorsed this decision, and in the middle of the afternoon Sally walked out of Chester station to find Owen's van, and Owen in it, waiting for her.

"She gets on with it," he said, when she told him what Eve was doing to put everything in place for Anastasia to come out of hospital. "Good person to have around. If you can put up with her."

"I can put up with her," said Sally.

"Yes. Two reasons: one, you're a naturally nice person; two, she doesn't see you as a threat or a challenge."

"I'm not sure what you mean."

"Exactly. She can afford to be nice to you because you are too nice to imagine being a threat or a challenge."

When they arrived at the yard, Sally held her arms out and Trompette walked right into them, leaned the whole length of her young, firm body against Sally.

"I'm glad you've come," she said at length, and pulled away to lead Sally onto *Grimm*.

Sally had been apprehensive about this moment, not helped by Eve. "It'll be sordid," she said. "Be prepared."

It was not sordid. It was designed with the sleeping areas at the rear and the kitchen at the front, the reverse of the *Number One*'s layout. At the bottom of the steps down from the rear deck was a cabin with two upholstered benches, one either side of the gangway. At night, these could be pushed together and made up as a double bed. On one was a pile of bedding, neatly stacked. Everything else in the space was equally tidy, Sally realized, when she had overcome the shock of how much stuff there was, in contrast to the austerity of the *Number One*. Boxes were lined up underneath the bunks; a sewing machine sat on a shelf across the end wall; a wire ran above one of the beds from which hung garments, on hangers, many of them the sort of thing Trompette had sold to Misty of Misty's Cave in Birmingham, some of them Trompette's own. They moved slightly in the breeze from the open hatch, a forest of shapes, colors and textures that made Sally think of seaweed fronds in a rock pool. The floor, the bedding, the windows and the clothes were scrupulously clean. Sally was aware that Trompette was watching her; she, too, must have been apprehensive about this moment.

"Trompette's cave," Sally said. "It's lovely."

The shower and loo came next and then another cabin that was a closer match for Sally's fears. It also had two benches and was full of stuff that was obviously Billy's: musical instruments, strange and unsettling objects wrought in metal or woven from string, black plastic boxes with wires wrapped round them, piles of clothes and unsavory blankets and rugs. But this cabin, too, was clean, and Trompette had piled up Billy's belongings as neatly as the quantity of awkward items allowed.

"Billy's cave?" Sally said.

"Billy's things," Trompette said. "I tidied up. Usually, I can't. He won't like that I have. But I like it."

The kitchen, after this, was unsurprising. Clean, tidy but with an excess of things that Anastasia would be horrified to see. A table was fixed against the wall with a bench either side. On the table was a square parcel wrapped in tissue paper.

"This is for you," Trompette said, placing a finger on it.

Sally sat down on a bench and drew the parcel toward her. The tissue paper had been shaped into a sort of envelope which was formed without the use of sticky tape. Sally undid the folds carefully, avoiding tearing the paper. She was enjoying the perfection of the package as much as she was looking forward to the contents. At last it opened enough for her to be able to glimpse the blues, greens and scarlet of the piece of knitting Trompette had been doing when they moored near Birmingham. She was speechless with admiration for the beauty of the thing Trompette had created. The kimono-style jacket hung in elegant folds if held still but, at the slightest movement, shifted to reveal a flash of color, a perfect curve, then fell again into its natural shape.

"Oh, Trompette," Sally said.

"Put it on."

Sally was wearing a T-shirt and jeans and assumed the cardigan would look incongruous with so ordinary an outfit, but when she had stood for Trompette to smooth and twitch and pronounce it all right, she was allowed to go back to the shower where there was a full-length mirror, and found out she was wrong.

"I love it," she said to Trompette. "But I said I'd buy it. How much do you want?"

For the first time, Trompette looked like the child she so nearly was. "Why do you have to spoil it?" Her face became red and petulant and she squeezed her hands into fists. "It's for you. It's a present. I did it for you."

Sally took one of the balled-up hands.

"I'd much rather have it as a present," she said. "It makes it so much more special to me. I just didn't want to assume."

Trompette pulled her hand away, composing herself once more into her normal, controlled manner.

"It suits you," she said. "I knew it would."

When Sally went into the shed to see the *Number One*, out

of its element but monumental in elevation on a cradle, Owen thought so, too.

"My word," he said, removing his gauntlets and his goggles, and touching the fabric, "that suits you."

That night, snuggled up on the benches in the rear cabin, in the dark, Trompette told her what had happened in Birmingham. In the early hours of the morning, they had set off after Thad and moored alongside him. He and Billy went out together and Trompette went to bed. She was woken in the night by Billy clearing all the hiding places of drugs and telling her he was sorry. Thad was dead, he said, killed in a fight with whichever gang had come off worst the night before. He was going. There was nothing she knew, or had on board, to implicate her in the crimes that had been committed. The next time she saw him was in prison.

Grimm, and Trompette, had been thoroughly gone over by the police. In the end, she had most difficulty convincing them she was over eighteen, but once they had accepted that, they left her alone. She had spoken to the lawyer appointed to represent Billy. He would be in jail for a number of years, if found guilty. The lawyer was noncommittal on his chances of being found not guilty. Like herself, Eve and Anastasia, Sally thought, Trompette was suddenly in a position of having her way of life tugged out from under her. Only, unlike them, she had most of life ahead of her and no resources. But despite this, or maybe because of it, once she had told her story, Trompette dropped off into a deep and apparently undisturbed sleep.

Eve arrived at the yard in a car she had bought, and which Owen seemed to think was a good buy. By this time, Sally and Owen had planned their route back to Uxbridge with the *Number One*, and timed it at three weeks. They used the map Anastasia had pinned up on the wall and used the hours' travel time it gave them for each section.

"It'll be wrong," Owen said. "But not that far wrong."

Via Middlewich, Stoke-on-Trent, Great Haywood, Fradley, Tamworth and then Braunston; from there, they would follow the same route they had used on the way up. It was 200 miles and there were 189 locks. The last piece of planning—who would be staying with Anastasia—they left until Eve arrived. Sally had assumed Trompette would leave *Grimm* at Owen's yard, travel at once to Uxbridge and be there until she and Eve got back with the *Number One*. But neither Trompette nor Owen thought this was a good idea. Trompette wanted to keep close by the only home she had, and Owen was reluctant to let *Grimm* occupy space he could be using for people who would pay him. So both boats would be making the journey, in tandem. Only one person per boat, Owen pointed out, was strictly necessary in a convoy, and they could take turns to spend time in the flat.

Eve agreed. They should take it in turns, she said, to look after a woman who would undoubtedly be grumpy and rude and uncooperative. Owen announced his intention of going down the next day to extract Anastasia from the hospital and install her in the flat. He could spare three days, he said.

"Are you sure?" asked Sally.

"Yes," Owen said. "Technically, she is my responsibility. And practically, she is more likely to do what I tell her."

It was a relief to Sally to go to bed in her own narrow little berth on the *Number One*, back in the water with every chip

and scratch painted over. Although in theory she'd had a bed
to herself on *Grimm*, Trompette had had a tendency to shuffle
her half of the double across and snuggle up. Sally had felt short
of sleep, and breathing space, and oppressed by the profusion
of things.

9

To Uxbridge

BY THE SECOND DAY, they were on the Middlewich Branch, which linked the Shropshire Union to the Trent and Mersey. Eve concentrated on the experience of traveling. The rhythm of movement along a canal, the tramp of feet on the towpath like a song without notes. This was not about the destination; the point was the traveling, at a speed that allowed change to occur at the rate of one hundred yards every minute. Or less frequently. When the boat was stationary, change occurred only as the wind blew and shifted the pattern on the water's surface. She'd never noticed this before. She had never noticed how many unexplored paths there were leading off from the canal, visible only as a footpath sign, a short stretch of lane crossing a bridge and plunging at once round a bend and out of sight.

She pointed this out to Sally, perched beside her, wearing the remarkable cardigan.

"Would it be fanciful to say I am noticing this now because we are so close to having to choose which path to take?"

"Of course not," said Sally. "And if it is, you go ahead and be fanciful."

"Unfortunately, we don't have any data to tell us which path is worth exploring," Eve said. "If only we had time to stop and explore."

"That's more like it," said Sally. "Keep a grip on the facts."

They passed a cluster of buildings, alone in a clearing, close to the canal's edge. A square house, a line of what could have been stables or storage sheds, all built of brick and looking as if they had been only recently abandoned; the house surrounded by cultivated plants untended and overgrown; the sheds with a window broken here and there but a pile of logs stacked neatly beneath a tarpaulin not yet shredded by the wind.

"Look, look!" said Eve. "Wouldn't that be a project? Think what we could do with that—tidy it up, offer moorings, a café, B&B, day trips—what do you think?"

She had throttled back to give herself more time to look and the boat was drifting in the wind.

"I think you're at risk of running aground," Sally said. "And who do you mean by 'we'?"

"I don't know. It just looks like more than a one-woman project."

They had drifted past now and, as Sally had predicted, when Eve opened the throttle and tried to move forward, the *Number One* was caught in shallow water on a patch of reeds. It took them ten minutes with the pole and much maneuvering to regain the central channel. Trompette, on *Grimm* behind them, held back throughout, keeping her boat neatly central between the banks. She made no effort to come closer and help.

"I'm glad she's your project, not mine," Eve said. "Or don't you think she's a problem?"

"She is, but not your kind of problem. You like problems that can be sorted out by the application of logic and by taking the right steps. I'm not sure what the answer is, for Trompette, but I'm not looking for a fix, just to make a difference."

"Lucky for her she found you," said Eve.

"I wasn't criticizing you."

"I know. And I wasn't being sarcastic."

They started early each day and traveled on into the evening, aiming to reach Kidsgrove by lunchtime on the third day when they were due to meet Owen. There was a series of locks called, so the book (and a chatty fellow sitting with his dog on a lock gate) told them, Heartbreak Hill. There were eighteen locks in a four-mile stretch, and although the map showed these as double, they were two individual locks, side by side, so it was twice the work for whoever was not driving, operating two locks at once.

They dished up the remains of such food as they had on board because Owen was in a hurry to get back to the yard and Eve needed to set off for Uxbridge to relieve Jacob before Anastasia became too acidic for even Jacob's sunny nature to bear.

"She's at that moment when she's been thinking, 'Thank heavens that's over,' and then she realizes that of course it isn't. Now she's faced with the beginning of what comes afterward. If you know what I mean."

Sally and Eve both did.

"You mean," said Trompette, "when Billy's trial is finally over and he gets convicted, it won't be the end. It will be the beginning." She lifted the hem of the smock she was wearing and wiped her eyes. "Poor Anastasia. She won't know how to be anyone except the person she always has been."

"She'll cope," said Owen. "You will, too, Trompette."

There was somewhere Sally needed to be the next day, but first they had to go through the Harecastle Tunnel. Nearly as long as the Blisworth Tunnel, but only one boat's width and low enough that hard hats were recommended. There was a convoy system in operation, and they were given a safety briefing before setting off. If this had been her first experience of tunnels, Sally thought, as she set off in front with the *Number One*, she would have been comforted by the impression that they were not alone or having to create their own rules; but once she was inside, it was considerably more frightening than Blisworth. It was not so much a tunnel as a sewer, so low was the roof, so close the side walls. At first, she was shrouded in a fog of fumes from the boat in front, which was an unhelpful reminder of the story Billy had told about the Blisworth, but then, with the convoy inside, the ventilation fans started up with a noise like a tumble dryer. Sally concentrated on maintaining the gap between herself and the boat in front, as directed, and on ducking to avoid the bright painted arches that were the lowest point, and on thinking of nothing but these two tasks.

She looked back when she had cleared the entrance to check on *Grimm*. Trompette was wearing something white and tent-like, and as she neared the mouth of the tunnel, *Grimm* and its helmsman could have been a thing of horror, not wholly real nor insubstantial enough to be dismissed as a dream. Out in the open, Trompette peeled off her cape and was as neat, as un-moved as ever.

SALLY WOKE UP MISSING DUNCAN for the first time since she left 42 Beech Grove. The absence of the person she had lived so closely with for more than twenty years was suddenly so obvi-ous she was surprised she had not felt it before. How could she have gone from knowing everything—which shirt he would be wearing next day, whether the patch of eczema on his wrist had flared up, what he would be eating tonight—to a complete absence of knowledge, and not felt the gap?

Noah sniffled and she remembered her responsibility, in Eve's absence, for the animal. She thought, as she pulled on her jeans, that she had woken aware of a lack of Duncan because she had been dreaming about him. And she had been dreaming about him because she was about to see him. He was coming to visit her on the *Number One*. By invitation.

Sally remembered Lynne the hairdresser's reaction to the news she was separating herself from Duncan, her expectation that there would be emotional fallout. There had been very little strong emotion in her marriage, she thought, looking back, but that didn't mean Duncan would be accepting the new situation with the sense of liberation she was experiencing. The gap she had left behind could be an abyss, for all she knew. She sus-pected it was not like that; nothing Duncan had said or written since she'd left led her to believe he was finding it hard to cope, and the idea of Duncan in despair, looking at the washing line and wondering where there might be a sturdy enough hook or beam more than six foot off the ground, was enough to make her smile. Which she should definitely not be doing. To have given him even a day or a week of misery was something she had to regret, even if, as she so fervently hoped, he would find out soon enough that this was not the end of something wonderful but rather the start of something potentially better.

She sorted Noah out. She appreciated his tolerance of her, fourth best as she clearly was to Anastasia, Eve and Owen, and was tolerant in return. After breakfast with Trompette, who had agreed to keep *Grimm* moored a little distance away and to stay out of sight, she walked up to the turnoff on the road over the canal, where she had told Duncan to park. She took a book. Sat on the grass and opened it up. Her phone beeped. He had sent her a text message telling her when the satnav estimated he would arrive. She shut her eyes and wriggled her back against the tree supplying her with shade.

There were no more texts, so she guessed the satnav had been accurate. She was standing in shadow and was able to watch Duncan drive up, turn the engine off and open the door without him noticing her. She stepped forward, as he stood up, phone in hand.

"Hello there," she said, and he jumped.

"I didn't see you," he said. He looked up and down the road, on which no buildings were visible as far as the bends at either end. "How long have you been waiting? You shouldn't stand around in turnoffs, you know. You're making yourself vulnerable."

"Oh, Duncan," she said.

She had worried about how the greeting would go. Should she kiss him, expect him to kiss her? But this exchange had allowed them to be into a post-greeting place without a stumble.

"This way," she said.

She tried to see the canal, the boat, the situation, as Duncan was seeing it, thinking how he would describe it, later, to whomever he was talking to in her absence. Of one thing she was sure: he would be talking to someone.

The boat looked sparse. Although it was clean, the sunlight falling through the portholes onto worn, scuffed surfaces made it look dingy. Duncan was neither tall nor particularly fat, but filled the space in the cabin as he stood waiting for her to tell him where to sit.

Then Noah wriggled past Sally's legs and displayed some pleasure at the sight of Duncan. Duncan had always responded positively to other people's dogs but the question of owning one had never arisen. Because of her, she realized now.

"Where's, um, what's-her-name?" Duncan asked.

"Eve. She's back in Uxbridge, looking after Anastasia."

"That's the boat's owner, right? Strange name, Anastasia. Is it Russian, do you know?"

"Not so far as I'm aware. I've never asked."

She made them coffee, while Duncan looked around, opening doors, pulling down flaps, commenting on what was neat, what was missing, what he would think about doing with the space if it was his boat.

"I can't imagine you wanting to live on a boat," she said at last.

"No, I wouldn't. But do you? And if not, where do you want to live? Isn't that what we're here to discuss?" He said this as if she had been the one who had failed to approach the topic in a straightforward, businesslike way. It was curious, how exactly like himself he was, how not one of the things he had said since switching off his car's engine in the turnoff had struck her as being unexpected. Which, after all, was not surprising. They had been together half their lives. The difference was not in him but in her. She was, for the first time in years, listening attentively to every word. And hearing it, she began framing the responses she had always avoided framing. Now she wanted to point out how he was formulating opinions as he spoke, taking no time to understand his own point of view, test the limits of his knowledge before opening his mouth. How he was looking at detail, never at the whole. How this did not stop him drawing conclusions which implied the truth-according-to-Duncan was a universal truth.

She had never said any of this when they were first married, because she had not understood exactly what she thought and could not have articulated it if she had. Later, she had understood and had entered the conversation with a view to challenging Duncan's assumptions, introducing an alternative angle, or moving the topic on to what she thought would be a more fruitful or interesting area for discussion. It had been frustrating. So she stopped listening. She allowed the rattle of Duncan's words to roll over and past her.

Of course, there were times when they had truly talked to each other, on topics that mattered. He was not a foolish man, not unfeeling, unsympathetic, self-centered, vain or touchy. He was someone she had married because she thought he was the husband she wanted. (It had not occurred to her that she might not want a husband at all.) What he did not have was stillness and depth, and the half an hour he had spent on the boat so far had reminded her what living with his noise and triviality had cost her.

"I don't know where I want to live," she said. "Except it isn't 42 Beech Grove."

An expression crossed Duncan's face that she realized was irritation. He was a man capable of being irritated, even easy to irritate, but he had never before shown any irritation toward her. He hadn't had to, she thought. He had only had to smile and soothe and be a little patronizing and she would back away from any potential argument, not bothering to stand up for herself. Conflict had been almost entirely absent from their marriage. So in this flash of exasperation, she recognized a shift. He, too, had looked beneath the surface of their life together and found her, as she had found him, imperfect. This was an exciting development. All her fears for this meeting, that it would be platitudes coming down like stair rods and she would have to use all her fortitude not to raise the umbrella of indifference against them, vanished.

"I guessed that," he said. Then made a series of pouting, sucking movements with his lips. "Can I take it you also don't want to live with me?"

"I haven't changed my mind," Sally said. "If anything, I'm clearer now that being married to each other is not the best thing for either of us. What do you think?"

It was as if she had given him the cue to a line he had rehearsed but did not know how to introduce. He looked happier at once.

"I have to say," he said, "I have been doing a lot of thinking along those very lines myself. I've been thinking about it and then talking it over with Ffion." Of course you have, Sally thought. Ffion lived next door and was a collector of other people's stories, which she dramatized and used as social currency to create status for herself in the community. "She's been very helpful, actually. She's really helped me sort out what I feel, just by listening to me, mostly, and throwing in the odd word. The truth is—I hope you realize I'm not trying to be hurtful—I never felt you did actually listen to me. You were always a bit slow to pick up on what I was saying and to give it a bit of a bat back and forth, so to speak. I know you're cleverer than I am, and I admit I sometimes felt as if you weren't responding because you could see so many more sides to a thing than I could—you know, see the back and the sides while I was standing staring at the front."

Sally was surprised to find he understood this, but more surprised by another part of this speech.

"What makes you think I'm cleverer than you?" she asked. "You're the one with qualifications and a job that needs you to apply your brain."

"Oh, yes, but that's just knowing facts. I've always been good at learning facts and fitting facts into patterns. But when it comes to ideas—what would you call it, concepts?—well, I think you're well ahead of me."

"I didn't know you thought that," Sally said.

"I did and I do and I've often had the feeling you might hold me in contempt but then I'm not the type to brood or dwell on things and I do tend to the positive outlook so I've always reminded myself how you've never actually argued with me and you seemed to be happy and . . ."

"I don't hold you in contempt," Sally said. "But everything else you're saying is right. I didn't bother to argue with you even when I didn't agree with what you were saying, and I'm not sure that was fair. It was the same as ignoring you, and I suppose that is treating you with contempt. If I agreed to come back and try again, I can't promise to be any different."

"That's the point, you've seen our marriage front, back and sides, haven't you? While I've been looking at the, what's the word, the façade."

"I don't think I did so consciously."

"No, but you see, you have understood it when I didn't, and you've done us both a favor. You've helped me look at it in the round, so to speak, and that's been a good thing. What I've seen, since you've been gone, talking to Ffion and to Laura in the office, who's a really good listener, is that the life I was leading wasn't as good as I thought it was. We spent our free time, now that the children have gone, looking after the house and the garden. Well, I'm here to tell you I don't want to do that anymore."

"What does that mean?" she asked.

"I want to sell the house, split the money and use my share to buy a flat in town. I want to enjoy myself."

Sally wondered who he would be enjoying himself with— Ffion? Laura? Because she knew Duncan well enough to know that he could not enjoy himself on his own. She hoped he knew that, too, and had already lined up candidates to be on the sofa at the day's end.

"I understand," she said.

"But what about you? You don't seem any clearer now than you were before you left. What will you do? You'll have half the proceeds from the house, of course, and half our investments."

Sally asked him how much that might be and he told her. It was more money than she had imagined. The area they had bought in, Duncan explained, had become more and more desirable. The mortgage was a fraction of the value.

"You could buy a barge," Duncan said, "like this one. There'd be money left over to live on if you didn't want to go back to your job. Or you could find a job in another part of the country where houses are cheaper and buy a house."

"Please," Sally said, "please stop speculating on my behalf. I can work it out for myself."

Duncan fidgeted. "I suppose if we were to go for a divorce you might be able to claim a share of my income, or my pension. Is that what you're thinking?"

"No! What you've suggested sounds so simple, and as you've paid more of the mortgage I think it's more than fair."

"There's your individual savings accounts, too," said Duncan.

"Stop it at once," Sally said. "Do we need some agreements drawn up?"

"Yes, I've consulted with a solicitor and . . ."

"Well, I'll wait for you to tell me where to sign." Behind Duncan's head she could see the sun sparkling on the water, see the trace left by a duck coming to investigate the boat. She could hear Noah snoring and feel the roughness of his flank against her foot. She was in free fall; soon she would have to pull the cord to activate the parachute, choosing a spot to steer toward for a painless landing. But for this moment, she could enjoy the sensation of having jumped out of the plane and having nothing holding her back.

She had to give Duncan lunch. She had to endure his first experience of the boat's lavatory and his views on that experience. That he was as relieved as she was that they had come to so agreeable a view of their jointly separate future was evident in his ebullience, his need to comment on everything.

"All good things must come to a Brussels sprout," he said, back at the turnoff. "As they say."

"Indeed they must," she said, and hugged him. After a moment of surprise, he hugged her back. They did not attempt a kiss.

ANASTASIA WAS OCCUPYING TOO LITTLE of Eve's time, during her spell as carer. She suspected Anastasia was keeping out of her way; she recognized she was brisk to the point of bullying, in comparison to Jacob and Vic, who seemed to be around more than she had expected them to be. All this gave her time to think, and she thought she needed a plan. Being back in the flat reminded her of the way she used to operate: an end was in sight and therefore a new beginning had to be formulated, as, in her old life, she had begun to think about the next project before the current project was fully wrapped up. She should by now have some parameters, a vision, a handful of key deliverables jotted down on a sheet of paper. Probably a couple of visuals that represented the point of departure and the distant destination, or that conceptualized the territory the new project would be aiming to occupy with reference to existing fixed points in the company's business and in the marketplace. Now was the time when decisions would need to be made. But she had insufficient data. She liked to start without considering the detail, but with enough information to pin down the options.

Some days ago, she had received an email from someone she had worked with in the past. He had mentioned a new project and invited her to phone him.

His name was Juri, and he was Finnish. He had worked for
Rambusch, but only briefly, because he'd never learned to appreciate the banter, with its cheerful crudeness and edge of aggression. He tried to ignore it, telling Eve, in the early days of
his employment, that he hoped hard work and achievements
would be effective in securing respect, which he equated with
a silencing of the needling laughter. She knew it wouldn't. On
the contrary. She pointed out to him that the level of abuse he
was experiencing, masquerading as good humor, was a form of
respect. If he had been no challenge, no better than competent,
he would have been, if not left alone, at least only intermittently
noticed. As it was, there was a frisson of fear running through
his peer group's treatment of him. Not only was he highly competent, and ambitious, but he was both taller and better looking
than most of them. Doing the job better than they were, on top
of this, would make life unbearable. He couldn't understand
this distorted logic, so she was not surprised when he moved on.

Nor was she particularly disappointed, though he had moved
in with her shortly after joining the company because she appreciated those things that upset her male colleagues—his
good looks, his height. And of course, his intellect. It had felt
like love, for a while, but this was an emotion she had always
struggled to sustain. She found it difficult to overlook the
negatives. By the time he left, and despite the physique, good
looks and remarkably astute brain, she was beginning to dread
the evenings and weekends spent in the company of someone
for whom nothing, however absurd, was a joke. But they had
stayed in touch. They had met from time to time at conferences and exhibitions. He had congratulated her on her rise
through the company's hierarchy. She had congratulated him

on his marriage (to someone small, serious and Finnish) and his successive successful projects for increasingly impressive international organizations.

When she had opened the email asking her to ring him, she had been disturbed by the idea. She knew that if she had phoned him, she would have become excited about the project and she wasn't then ready to be excited. Now she was. So she rang him.

Eve and Anastasia were invited up to Jacob's flat for dinner. Jacob had cooked the whole meal from a book by Nigel Slater, which he said was easy to follow. It was a better starting point for a newly interested cook, he said, than the one he'd sent her, but he had wanted to show her how interesting cooking and cookery writing could be. The food was delicious. It took some while to eat and some more while to talk through the ingredients and the recipe. The wine, chosen by Vic, was too good to leave any in the bottle, and Vic himself turned out to be a witty raconteur after a glassful, so there was never a moment when Eve could let her mind wander back to the conversation she had had with Juri. Then when they went back downstairs, Anastasia seemed to take a long, long time to prepare for bed and Eve, worried about her, sat up listening to make sure she had gone to sleep and that the noises of Anastasia sleeping were only the usual noises and nothing more alarming. It was after midnight when she finally relaxed, and she was too tired to structure her thoughts so she didn't try.

She drew, on a piece of paper, the alternative circles into which she might choose to put a foot. Each circle had a focus, people and places. The first had the *Number One*, Sally and Anastasia, Chester and Uxbridge. The second circle had Project Prospero, which stood for an energy infrastructure as yet undelivered but not completely undefined, Juri's name, and those of a few other people she had met or worked with in the past; it had Uzbekistan and the UK, undefined. The third circle was the least well populated. The focus was a job; more research needed to identify what jobs might be available, where, working with whom. Juri had given her the name of a headhunter, and so the first step was to make another phone call. Only not at one o'clock in the morning.

She looked at her circles and then drew a timeline underneath them, from this evening, here in Uxbridge, for the next six months. She needed to redraw the picture with the circles on the timeline, checking the overlap, marking the decision points, highlighting the steps needed to acquire the detail necessary to make a decision, to eliminate or to keep. Only not tonight.

ANASTASIA HAD AN APPOINTMENT WITH the specialist. Sally took her to the hospital in Eve's new car and left her at the entrance while she found a place to park. When she returned, she found Anastasia had not gone on to where the clinic was being held, but had waited for her, perched on a chair by the automatic doors which opened and closed as the flow of the sick and the apparently well never ceased.

"All right?" Sally said.

Anastasia nodded. "I need you to come in with me," she said. "I didn't want to get hustled in before you turned up."

"We'll do this together," Sally said, and stood near enough for Anastasia to hold her arm, if she needed to.

When they reached the waiting area for the clinic, Anastasia was taken away to be weighed and have her blood pressure checked.

"Why do they do that?" she said, sitting back down.

"Collecting statistics?" suggested Sally. "It's vital to have data. Eve says so."

Anastasia snorted.

The consultant, when he called them in, was indescribably clean and pleasant and authoritative. This was obviously not the first time he had met Anastasia, and he treated her as if he knew and liked her.

"I won't ask how you are feeling," he said. "But I expect you to tell me if anything is bothering you."

"Get on with it," said Anastasia.

The news he gave them was better than Sally had feared but worse then she had hoped it might be. The operation had, their analysis told them, removed the cancerous cells, but because of the extent of these cells and the location, he wanted to follow up with a course of chemotherapy. Six sessions, one a week for six weeks. This meant—Sally wondered if he was frank with patients less indomitable and forthright, which was likely to be all his other patients—that she would spend a couple of days every week feeling sick. How sick he couldn't say, as different people responded differently, but she would, at the very least, feel unwell. The treatment was debilitating and it would take her some time to recover. After six months, they would do a scan and if that was clear she would be called back for scans once a year until they were satisfied.

"I see," said Anastasia. "So you want to rough me up some more before you spit me out and let me go back to leading my life in the way I choose to lead it."

"Yes," he said. "I want to hold on to you for a while longer in the hope that I never have to see you again after that."

"I don't want to see you again, either, but I can avoid that by dying, without bothering you further in the matter."

"Don't do that," said the consultant. "You'll mess up my statistics."

They hardly spoke on the way back to the flat. Anastasia, as she had done on previous days, went and lay down for a couple of hours. Sally listened for evidence she had gone to sleep, the whistly snores she associated with Anastasia sleeping, but heard nothing. Still, after the two hours were up, Anastasia got up and came through to sit on the sofa and drink a cup of tea.

"The medical profession don't think the fridge is damaged beyond repair," Sally said.

"No," said Anastasia. "That much is clear. I just have to decide whether I want to go through the process of having it repaired."

"I understand."

"I'm glad it was you with me today," Anastasia said.

"Eve would have understood, too."

"I know. But she would have wanted to talk about making a decision, and I'm not ready to do that."

Before she left, to be replaced by Trompette, Sally said:

"You may not be able to work the locks on your own anymore but that doesn't stop you living on a canal."

"I'll take into account that you said that."

"And there is no point rejecting the treatment without first finding out how bad it is."

"I'm afraid you're probably right about that."

TROMPETTE: Sally?

SALLY: Is everything all right?

TROMPETTE: You'll never guess what's happened.

SALLY: Well, you'd better tell me, then.

TROMPETTE: Arthur's turned up.

SALLY: Oh? Is that good news or bad news?

TROMPETTE: It's good. I was really worried about her after the first chemo session. She wasn't particularly sick or anything but she was so miserable. It felt as if she was thinking of giving up. I mean, Anastasia, giving up! I was really frightened.

SALLY: And she isn't now? Looking as if she's about to give up?

TROMPETTE: No. Arthur sort of bats everything she says back at her. I'd been out shopping so I wasn't there when he came, and they seemed to be in the middle of an almighty row when I got back. Only Arthur was being the strong, sensible one and Anastasia was doing the shouting. Except she can't actually shout—she hasn't got enough puff—so she was sort of whispering fiercely.

SALLY: Goodness!

TROMPETTE: Yes. Anastasia told me to run along and bother Jacob and leave them in peace, so I did. When I went downstairs again, Arthur was singing to her and she looked positively peaceful.

SALLY: How long is he staying for?

TROMPETTE: Well, that's the point. He says he can stay
for a couple of weeks, so I said I'd go back to the boat
and they told me not to. I'm not sure they want to be
alone together. War might break out, or something.
So I said one of you two would be coming as soon as
I left anyway, and they didn't seem to think that was
a good idea, either. They want me to stay until you
both get here with the *Number One*.

SALLY: Yes, I can see you'd be easier to have around
than either of us.

TROMPETTE: You mean, I don't really matter.

SALLY: That's not what I'm saying at all, my dear. But
you're more restful, less likely to provoke an argument by expressing your own opinions. So do you
mind holding on? Have you got plenty of wool?

TROMPETTE: Lots. I can stay here and knit. I don't
mind. And if they start fighting I'll go upstairs and
get Jacob to make me some chocolate brownies.

SALLY: Trompette, you're a treasure. Let me know if
things take a turn for the worse.

TROMPETTE: I will.

THEY WERE BACK ON THE canal they had traveled along going
in the opposite direction all those weeks ago. Sally on *Grimm*,
Eve on the *Number One*. Too far apart, as they pressed on, mile
after mile, to share their idle thoughts as they had done the last
time they passed this way.

They went through Blisworth Tunnel, the *Number One* in

the lead as it had the better, brighter light. Eve remembered how anxious she had been, on the previous trip, and how Arthur had played a tune on his harmonica. Arthur. Alone on the *Number One* the previous night she had taken out her plan with its overlapping circles and crossed some things out, adjusted the timeline, begun to map a few actions along the way. Forget Arthur. He might fit, he might not. But first, she had to talk to Sally.

"I've been thinking," she said, when they were sitting waiting for the shepherd's pie that Sally had made to cook.

"Not much else to do," said Sally. "Tell me what you've been thinking."

"That I will take the Project Prospero job."

"I thought you would."

"But also, I will buy a house. Now what have you been thinking?"

"I've been thinking I might buy a house or I might buy a narrowboat."

"Where would you buy a house?"

"By a canal, obviously. With a mooring, if I can afford it."

"Well," said Eve. She could feel the color rising in her face, something that had not happened to her for so long she had almost forgotten what it felt like. She had not been so nervous since the days when, being young, other people's reactions to what she said felt to be of critical importance. "I won't need to live in the house I buy all the time. And I don't mind where it is as long as it's within reach of an airport."

"Go on," said Sally.

"So. We could pool our resources. Buy a house, and a boat if we can stretch to it. It would have to be a big house with enough space and ways in and out so we wouldn't have to be living together when I'm home. Only, I'd have somewhere to come back to where I wouldn't be alone."

Sally touched her hand. "We'd need space for at least two boats, don't you think?"

"Have you thought all this, too? A house by a canal which is a home to us both, and somewhere for Anastasia and Trompette to moor up?"

"It had crossed my mind. It would have to be near Chester, if we want Anastasia to be close to Owen."

"The Middlewich Branch."

Eve stood up and did a sort of jig in the narrow space between the table and the wall.

Sitting down again, she said, "You're like a gelling agent that bonds molecules together. The rest of us are all separate particles, but you can cement us together."

"Doesn't Anastasia do that?"

"You remember you told me Owen said she tried not to have too much influence over him when he was growing up. She stands tall and strong and she's an inspiration to other people, but she doesn't reach out and draw them to her like you do."

"You're the hand truck."

"The *hand* truck?"

"You move things forward."

"Can't I be something more elegantly engineered than a sack truck? A transport hub?"

"All right, I'll agree to conveyor belt."

When they had eaten the shepherd's pie ("I wonder if a dash of Worcestershire sauce would help the flavor?" Eve said), Sally said:

"You'll be sitting in a departure lounge listening for flight announcements and I'll be sitting on the canal bank listening to a moorhen calling for its chicks."

"Or," said Eve, "you'll be scraping the ice off the cap of the water tank and trying to feel your fingers through your gloves, and I'll be sitting in the warm with a cup of coffee in my hand, watching the snow falling."

"I'll still be the lucky one."

"Lucky for me I met you."

"Lucky for me I met you and Anastasia."

"Lucky for Trompette she met—"

"That's it. I'm off back to *Grimm* for some sleep."

"We can make this work, though, can't we?"

"Well, I know we're all made up of matter and are subject to the laws of physics," Sally said, "but even if we can't, strictly speaking, have free will, we also can't predict how other people will behave."

"Annoying, isn't it?" said Eve.

IT IS RAINING AND THE windows of the narrowboat *Number One*, moored on a wooded section of the towpath in Uxbridge, are steamed up, rendered opaque by the breath of six people and a dog packed into the kitchen. The folding chairs from the front well have been brought through, and Arthur is sitting on one of these in the doorway of the middle cabin, looking like a man who has an escape route uppermost in his mind. On the other, tucked in the space between the sink and the cooker, Trompette sits, knitting, looking down at the work in her hands. The four spaces round the table are occupied by Anastasia, Sally, Eve and Owen. Noah is under the table, nose on paws, watching the movement of their feet as they shift position in their seats, either because he hopes this will yield some clue as to the outcome of the discussion or because he is worried that one of them will tread on him.

"We need to know," Sally says to Anastasia, "that you're prepared to carry on making an effort not to die."

Anastasia looks ill. She has cut her hair even shorter than normal, expecting it to fall out, and has lost weight. These two changes combine to give her a craggier but more regal appearance.

"I've been through all that," she says, "with Arthur."

They all swivel round and look at Arthur. He takes out his harmonica and plays a tender, lyrical little tune.

"That's all right, then," says Sally. "So, you should know, Eve and I have a plan."

"Not another Easy Plan," Anastasia says. "Because it isn't going to be easy."

"It can't be an Easy Plan," says Sally, "because I have abandoned all pretense of being Yasmin, so we are short of a Y."

"If Trompette is part of the plan now," Anastasia says, "it will have to be the East Plan. I don't think I like the sound of that."

"Or the Eats Plan," says Trompette.

"What about me," Owen says, "and Arthur? What if we want to be part of this plan? We'd have too many vowels. Not enough consonants. We'll have to use surnames as well. What's yours, Trompette?"

"Stop it, all of you," says Eve, raising her voice, waiting until they are looking at her. "I have a name for it. It's Plan Number One. And I know it is going to work."

Acknowledgments

I appreciate the skill, support and enthusiasm of the team at Transworld, especially Jane Lawson, Alison Barrow and Kate Samano, and at Flatiron, New York, especially Caroline Bleeke.

I am grateful to my early readers, Fiona Clarke, Rebecca McKay and Felicity Zeigler, to Paul Youngson and Mary Wooding for practical guidance, and to Elizabeth Crowley, Bev Murray and Ceri Lloyd for encouragement.

I am indebted to a number of excellent books on the history of the canals and the lives of those involved with them, then and now. In particular: *Water Ways: A Thousand Miles along Britain's Canals* by Jasper Winn, *Barging Round Britain: Exploring the History of Our Nation's Canals and Waterways* by John Sergeant and David Bartley, *Number One* by Tom Foxon and *Narrow Boat* by L. T. C. Rolt. The vlog at www.cruisingthecut .co.uk was also useful, and the Nicholson Waterways Guides were indispensable.

The Narrowboat Summer
DISCUSSION QUESTIONS

1. Discuss Eve's description of life on the *Number One*: "Eve concentrated on the experience of traveling. The rhythm of movement along a canal, the tramp of feet on the towpath like a song without notes. This was not about the destination; the point was the traveling, at a speed that allowed change to occur at the rate of one hundred yards every minute." Have you ever experienced travel like that? What unique insights does it offer?

2. Sally describes the narrowboat community as being "rooted in a geography that was defined by its distance end to end rather than by boundaries round a fixed center." How does that geographic orientation affect life on the canals and the relationships that develop there?

3. One of the unexpected joys of narrowboat travel for Eve is that all of her problems are immediate: "As long as she needed to think ahead only as far as the next tap, the next locks, the next mooring, Eve had no room to worry about the next month, the next year." How is life different for Eve and Sally on the *Number One*? Do you see the appeal of that lifestyle? Could you imagine yourself doing what they did?

4. Is the "Easy Plan" that Eve, Sally, and Anastasia come up with actually easy? Discuss the ways in which it is both easy and difficult for each of them. How do the three women approach the big decisions they face in this novel? Is there an element of randomness inherent in decision-making?

5. When Sally's hairdresser asks why she is divorcing Duncan, she replies, "It's sometimes harder to endure the everyday than it is to cope with a big trauma." What do you think she means? Do you agree? What do you make of her reasons to end her marriage?

6. Sally has a camera with her on the trip but reflects that "taking photos as they traveled in the *Number One* was as unlikely as taking photos at her kitchen sink. This was not a holiday. It was life, going on in unrecorded moments." What do you think she means? How does her perspective bump up against our current social media culture in which everyday life *is* often recorded in photos and text?

7. Billy says of Trompette: "She saved my life and so we are bound together for eternity. I cannot leave her because I owe her too much; she cannot leave me because she has taken to herself the responsibility for my well-being." What do you make of their relationship? How does the idea of holding responsibility for someone else's life run throughout this novel beyond Billy and Trompette?

8. Sally reflects: "After all, was it not important to change every aspect of her routines? How else would she be able to identify those hooks and burrs that held her, like the flag on a flagpole, free to flap about but not free to drift or soar?" Do you agree that sometimes it's necessary to change everything in your life? Have you ever had the opportunity to do that, or have you dreamed about doing that? Discuss.

9. For Eve, life on the *Number One* helps her understand the ways in which her highly structured life both benefited and hindered her: "Previously, any change she had made had been within a structure she understood; it was not until now, on the verge of changing everything . . . that she understood the boundaries that had enabled her to make decisions easily, because the choices were limited and familiar." Discuss the advantages and disadvantages of structure. How important are boundaries or a lack thereof in your own life?

10. Over the course of the novel, Billy tells several stories on the canal that are often a mix of fact and fiction. He describes his stories as capturing "a version of the truth . . . A storyteller's version." How can truth be different from fact, especially when it comes to storytelling (and novel writing)? What purpose do Billy's stories serve in the narrative?

11. What do you make of Anastasia's relationship with Arthur? Were you surprised by the nature of that relationship when it was revealed? What about Owen? Discuss the different kinds of family relationships

we encounter in the novel. How are those similar to and different from the friendships?

12. Sally and Eve both read Arthur's book recommendation, *Mr. Lucton's Freedom*. What does the novel mean to each of these three characters? Discuss the book's "optimistic" message: "It was good to leave, but there is pleasure in going back." How does that idea hold true (or not) for the various characters in *The Narrowboat Summer*?

13. After they've known each other for several weeks, Eve tells Sally, "You've turned into someone else entirely." When Sally disagrees, Eve revises: "You are the person you've always been, but that person is only now rising to the surface." Do you think Sally, Eve, Anastasia, and Trompette change over the course of the novel, or do they simply become truer versions of themselves? Is there a difference?

14. What do you think Plan Number One will entail? What does the future hold for these characters? Which character did you feel most drawn to and invested in by the novel's end?

About the Author

ANNE YOUNGSON lives in Oxfordshire with her husband. *Meet Me at the Museum*, her debut novel, was short-listed for the Costa First Novel Award.